LONESOME ANIMALS

LONESOME ANIMALS

| A NOVEL |

Bruce Holbert

COUNTERPOINT · BERKELEY

Library of Congress Cataloging-in-Publication Data is available.
ISBN: 978-1-58243-806-1

Cover design by Michael Kellner
Interior design by: Neuwirth & Associates, Inc.

COUNTERPOINT
1919 Fifth Street
Berkeley CA 94710
www.counterpointpress.com
Distributed by Publishers Group West

Printed in the United States of America

10 9 8 7 6 5 4 3 2 1

For Holly, Natalie, Luke and Jackson

The author would like to acknowledge Dan Smetanka, Janet Rosen, and Sheree Bykofsky for shepherding this work to publication, and Max Phillips, Chris Offutt, Elizabeth Mc-Cracken, Charles McIntyre, John Whalen, Melissa Van Beck, Desi Koehler, David Hamilton and Bob Ganahl for their support of his work these past years.

We are lonesome animals. We spend all our life trying to be less lonesome. And one of our ancient methods is to tell a story.

—JOHN STEINBECK

Strength is just an accident arising from the weakness of others.

—JOSEPH CONRAD

LONESOME ANIMALS

There was, even in Russell Strawl's time, the myth of the strong silent man of the West. The reverse was closer to the mark. Geography and miles keep people few and far between, even in settled times. Their minds combat the silence and isolation inherent in such spaces by supplying their own narrative. The sound fills the waking hours and intrudes upon any dream they might recall. The remoteness in their gaze, the hesitance in responding to any word put to them, is neither contemplation nor the weight of seriousness nor peace nor solitude nor even alienation upon their souls; it is the jar of another's words piling into the torrent of their own.

For ten years preceding his marriage, Strawl policed the upper Okanogan country. In that time, he arrested 138 Indians, ninety-seven white men, and one woman, who nearly shot his hat from his head as he tried to talk her out of a pistol. He killed eleven men in flight because the circumstances made returning them alive too much trouble. Three others he killed returning fire, and one he beat into a moron with a blacksmith's hammer.

He deposited his checks directly into the army bank, and that kept him from drinking them up in the early days, though after a year, the work occupied him more than any tavern might. The

Lord above filled the holes in the Sunday morning believers; the law began to do the same for Strawl.

Strawl could smell a guilty man—perhaps because the odor was familiar. He could predict which rise he might pursue for his stand, because he himself would have chosen the same. In a person's face, he recognized the seed of acts before he who owned it might. Among the stories told about him are those in which he announced to a suspect hoping to disappear in the hollow of a thicket: "You are considering the distance between yourself and the brush and whether I can get a round in you before you reach it. It is a good bet for you, nearly fifty/fifty. And once you are in the trees, well, your luck may hold for who knows how long. But then I will kill you instead of arrest you, which is simpler for me and requires no paperwork or trial. It's up to you. If you've a weapon, you might even get a round into me, though no one has managed yet, and if you have a brain in your head, you know who I am."

And the pursued would consider his chances while Strawl opened his revolver and spun the cylinder to make certain each round remained in its place. He would likely fire one into the terrain above, raining dirt upon his man. Then he would linger silently, ignoring the conversation his suspect might employ to buy time or stave off boredom. Most instances, less than five minutes and his man would surrender his weapon from the brush. Strawl would treat him kindly with the cuffs and rope and help him to his mount if he possessed one.

Some took hours, however. Strawl ate his supper and smoked cigarettes, then let The Governor drink from the coffeepot. If it was cold, he'd build a fire with as pitchy a fuel as he could find. A few patient enough to manage twilight threw insults at him as the light thinned upon the horizon. In the early years, he prepared for such contingencies by keeping the wind at his back, then lighting anything between himself and his quarry that took a match. Or if the ground was steep and the country right, he would lever boulders free with a bar and roll them onto the suspect's position. Later in his career, waiting lost its capacity to entertain him, and, after an hour, he grew annoyed and threw army surplus hand grenades or smoke ordnance to move the conversation forward.

His facility to stash heart and soul in a saddlebag and his man's inability to do the same separated him from his prey; there was little human in it. Yet Strawl believed the state of every mind was thus and saw it as the central truth around which each man orbited, not considering the possibility that the star that held him in its gravity may not be a star at all, but a black planet and he a trivial moon, circling it.

The moments when Strawl crashed against a door and spilled into a room, or knelt under a pine's shadow outside a fire's fitful light, every second belonged to itself and what occurred within it either informed the next or did not. Some appeared to blend like a painting's oils, a pleasant serendipity, while others existed apart, as those on the pallete, the same colors a useless collision of time and reason.

Justice was just a coincidence within the bedlam, a moment that when separated from the whirlwind turns simple enough to take on fairness's guise. Prosecutors argue the malice in a thunderbolt; defense attorneys the inevitable forces of the jet streams and barometric pressure and condensation and topography. Given the proper atmosphere, a tornado resided in each of us; only our circumstances differed.

Sympathetic as the latter's pain and damage might be in an acquaintance, a judge and gavel encouraged an ordinary person toward clarity. Jurors will avail themselves of any opportunity to hunt meaning in the dying winds and withdrawing rain inside a courtroom. Strawl had witnessed them rule more than one innocent man guilty just for a reprieve from the moral ambiguity outside the courthouse walls.

Strawl, however, remained in the comfort of the storm, and he thought himself content.

When a woman, the only one Strawl ever desired beyond the natural stirrings flesh is slave to, pierced that narrative for a time, it seemed evidence that nature, judgment, and good fortune had finally taken Strawl's side. Women were not foremost in his thoughts. Church girls tended soldiers' barracks, and on occasion the grocer's daughter—Emma Everett was her name—visited Strawl's billet to open the windows and trade out the bedding. She had a fine, straight nose and long, dark hair and possessed little of the formality that set him off of most women.

She approached him in September. The air was heavy with dust and harvest chaff holding the light. She wore a long dress, thin enough to reveal the shadow of her legs in the lowering sun.

"Would you enjoy a hale and hearty walk?" she asked him.

"I traipse around all day long," he said.

She cocked her head and blinked her eyes at him, then puffed up her lower lip like a child.

She extended her hand. He stood, but didn't take hers, so she slipped it under his elbow. Dusk cloaked half her face and, in the shadows, he enjoyed her nose and thin lips and teeth slightly bent inward in a manner that the old women used to say came from keeping on the tit too long.

On a bluff that overlooked China Bend, he sat in the damp grass and listened to the crickets rake their bellies. Emma bent to one knee with him. Her shoes were within his reach. He wanted to bend and clean them with his handkerchief.

"I'm working at the grocery," Emma said. "I see nearly everyone in the county except you. Would it slay you to stop once in a while?"

"Commandant does the shopping," Strawl said.

Her brow creased and she frowned.

"I'm not much for conversation."

"Is it because people lie to you in your job?" Emma asked.

"I have heard some whoppers," Strawl chuckled. "Words turn just noise after a while. I suppose if a house was burning, 'fire' might be handy, but not nearly as much as a bucket of water."

"So those books on your bed stand, they must raise quite a din when you open them." Strawl loved books. They were closed loops. He wondered if she was poking fun at him.

"Why'd you haul me up here?" Strawl asked.

"Because I didn't think you would."

She bent and kissed him and her face erased the sky. She closed her eyes and her face turned blank as a piece of paper waiting for his writing.

He held her head in his hand, pleased with the weight, then put his face to hers and their lips clobbered awkwardly. A drop of blood stained one of her front teeth. She kissed him again, and he tasted her blood in his mouth. Afterwards, he gazed down at the clear part in her hair and the white skin and her forehead and nose underneath. She turned her head up to his and he set his lips to hers. She parted her mouth like she was drinking from a stream and he felt his do the same.

Emma took one of his hands and laced both hers over it. He clamped her wrists and pulled her toward him until she was stretched enough to kiss. Sweat stung his scalp. Her nose flared and her lungs filled. He found her dress buttons with his fingers. Hers fluttered on the backs of his hands like tiny birds. "Oh," she said. "Oh."

He stared at her breasts loose under her camisole. "I don't know what to do," he said.

She took his hand. "Please don't think I do. Know what to do, I mean."

"I will think whatever you want me to," Strawl said.

She laughed a little. "Not knowing. That's better than flowers or ribbon or perfume, really."

⁎⁎⁎⁂⁎⁎⁎

The second year of his marriage, Strawl tracked a bad half-breed for a month. The man's path included a girl not more than fourteen raped with a tree branch and another, only a little older, beaten nearly to death then violated with a broken pool cue. His third woman, he took a breast as a trophy.

The first woman had been conscious enough to offer a fair description: brown hair, cut with bangs in the front, a mustache, wiry strong. The second added he blinked too much. Even the third, in death, contributed the bloody red handkerchief that a man named Reynolds—who fit the rest of the descriptions—was known to favor. Strawl found him at the Red Garter in Coulee Dam sharing a pitcher of beer with two ranch hands between alfalfa cuttings.

Strawl shot out Reynolds's knees in the chair where he sat. The ranch hands scurried under a pool table. Strawl approached Reynolds, stepped on his wrist and put another bullet through his palm, then did the same to the other, leaving the ring finger dangling. Finally he hauled Reynolds by the ankles outside where he tied him to his horse and fired a round into the air. The horse bolted over the steep, paved road, Reynolds's head whacking the asphalt each step. When the horse tired, Strawl shot into the sky again and the horse barreled onto the highway where he was fortunate to dodge a freight truck. No luck saved Reynolds, whose head smashed like a melon under the Studebaker's wheels.

For two months following, nearly every morning, Strawl and Emma woke to cut flowers on their doorsteps or fruit breads or a string of cleaned trout or a calf's liver. Emma cooked or sliced each gift from the porch and invited neighbors to meals, serving them grand dinners that she allowed Strawl to enjoy by carrying the conversation, occasionally hauling him by callused hand into the kitchen where she shut the door and hooked the lock into the hoop and tongue-kissed him and banged her hips into his until both their faces flushed with ardor.

Seven weeks later, he encountered a pervert suspect on a Nespelem street. The man drew his weapon like he was Jesse James himself and Strawl twisted out of the bullet's path behind an elm. The pervert let off another round. Strawl saw it leave the barrel and the smoke following it. He dropped to one knee and heard the bullet thump into the withers of an Appaloosa brood mare tied to the livery post. The horse reared and dragged the shop's porch into the street. Strawl rested his right wrist on his left and squeezed his pistol's trigger. The bullet took the man's testicles from his lingam. His pants leaked blood like he'd pissed himself red and both hands covered his plumbing like he might still mend. Strawl belted the man's pistol and removed a knife and razor from his pockets, then walked to the stockade, where he ate a late lunch and afterwards sent a pair of corporals to collect the man, who lived to stand trial and serve twenty-three years in Walla Walla breaking granite to gravel to pave farm roads.

One of the girls the man had victimized stopped by a week later with a jar of apricot jelly. "I slept three nights in a row now," she told him. He said nothing, but Emma cried, and that night she pulled him to her like a hungry she-wolf and didn't turn loose until the moon crossed half the sky. Strawl felt close to heroic.

Emma informed him she was pregnant six weeks later, and he felt he had arrived in a strange country that he'd set out for but never expected to reach. Someone invited him to join a church. Emma was included in a fashionable quilting circle and the commandant suggested Strawl spend more time at his desk. He put his savings into a plot of land across the river and Emma began sketching house plans.

His daughter arrived healthy and they named her Dorothy, though she soon became Dot. Emma clucked and hummed to the baby all hours, but to Strawl the child turned frustration. He found no edge to an infant he could grasp, and she became as foreign to him as the moon.

Narrative could not reside in such routines, though, despite the fact most of living did. Strawl's wife knew his twisting his hands and worrying the windows for what they were: foreshadows of an escape from her and his daughter for his work. They were no more interesting than a field to him. A description of a man and a litany of his crimes, though, made for a story that he, in those days of righteousness and ignorance, could end and rely upon as argument that the world contained patterns and logic and, if not justice, then at least retribution.

The habit, however, required being alone, and the isolation drove his mind into his skull like a mussel into a shell. In his isolation he concluded each person ground the gristle and meat of his days and events and emotions into a meal he could feed himself and not feel empty. A person's worth came down to his talents as a butcher; some cut and boned their hours and years without reckoning and wondered why they encountered blood at all, while others acknowledged themselves as the source of both the killing and the sausage.

He was mistaken of course.

When he was assigned what would eventually be called the Box Canyon Massacre, he had not yet surrendered his ignorance or his bliss.

Box Canyon was north, and north was a direction like Hell was a place. Property lines and boundaries between counties or countries remained rumors. No one knew where Up North started and where it left off, but they were certain that it held all that white people feared and the little left they didn't understand. Any disturbance that remained a mystery beyond a month the army relegated to that particular compass point, and when county and state police took up the army's duties, they found it just as handy. Strawl had apprehended men in the north country, which was filled with mountains and trees and rock you found any other direction; the only difference was a later spring and earlier fall and a few wolves and panthers. The Indians knew this, but the BIA cops still attributed crimes that they themselves were accessories to or those that they were too indolent to investigate to that bearing.

The Box Canyon Massacre took place neither in a Box Canyon, nor was it a massacre. A family of Methow with no reputation for trouble left the reservation to pick huckleberries in the Okanogan foothills. A cattle rancher named Doering accosted the spindly group as they crossed his rangeland. The Indians quickly agreed to divert along a county road. The rancher, though, being German, possessed a bit of the Hun, and he shot the old grandfather who spoke for them in the shoulder. Horses reared and riders fell and, in the melee, the rancher broke his neck against a tree stump, and his straw boss's thigh took a bullet—likely from Doering's rifle, facts would later determine. The Doering widow, however, insisted it was murder, and the superintendent of police summoned Strawl to clear it up.

The Methows knew enough of military justice to recognize their best chance lay in the high timber. They bolted for the deepest country in that portion of the state, north of Aeneas and beyond the Kettle River toward Curlew and the Canadian border. Severe as a steeple, all except the frost line remained canopied with pine and birch and aspen and tamarack, making tracking dark and humid, even midday. Add that to the carpet of ferns and brush that grew in such habitat and it was slow travel. It took Strawl six days to close on the group enough to hear them and another two days for a sighting. They labored across a trail that led around Chesaw Mountain, bearing their belongings on packboards and a travois. Above and below, sheer granite cliffs sparkled like fresh water.

Strawl worked himself ahead of them at the foot of a talus slide. When they were within his sight once more, he fired a warning shot into the rocks above as was his habit when he wanted to stop a suspect he knew was already afraid. The gun belched sulfur and a smoke wisp and the report echoed against the rock. A second of silence passed, one that, looking back, should have made him uneasy, as the women should have at least shouted in surprise. A rush of stones followed. One tumbled through the trees a hundred feet below, scalping saplings and bushes in its path. An old woman wailed. The family had bolted in their fear and collapsed a soft part in the trail, Strawl surmised. As he approached the little band, he saw checked shirts and wool blankets scattered among the rocks along with stockings and unmatched shoes. Ten feet beneath the trail, he discovered the father and his son, half buried with stones.

"How did this happen?" Strawl asked.

The old woman flexed her forefinger as if it were pulling a trigger.

"I didn't shoot them," Strawl said.

The old woman shook her head. She pointed to the rocks above.

"Goddamnit, that's not what I intended!" Strawl shouted at her.

The woman looked at him as if he were a tornado or a thunderbolt or a killing freeze.

Strawl removed the stones covering the bodies. The father's skull was a leaking gourd and his shirt spattered with his own grey brains. A boulder had blasted the boy's chest with such force it parted his ribs and sternum and tore a strap of flesh a foot wide and twice that long. Under, his heart and part of a lung sucked for air and floundered until they ceased their toil.

Suddenly, a girl cried out in Salish and scurried from the trees beneath them, half naked, dotted with welts. She raced through the stones and fell upon a pack, tearing at the rawhide straps.

Strawl had prepared for her to rise with a gun. But she held in her hand, instead, only a skinning knife. Relieved, he cried out in her language to put it away. She blinked at him, understanding the words but not how they could be from him. Then she drew the blade across her throat. Blood arced from an artery and the scarlet spray pocked her skin and the rocks beneath her. She dropped to one knee. The blood poured from her like she'd opened a spigot. By the time he reached the girl it was thick as syrup.

Strawl sat on a flat rock and watched her die. He was too weary to speak. He remained where he was through the day's heat and into the cool evening. He possessed no compass to direct him from this place and no heart to beat blood into his muscles and press him forward if he had.

He carried the bodies into a draw, where the dirt was softer. There he dug three graves. He let the old woman sing, then filled them. It was nightfall when he finished. He offered the woman passage back, making it clear she would ride his mount, but she was determined to stay and he could produce no convincing argument otherwise in her language or his own.

Rumor and the Box Canyon newspaper reports cemented Strawl's reputation with criminals and the general public alike, and, though those opinions originally diverged, time would eventually wind them into a braid.

Ten days later, Strawl cooked breakfast, as he did each morning he wasn't pursuing suspects. The skillet snapped with Polish sausage and he added three eggs. Emma puttered behind him, organizing canisters and setting the table. The child slept. Ordinarily it would have been a sweet moment for them, yet when he asked Emma for the peppermill and she dallied to finish lining the napkins with silverware in the proper order, Strawl clanked the pan with the metal spatula and said again, "The pepper." Emma crossed her eyes at him testily, and he lifted the cast iron skillet, sausage and all, and drove it into the side of her head. Sausages scattered across the floor and grease, blood, and cerebral fluid clotted her hair and streaked her face.

She staggered, blinked her eyes at him, then collapsed onto her side and seized. Strawl took her head in his hands and watched her pupils black the hazel from her eyes. The child, four years old, fussed in the other room, then found a toy and quieted, until a neighbor shielded her eyes and packed her away.

Emma breathed for two more days, then did not.

Strawl confessed to the commandant and insisted on a trial and prison. The commandant wrote Emma's death up as an accidental fall and ordered her buried without an investigation. He promoted Strawl to captain, but Strawl resigned his commission the next day and remained AWOL throughout the remainder of his stint, taking contracts on men from the state and later the feds.

He put Dot in his bed and she slept under his unfurled arm, but he did not rest. The third day, he farmed her out to the most pleasant neighbors and soon was absent entire seasons, just his bedroll and Isaac Stevens. He could tolerate only silence for weeks at a time, though it wasn't the kind conferred upon so many men a generation younger than he, who drew their stoic qualities from dime-store novels and the picture shows. Strawl's stillness was not a heroic choice; it contained nothing resembling assurance or calm; it was its opposite: a smoking, frozen bewilderment, or, when driven past tolerance, a mustering of powers so unhinged from will or belief, so purely sired in what was before him and his blindness to it, as to be monstrous.

It seemed to him he'd gotten living backwards, that the years were stealing wisdom from him rather than delivering it. He recognized what anyone in police work must: in even the most virtuous life, anarchy lay, like a live round, bolted and chambered, and at any moment the firing pin could fall upon the casing and thrust the spinning lead in any direction.

Those years, the only words he heard directed him toward his man or lied to steer him awry. Traveling aboard a breathing animal, he matched its breaths with his own, the only tastes in his mouth the remains of a meal from an army tin or something he'd killed an hour before, his mind emptied and filled with all of what surrounded him, and he sought from it nothing but its silence. Yet his ears denied him even this small favor, for no man is permitted that kind of quiet.

ONE

The Omak Stampede was only another rodeo in those days and Omak just another lumber town. The year of the Crash back east, the mill owner's wife, along with her women's group, pressed her husband and the cattle barons and city fathers to adopt ordinances closing the taverns at 9 PM, and the sheriff was ordered to accost Indians and drovers for vagrancy if they had less than ten dollars on their person.

In the late summer of 1932, two eateries shut their doors and all three taverns, including The Lucky Seven, which served as city hall. Ranch hands traded their callings for dam construction in the coulee and payday whorehouses. The alfalfa second cutting was left standing as no one remained to operate the swathers and balers, let alone buck and stack the bales. The city fathers

concluded the winter following that, though the women were fine
ladies and the five churches' bells tolled a refined melody Sunday
mornings, none were likely to turn their righteous efforts to peddling flour or fence wire or nails or hammers or supply the man-
power to drive them.

The mayor, who drew the black lot, traveled to Nespelem and
promised the tribe a rodeo with longhouses and stick games and
Wahlukes and a powwow if they would consider coming in for
a community fair. An Indian woman named Pence mentioned
moving the Keller downhill races to the Okanogan sand hill. Six
months later the inaugural Omak Stampede Rodeo and Suicide
Race crowded the town with enough broke drifters and cowhands
to tend the ranches through spring.

Strawl was a horseman of some repute and a lawman of more
renown, though much of it had been fostered in infamy. Nearly
sixty-three, he had been invited to join the melee. When he declined, the fair's committee offered to name him parade marshal
and, when he again begged off, the city council asked him to fire
the starter's pistol for the first night's race. He agreed to attend on
the condition that there be no public announcement. His reason
was hardly modesty. His reputation was such he would be noted
by any he encountered, whether he mounted a pulpit or rode in a
convertible automobile. It was also such that half the crowd possessed reason to kill or maim him, some beyond even grudges, so
he determined to make it as difficult as possible.

Near sunset, half an hour before the race found him with a
group of doddering septuagenarians, smoking beneath a tremen-
dous oak at the race's beginning point. Though ten years their
junior, his pigeon toes and inward nature folded his shoulders and
shrunk his stature, not unlike the others. In his law days, the pos-
ture made him appear earnest and simple, a guise he employed to
combat the lies of suspects or those close to them.

Old Belsbe coughed an awful hack. He had been ill for two months, though there was nothing other than the sniffles going about. It was likely the men around him had stood at his wedding and certain they would carry him to his rest, but without a son to take on his ground, his widow would be compelled to auction implements and all. Huddled in their snapped shirts and bolo ties, they calibrated Belsbe's days and their own assets and those of the others.

Ground was truth past title and deed, past the addition or subtraction or algebra or calculus they learned in school or the god they learned in church or the trite history lesson a politician might use to lever a vote, a truth so inarguable it required no faith at all. Ground simply was. Strawl's own five hundred acres he'd bequeathed early to his children—a mistake slowly bankrupting him, though dirt and its flora knew no difference.

The participants in the race had begun to separate themselves from the crowd. They swapped whiskey bottles and laudanum in a tight group, while below the rodeo announcer delivered scores on the last few bull riders and chided the clowns draped on the stock chutes. Laughter and talk and periodic applause wafted up the embankment along with the smell of the frybread in the concession cooker grease.

Strawl checked the blank rounds in the starter pistol, then examined the course, which opened with a leap onto a sixty-two-degree grade that hurtled a hundred yards into the Okanogan River. Once man and horse were across and up the bank, they labored a hundred-yard incline into the rodeo grounds.

As the events in the rodeo round wound up, the announcer directed the audience above and behind the north bleachers. Lights mounted to the poles that lined the course suddenly blinded the onlookers. Horses, turned blanched as the moon, reared and wheeled. They grunted as the last of the riders cinched their saddles. One began to nicker and fight its bridle. The other animals responded until the whole field was astir. Riders yipped, armed themselves with quirts, and tied leather pouches filled with gravel meant not to stir their mounts but beat passing riders.

The mayor nodded toward Strawl, who lifted his arm and squeezed off a shot. Animal and man leapt at the bluff and piled as one down a hill too steep to hold plant or seed. In a breath, half the riders covered the two hundred yards to the water. The rest remained in the fog of men and horseflesh tumbling toward the Okanogan River. Those still aboard their mounts floundered through water, swam a few yards, then lumbered into the rodeo grounds, which were once again filled with sound and light.

The other riders littered the grade and nearest bank, hobbled with broken ankles, dislocated shoulders, cracked ribs, and cracked skulls. Their horses drank at the water's edge as if suddenly and quietly pastured. Three tested broken legs, stunned that something as certain as a bone could be so quickly cast into doubt. Later, in the rendering yard, they'd be put down for pig feed.

The crowd quieted. The temperature was stifling, and Strawl's duties as honorary marshal were finished. He started a second cigarette and admired the orange ember cooking the paper. In the clear sky, he could discern the constellations. They were all that was left of his mother's teachings, stars in the sky that someone once thought made pictures.

Strawl searched for the Rotarians and his check. They were uneasy in his presence and wouldn't keep him long. In his police days, when their tone bent toward haughty, Strawl would soon follow with a stop at their businesses, one of their children in tow. He'd confide evidence of their daughters letting lowlifes into their pants or their sons stealing skin books for self-abuse. Not crimes, he'd say. Just unbecoming. Not what a community man would want out.

The old-timers drifted toward a stand that hawked cold drinks. One wiry man remained, slight of build. His hand smoothed his long mustache and his blue eyes blinked in the dusty air. He wore a grey county sheriff's cap.

"Well, I guess you know why I am here," the man said.

"You're going to offer me some work, Officer Dice. Or arrest me."

"Both possibilities have been discussed."

"And?"

"The former. We want to contract you."

"Why waste the time and the money? The reservation is across the river from you," Strawl told him.

Dice remained quiet.

"And it's not your jurisdiction."

"No, it's not."

"Let the tribal police hunt him."

Dice looked into his hands. "It's more complicated than that."

Strawl laughed. Dice was sheriff of the neighboring county but rarely absent from his office except to walk across the street to town hall and lunch with the mayor. At his insistence, his picture appeared in the weekly papers next to the crime blotter, though he had investigated nothing rougher than a trespassing since succeeding Strawl as sheriff. Even when Jasper Sampson was arrested by vigilantes for burning outbuildings, then lit his jail cell on fire and cooked himself; Dice let a federal man clean it up. It wasn't that he had no stomach for the work; he saw no profit in it. Hiram Evans meant to give up the State House the following winter. A well-meaning neighbor had approached Strawl himself about an appointment to the position, but Dice wasn't waiting for encouragement.

Strawl hollered at a passing boy.

"Bring me a cold drink," Strawl told him. "Be quick."

The boy pointed at himself. Strawl nodded.

"Yes sir." The boy turned for the drink stand.

"You didn't give him any money," Dice said.

"He'll be glad to treat."

Dice watched him go. The rodeo below was breaking up. Strawl listened to the audience's steps clatter the bleacher planks.

"You hunted George Taylor," Dice said. Taylor was a bank robber after the Great War. He stuck up two Spokane Old Nationals in one day. A week after, Strawl discovered his abandoned sedan at Leahy Junction. He borrowed a mount and followed him north as far as the Columbia, then east through the reservation. Finally, he killed Taylor through a line shack window while the man fried bacon at the woodstove.

Dice stuck his hands in his pocket.

"Put the State boys on the bastard," Strawl told him.

"They been," he said.

"They got to have a lead or two then."

"Not a sniff."

Dice paused and lit a cigarette, then offered one to Strawl, who declined, as he was still working on his own.

"Heard you got you some help," Dice said. "Hired man?"

Strawl shook his head. "Dot's husband."

"I thought he was educated?"

"Can't eat a sheepskin."

"Them shysters back east wrung us good, haven't they?"

"My meals are still arriving regularly enough," Strawl said.

Dice drew from his cigarette. His pinched face pinked in the glow.

"That dam coming along?" Strawl asked him.

"Now that Roosevelt has shook Congress by the collar."

Roosevelt was a liar, but good at it. He'd requested money for a high dam in Grand Coulee, like Hoover's, but Congress had only funded enough for a low structure. Roosevelt ordered the engineers to go ahead with the original proposition anyway, then told

Congress to either finish the chore or explain five million dollars for a dam that stopped no water.

"Workers thick as ants on an anthill is what I've heard."

Dice nodded.

"Registered voters all, I presume."

"Soon as they cash their checks."

Strawl leaned into the oak. The striped bark pressed lines into the skin on his arm.

"Would you consent to examine a body?" Dice asked him.

"Where?"

"Truax's meat locker."

"Family don't mind you keeping him in a cooler?"

"Storing him isn't nearly as cruel as killing him was."

Strawl had planned to cross the river to Nespelem in the next week to sharpen saw blades at Clara's Mill anyway. Visiting the butcher wouldn't put him out. "I'll look at the body," Strawl said.

The boy returned. He handed Strawl the paper cup and Strawl took it and drank.

Dice tossed the child a quarter and the boy looked at it. "You want some, too?" the boy inquired.

Dice shook his head. The boy vanished.

"You got a kind streak for children?" Strawl asked him.

"I'm happy to treat, too," Dice said.

Strawl blew a cloud of cigarette smoke his direction and watched him blink.

"We've got three counties that meet within fifteen miles of one another," Dice told him.

"Well, you all put your heads together, then."

"There's money in it is what I'm saying. Might be handy."

Strawl turned the cup in his hands.

"How's that wife of yours?" Strawl asked him.

"She's nothing to this affair."

"Affair," Strawl said. "A word that fills both barrels, doesn't it?" He turned the paper cup until he found its seam, then slid his thumbnail under the corner and began unraveling the coating. "How long have you been copping?" Strawl asked.

"Including time as your deputy, ten or twelve years, I guess."

"In all that time, you ever once know anyone to twist my tail?"

"No," Dice said.

"Or herd me like a woman."

Dice shook his head.

He spat on the ground and smiled hard. "You think when I left that badge in the drawer, I left what was behind it in there, too?"

Dice extinguished his cigarette into the heel of his boot, looked at Strawl one more time. Dice had shoved too hard, coaxed too little, and Strawl waited to see if he possessed sense enough to retreat. And when he turned and walked back to his car without a word, Strawl gave him credit at least for that. He watched the patrol car pull away, a boxy Chevy magazine ads claimed delivered eighty miles an hour on a straightaway.

TWO

The following morning, Strawl arrived at Thacker Ferry just after dawn. He drove his trap wagon, a flatbed pickup. On the undercarriage, iron forks extended beyond the grill. They braced a hundred-pound bar on which Strawl had bolted a cable winch. He replaced it with a snow blade November to March.

Young Bill Thacker, Wild Goose Bill's son, picked at his breakfast on board the boat. A late riser and a drinker all his waking hours, Young Bill was worthy of remark, but he was never a shade to Wild Goose Bill, who had established the ferry for the army, which drove the Salish tribes through the Big Bend country to the Okanogans and back again until the federals settled on the reservation boundaries. Bill turned a profit, but he gambled and drank with anyone so inclined, which kept him from gathering the riches he might have. He'd earned his nickname for a drunken Thanksgiving hunting expedition that ended in him poaching a farmer's pet goose, then claiming he'd seen it walking toward Canada to migrate. He was killed finally in a gun battle over a woman he had determined to take as his wife, though the idea wasn't fondly received by her or the boy she coaxed into being her champion. The woman was shot twice through the arm by Bill, and the boy and he swapped enough lead to put them both beyond a doctor's care.

Young Bill wiped his chin and rose from the table, then pulled on his oily duster and wide-brimmed hat, beaten from crossings under weather less fair than this morning's. He unchained the gate and Strawl drove the truck carefully over the metal ramp onto the barge. Bill tugged at a come-along pulley and the heavy ramp rose, shifting the ferry forward in the water. He untethered the ropes from the poles driven into the river bottom on both sides and the current pushed them toward the downstream pilings, but Young Bill gunned the diesel engine and squared the ferry with the cable strung to the opposite bank. He tugged a rope starter and another, smaller motor caught, which turned a pulley. When he locked the crank into place, the spool took the cable slack with a lurch, then commenced to drag them across. Two seagulls rose at the sound, but a family of ducks simply separated and let the ferry pass.

At the opposite landing Bill opened his ledger and added the trip to Strawl's tab, then eased the ramp onto the sandy bank. The road rose out of the canyon, carrying Strawl again into the Okanogan country. Judged by beauty, it was far superior to Strawl's own ground. The slopes to the water were grassed with bluebunch and broadleafs like balsamroot and wolfweed. Alder and cottonwood dotted the bluffs and draws. He could smell the pollen in the air, and the pine and fir pitch cutting it, reminding him of Indian medicine.

Above, in the flat meadows, a few farmhouses appeared, some painted and others abandoned, their sideboards buckled against from weather and neglect. Falling boughs had punctured a roof or two. The Indians had surrendered the dwellings after a final year of not harvesting enough to make expenses, or simply deciding to labor upon a farm they never desired, so they could pay bills for which they felt no responsibility, wasn't a bargain they were willing to enter into another year.

Other homes were scattered across the clearings beyond: poorer shacks and lean-tos, often walled with rusting tin or the hoods and hacksawed roofs of cars. Spoiling elk and deer carcasses hung from a few cottonwoods and locusts shading them. Two men spooned in a garden like dozing lovers. Grease darkened their checked shirts. One's head rose, and he shaded his eyes with his hand to watch Strawl pass. A barnstormer dipped a wing over the road, then climbed until his plane was a speck in the sky too distant for anyone but Strawl to hear.

The town was four streets with passable houses surrounded by another scattering of shanties extended this way and that, as shapeless as spit on a flat rock. White men, like the butcher, Truax, owned the hardware and the livery and taverns and grocery. Most had appeared on the reservation with nothing but what they could borrow or pilfer. Eventually, they took women, but on the reservation the institution of marriage was unhinged. The merchants refused to acknowledge tribal ties and the churches wouldn't wed heathens until they could read catechism. Ceremonies, licenses, preachers, and justices of the peace were tiresome formalities, shed for flesh and convenience. Courtship consisted of a man putting whiskey into his beloved until she either surrendered to or slept through his passions. Women changed hands like tractor parts, and often a pretty girl was more or less shanghaied into a man's house if her family didn't have the means or guns to argue. The

Catholic priest scolded his parish weekly over such indiscretions, but Sunday morning generally presented its own difficulties to the local population, and the few in the pews already abided by the Church's teachings.

Strawl waited while eight mottled cattle passed, steered with a willow switch by an overalled Indian boy. A half-pint yellow dog followed, tongue lolling in his mouth.

Inside the butcher shop, Truax cranked a pan full of hog scraps into sausage. He glanced at the ring of a bell attached to the knob and squinted, then blinked upon seeing Strawl. His hand moved into a drawer that held his pistol and a pry bar. Strawl had never had any legal truck with the man, but he'd left one of his brothers walleyed in a bar scrape. On the other hand, he'd once extricated Truax's youngest son from a larceny charge when the boy fell in drunk with a gang of no-accounts who robbed a mule and wagon from the priest's stable.

"Still keep the equalizers in the same place, I see," Strawl said.

Truax smiled. "Didn't recognize you, sheriff."

"Or maybe you did." Strawl laughed. He nodded at the meat and the grinder. "Better pepper it up good."

"I could grind horse hooves and beaver teeth with a little pepper, they'd eat it."

Truax washed his hands at the sink, then dried them on an apron hanging from the pegs. Over six feet and barrel-chested as a bull, he cut an imposing figure, despite the spindly legs supporting it.

"I was wondering how many before you'd show up."

"I'm not on the payroll," Strawl said.

Truax tapped the ashes from his corncob pipe and reloaded it. "I got some advice for who is." He puffed. "Catch the bastard or put a lot of barbwire between here and that dam."

"If the barbwire was manageable, we'd see it," Strawl said.

Truax nodded. "We might as well be Canada, now. Less they hear the better."

"Except if you got a killer amongst you."

"Shit," Truax said. "I don't know a worthwhile man over fifty who hasn't killed someone."

"You included," Strawl said.

Ten years ago, Truax's niece had garnered the attention of an older man who'd turned up with a broken skull soon after. Strawl had caught the gossip that Truax had offered the suitor honor or life, and the poor fellow had thought it only poker and bet his chips. But Strawl was fond of Truax and not compelled either way about the victim. He'd relinquished the case to the tribe's police, who, when no one squawked and Truax made good on a beer keg he'd offered as a donation, declared the death a suicide.

Truax's was not unlike most reservation crimes. Here, justice was less a blindfolded woman weighing a man's virtues against his sin than a poor shot occasionally firing a round into a fistfight to remind those brawling she could, if inclined.

"I told you I ain't working," Strawl said.

Truax spit into his sink basin and ran some water into it. "If it was plain murder, Dice'd stick to shaming us Sundays with the Methodists and invest in cemetery plots. It's not killings they got objections concerning. It's killings with style."

"This fellow have a flair for it?"

"Thinks they put corpses in museums, far as I can tell. See for yourself."

Truax opened the metal door to the locker. The room went white in degrees as he set a match to each hanging lantern. Blood from the slaughter room adjacent had worked under the wall. The cold room smelled like meat and metal. The light irritated dust motes into the air. A steer lowed in the corral across the street. Otherwise, it was silent aside from the ticking of the flames in each lamp.

The body lay on three two-by-eights that rested across a pair of metal carts. It was facedown and blue, not the tinge a white person turns, but the darker hue of Indian flesh in rigor mortis. The sternum had been sawed, not broken with an axe. The killer had then painstakingly sliced tracks for the ribs with what looked to be a razor and pulled them through the back flesh until they resembled nothing more than angels' wings. The scapula blades added to the effect, though no angel or its carcass was likely to be found with skin strips and the attached fat dangling into its empty body cavity like guttered candlewax or strands of colored sinew dangling from its wounds like frayed denim.

"Who found him?" Strawl asked.

"Mills. Tied his horse to the hardware rail and there he was."

"He around?"

Truax shook his head. "Skidding logs with the Canucks."

Strawl's cigarette was out. He patted his shirt, then pulled a leather bag from the pocket and a paper loose from its package. He sprinkled tobacco into the folded papers and twisted the smoke, found his matches, then set both on the metal counter.

"There a gut pile?"

Truax shook his head.

"Any blood at all?"

"Just where the body laid."

"How come you know all this?"

"Like everyone else, I came running when Mills hollered."

Strawl nodded.

"Why at the hardware?"

"I don't know. Seems to me him laid out like a turkey on a platter's more to the point."

Strawl examined the bottoms of the man's feet and his ankles and wrists. He'd not been bound or beaten. An incision above each ankle had emptied his femoral arteries. Dried blood knotted each shut. Another slit had opened the jugular and drained the skull. Each cut was clean and stitched with needle and thread. The victim had been hit in the temple with something sharp enough to tear his cheek to the bone and blunt enough to drive a dime-sized skull fragment into the only organ the killer didn't relieve him of. A spade point was Strawl's best guess. It wasn't an unusual weapon on the reservation; guns made noise and knives required close range and probably some acquaintance. A shovel would at least provide the advantage of surprise.

The blow may not have killed the man. Skull fractures rarely took lives and those that did took time. The brain might have hemorrhaged, but bleeders generally took a number of blows. The man's eyeballs were shot with blood as if he may have been strangled, but Strawl found no ligature marks.

He examined the body for an hour, then stepped from the locker back into the store. Truax continued to grind meat, the wheel squeaking each turn. Strawl considered the delicate cuts on the body: no skips, no slashes demonstrating doubt, nor hacks from anger, just work done well. The rest was lunacy or a sense of humor. The incisions were where the genius was. His killer had shucked himself of emotion for practicality.

"Hell of a mess," Truax said, behind him again.

Strawl nodded.

"Not your problem, though."

"Nope."

"Who'll take care of it, then?"

"No one."

The skin between Truax's eyebrows pressed together. He rubbed his forehead, folding his thumb and index finger over each temple. "Ain't nothing you can do?"

"Tribe's got its police. Maybe they'll get lucky. That's what it'll take."

"Redskins hunting a redskin," Truax said.

"What makes you so sure it's an Indian committed this crime?" Strawl asked him.

"They're the only ones with time to do it up fancy," Truax told him. "Rest of us got jobs."

Outside, the day's light blinded him, then a clanking engine and the whir of wings and flaps split the air. Strawl lifted his face toward the plane and spread his arms, thinking he might himself take flight if he took a notion, but he remained anchored to the earth, looking crucified by the plane's hurtling shadow.

Strawl's hearing was as constant as a hound on the scent and sounds to him were clear and separate as smells. He could recognize a footstep two miles off, and likely what made it, and he could do it in a rainstorm. Moreover, his head divided sounds until he had them situated as well as if he could see what was making them. But such a clatter melted his talent into a chaos of noise and undid his nerves.

He reclined upon a shaded bleacher seat until the plane lopped over them, then suspended above the hard dirt like it required a moment to become simple and machine again, then rattled to the ground, stopping near the tiny horse track's grandstand, which held twenty Indians and rounders, as well as Strawl, ready to replace one gawker with another.

The girl finishing her ride reported she recognized nothing from above, not her house, not the town. The river turned a drizzle.

"A wonder the birds don't get lost," Strawl said.

Their faces turned toward him. The crowd parted as he approached the airplane and its pilot, whom he showed his badge.

"Police business," Strawl said. It was a big place with few people and lots of cover if you could manage on your own, and many could. He had decided a look from above might be of use.

He labored over the wing and into the plane's cockpit. The pilot handed Strawl a set of smeared goggles that Strawl declined. The plane's pistons began to whir. The connecting rods ticked and the cam whined and the carburetor twisted air and gasoline to accept the plug's spark. The tires bounced on the hard dirt while the wings bucked the wind and gravity until the plane shuddered and with a tug, began to rise. They climbed slowly over the rooftops, checkerboard spaces between the dusty streets like the tartan wool in the mackinaw the pilot wore. The trees were upended cones and then circles that contained differing degrees of green.

The pilot banked over the town and the fairgrounds and the upturned faces. Strawl pointed him south and west. The pilot nodded and they traced the river's channel. Cataracts boiled in its black current. Later, in a smooth pool near Washington Flats, a flock of mudhens rose as one. They could have been a school of fish misplaced, like Strawl himself flying, but he likened them more to a symphony climbing the opening notes of the overture, the instruments synchronized in a way both natural and not.

The dam was before them, then, a scar marking the river's course, but a minor wound from this high, an injury one survives, one that adds to one's courage, or the myth of that courage.

Strawl directed the pilot to the other side, and they floated over the farm country like no bird ever had, low enough for Strawl to make out the shadow of the plane as it passed over the country. Almota was where he had imagined it, and the spring and canyon that bore his own name, and the Big Hole and each road that ribboned the farms as delicate as lace stitching. Cattle gazed up, stupefied. A deer herd, with the same unison as the birds before, broke from feeding in the wheat, leaping rock and sagebrush and barbwire all with the same grace, until the plane passed and they halted, continuing to stare at the sound of the engine.

They passed Osborne Corner and Pearl and the Troutman Ranch Road and Tag Ear Lake and Badger Spring and the Chalk Hills and then banked over old Fort Okanogan back toward the reservation, and Strawl could identify each tree and each bay in the river and each bend and ripple, and then Kartar Town and the lighter blue and green of Omak Lake's south fingers and the silver granite cliffs lining its north edge, flashing in the light.

Strawl motioned up with his thumb and the plane climbed until the whole of the country looked under a haze and he imagined he could see the earth's curve at the horizon. Beyond Bonaparte Mountain, they wheeled like a circling hawk across the unpeopled north, broken with rock and choked with brush and trees of all varieties native to this country. The only sound was the engine and the wind passing, and it had ceased to be a sound at all. Strawl realized his own talent was useless in this sky. Listening married a mind to this moment, then the next, and a sky was too large for an audible second to tick away and another to replace it. If he had ears, silence was all a god heard. Prayers and hymns and oaths and curses turned as repetitive and indistinct as raindrops against the river's surface. Salmon bucked two hundred miles of current, soundless as the dead, and trees rose a hundred feet without uttering a noise aside from what the wind pressed from their needles. Even time thinned to nearly nothing in the face of plain country. A thousand years and Babylon was only a word.

And Strawl possessed what was below like a god possessed his world; nothing in it occurred that he didn't recognize, and that was why the killings troubled him. A dab of wood smoke smeared the horizon. Strawl could smell it, too insignificant to be a wildfire and too grey to be part of the haze. He motioned the pilot that direction and they traveled ten minutes, though the smoke got no closer. He spied a boy driving a pair of roped goats up a path. The boy's face stared up, the rest of him just a dark, squat shape under it. He motioned for the pilot to press on, but he shook his head. Strawl showed him his badge once more, but the pilot pointed to the fuel gauge and Strawl nodded, disappointed to return to the prison of gravity and his spinning planet.

| THREE |

When Dice offered him the case files, Strawl understood his rationale for keeping the details out of the paper.

The first victim a Nez Perce man, about thirty. He'd been struck in the temple, as well, and though the body exhibited no wounds Strawl could associate with struggle, even a dying man would likely fight being castrated. The killer had cut the scrotum, emptied its contents, and later cured and tanned the empty sack, stuffed it with tobacco, and tacked it to the postmaster's house.

The second and third men were about the same age as the first. One had been discovered dangling from a rope in an elm in what passed for a park in Nespelem. Gutted throat to anus, he'd been cleaned like a fish, thoroughly enough that in the photograph sunlight seeped through the skin covering his ribs and spine. The murderer had broken free a bottom rib and skewered the man's liver upon it.

The third had been skinned. The hide—scalp and all—appeared one Sunday morning draped over the wooden billboard welcoming travelers to the Colville Indian Reservation.

The fourth, like the first, had been gouged through the privates. The photograph was just a bloody blur. However, a week later, a hairy band constituted from the man's pubic hair was discovered in the five-and-dime store in Mason City, ornamenting a ladies' hat.

Indians had a reputation for disrespecting bodies. Thirty years ago on the Plains, the Lakota and their like would take hair if they were too angry to think straight, and the bands in the Southwest were disagreeable in all kinds of matters regarding women and children. A thousand miles lay between them and this country, though, and, despite what Phil Sheridan and the missionaries thought, every Indian didn't need killed or saved to get along with white people. The closest the locals had had to a burr was Chief Bird, who was more politician than warrior and only rankled the government because he neglected to remain in one place long enough for the government to build a fence around them. In conflict, the local tribes were more inclined toward embarrassing an enemy than killing him. When they were amongst themselves, they would heist another band's horses and return them a week later painted blue or sneak into a sleeping camp and piss in the kettles outside a rival's tent. The worst Strawl had heard them do was, in the very old wars, capture a man and lop off his pointer finger, leaving him awkward drawing a bow, but alive.

Dice perched on the edge of his desk across from Strawl. Strawl tipped the folder at him. "How were they killed?"

"All with something blunt," Dice said.

"Same thing?" he asked.

Dice shrugged. "We weren't careful enough early on, I admit. Tribe caught the first one. A case of beer and a basket of chicken is their idea of police work. They didn't even know he'd been nutted until the sack showed up. Called us and Ferry County, but it was too late to figure much."

Strawl nodded.

"We got started earlier on the others, but as you can see, it did little good."

Strawl closed his eyes. The town had electricity and the glow from the bare bulb above turned the papers a blinding white. He squinted at the photographs one more time and rubbed his temple. Dice's office sat in one corner of the building and the jail cells in another. Strawl could hear a prisoner rise and take his breakfast, a bowl of mush that a passing deputy had delivered him. The man had been charged with assault, Dice had said, a crime generally ignored amongst laborers. Fighting was common between Okies and drifters and the Bureau didn't want to lose laborers. This prisoner, however, had belted an engineer. Dice would hold the man for a fortnight, when the judge would return and rule time served.

Dice put a plug from his tobacco into his pipe and lit it. Sweet-smelling smoke filled the room. "What's your price?" he asked.

Strawl tipped back in his chair. He'd heard talk that some men's souls were built to hunt others, just like some were constructed for crime, each minute adding a brick until they were complete enough to rob or shoot their way to the state prison in Monroe. It wasn't the blood Strawl missed or the idea he'd righted a person wronged. There was quiet on the ranch, but nothing approaching the serene. Between planting and cutting and tending the storage silos and the parts he either needed or was going to, his head was as full of noise as the radio. Most days he'd have liked to shoot a gun in the middle of it, just to enjoy the report in his ears.

"What do you think is behind most murders?" Strawl asked Dice.

"Bad tempers," Dice answered.

"Or bad cards," Strawl said.

"Or plain stupidity," Dice said. "Remember that Trust in Coulee City?"

"Yep." A would-be Dillinger had managed to get off with a suitcase full of scratch, but shotgunned a man on a constitutional that he worried might witness against him. The poor fellow was blind. The murderer hanged just a few months ago.

"What's under this one?" Strawl asked.

Dice studied him. "I haven't encountered a crime akin to this one," he said. He tapped on his pipe, then set it in the pie tin that served as an ashtray.

"Children," Strawl said. "Of all that might have undone me, who'd have thought it would be children." He chuckled. "Half the ranch. That's what they lost. That's what I'll take for salary."

Dice shook his head. "Too much." He puffed again, then spoke through gritted teeth clamping the pipe stem.

"I heard once that the best cop has to be half a criminal himself," he said.

"I hear the same of politicians," Strawl replied.

Dice laughed. A deputy walked past the office, returning with the prisoner's empty bowl.

Strawl rose.

"I can get you half."

Strawl leveled his gaze at the man. "Half just gets me half broke."

"You don't think much of the public, do you?"

"Not any more than I have to." Strawl took his bowler in his hand and rose. "Once more, good luck to you," he said.

"Should I arrest you and save a lot of trouble?" Dice asked him.

Strawl stopped for a moment, as if considering an answer, then continued out the door.

In town, he visited the grocery, filling Dot's list, adding a sack of candy for each of the girls and a lollipop as big as his head for the infant, to preclude him choking on it.

Like many of the ranchers, he concluded his visit at the lip of the coulee, gazing skeptically at the labor on the dam. It was the first Roosevelt president who had augured the future for them.

> Their barbarous, picturesque, and curiously fascinating sur-roundings mark a primitive stage of existence . . . and will pass away before the onward march of our people. The doctrine seems merciless, and so it is; but it is just and rational for all that . . . let [these men] share the fate of the . . . hunters and trappers who have lived on the game that the settlement of the country has ex-terminated, and let him . . . perish from the earth he cumbers.

This didn't keep T.R. from admiring the old-timers' character; indeed, he often imitated it, without a hint of irony or cynicism. Hunting as ritual and battling the indigenous people replenished the stagnant and cooling Caucasian blood with the truth violence recalled in the human soul, he declared. But by then Wyatt Earp was refereeing boxing matches and advising Hollywood movie directors.

If T.R. served as the West's prophet, his nephew, Franklin, was the prophecy manifested. Deified by the papers and itinerants searching out work (his framed glossy hung with the family pic-tures on the wall of every store and eatery within a hundred miles), he promised a concrete wonder to curtail the downriver floods and irrigate the state's desert center. The result, the papers trumpeted, would be a structure with enough concrete to build a sidewalk to the moon.

The river below marked the county line, and Mason City in the coulee's bottom straddled it. On the Grant County side was an army of tents that housed bevy after bevy of destitute Midwesterners ecstatic for their spot under the canvas and three squares. The project compensated them little past meals, but it seemed a fortune next to nothing. What they did hang on to they squandered in Grand Coulee's B-Street, which kept only one grocery store but three cafés-cum-cathouses Fridays and Saturdays.

Strawl rubbed his closed eyes. The town of Grand Coulee teetered on top of a flat bluff above the rock high enough to keep clear of the Columbia when it leaped its banks with the spring Chinooks. Churches pocked the town, and Sunday mornings, while the unfortunates camped below mustered breakfast over open fires and finished what whiskey remained and, after, concocted Heat cocktails of gasoline and milk and honey, the blessed and the faithful lined pews and lifted hymnals and sang—the women in earsplitting pitches and the good men in their bolo ties vocalizing little recognizable as music beyond the lyrics. They killed with alcohol and church bells, emptying a man's pockets Fridays and Saturdays and declaring it his own doing on the Sabbath. But that, Strawl knew, was only half of the truth. The other half was that drinking wasn't what made most men drunks; they were just pouring liquor into a hole in themselves, and it drained nearly as quick as it filled, which made it necessary to drink steadily or stay empty, which they refused to do.

The project had succeeded in shearing one portion of the coulee by dangling men in ropes and harnesses a hundred feet below the cliff's edge, where they set dynamite charges. After detonation, another crew with jackhammers would drop to beat the rock smooth. Below, others cleared the debris, raising the five-ton pieces of granite and limestone with long-necked cranes that deposited them into belly dumpers with wheels on both sides of their carrying compartments. The rigs bore the slag to banks to riprap the riverbank. It was silver and glinted like tin in the sunlight.

In the river itself, the contractors had fashioned a simple cofferdam with enormous timbers that resembled giant railroad ties. The contraption diverted a third of the current from the far bank. Inside the deep box, the men had scooped the river bottom until they encountered bedrock, then hammered it flat and drove steel rods into the stone to anchor the concrete pours. Lead pipes filled with river water crosshatched the space to cool the cement, a process that would otherwise take ninety years.

Strawl smoked and studied the laborers who scurried across the site like locusts from the Bible. Nothing below looked as it once did. Not even cities changed the country they occupied so. The killer had sprung from this hurried rush toward who knows what, and Strawl had killed or arrested anyone who might have been a brake on the wheel. He was liable as Roosevelt for what went on below.

He leaned back in the car's seat until the sun neared the west wall of the coulee and the whistle ended the shift below him. He heard the gravel turn and Dice's squad car ease to a stop. "Your place wasn't worth as much as I imagined," Dice said.

A mandible muscle under Strawl's jaw fluttered and cramped. He rubbed at it. "Took you all day to find an assessment on the place?"

"My clerk is a slacker."

"Good help is hard to find," Strawl said.

"Grant County agreed to split your fee, so I guess you're going to get paid, if you're still game."

To those county commissioners and city fathers who'd conjured this concrete idol, Strawl was as aboriginal as the natives he had penned up and more savage—a mean dog with nothing to guard, until, of course, another mean dog showed up.

Dice handed him a contract to sign. "You'll want to make it legal," he said.

When Strawl didn't move, Dice looked at him. "Second thoughts?"

Strawl shrugged. He could smell the sickening aroma of Dice's tobacco and wondered at what ugliness it hid.

"I don't have a pen," he said finally.

| **FOUR** |

The dawn sky was slipping to purple, and the cumulus clouds that floated over the horizon had tinged with the rose color Homer favored no matter what occurred beneath it.

When he had surrendered the road and copping for the ranch, Dot was eleven years old and a budding intellect, thanks to her school and foster parents. She had insisted on educating Strawl, reading aloud the *Iliad* and *Odyssey*. Afterwards, she explained the results of a battle or one god lining up against another. The characters made speeches and argued in their own camps more often than they swung a blade against their enemies, and as soon as Strawl took a rooting interest in one, he'd prove himself a fool. He did, however, favor the portion when Hektor returned to the walled city from the wars. His wife was holding their son, and when he reached for the boy—Strawl didn't recall his name—the child cried out and shrank into his mother's blouse. For the moment, it appeared there was nothing left for Hektor but to finish breaking their hearts and die. Then he realized the child's wide eyes were on the metal helmet and the horsehair plume rising from it. He removed the headpiece and the boy leaped to him, and for a moment they were happy.

Strawl heard the rap on his door. He twisted the knob of the kitchen table lamp and watched the flame climb the flue. At the stove, he lifted the black pot and poured a second cup of coffee, then set it across from his own. Mornings, the fluid greasing his joints congealed to something feeling like paste and the grit in it often halted an elbow or a knee altogether. He missed moving smoothly. Aside from his hearing, the only other physical skill he'd owned was foot-speed and he bemoaned the loss. An exaggerated instep left him somewhat pigeon-toed, fodder for mockery in country still negotiated primarily by horses and their bowlegged riders, until he reached twelve-and-a-half and the same muscles that set his knees akimbo suddenly turned him as fast as a colt. At local fairs, he whipped boys and men in both the straight sprints and on the horse track's mile oval, then bested them again in the stick relays, running alone. The sole contest he lost pitted him against a bicycle, and only after a mile and a half of wagers and shouting did he collapse and lose consciousness, waking to the barker passing horse dope under his nose.

Even the preacher had cited his mettle in a sermon, though the man had turned on him when he refused to race any longer, citing him as an example of misplaced vanity or pure pigheadedness. Strawl had no idea where one began and the other left off, and, though confused at the new huffiness directed toward him, possessed neither the feelings to suss it out nor the words to pose his bewilderment into a question, and even if he had managed one, he wouldn't have known where to submit it.

It wasn't much later that his father, with two in the cradle and three others younger than Strawl, had walked him to the end of the block. "Old Abraham had to sacrifice his firstborn, and I guess I do, as well," he said.

"God kept Abraham from it," Strawl corrected him. "He sent an angel."

His father had stared into the white sky and nodded. "Yes, but Abraham was blessed by God and founder of a nation. I don't see one coming for you and me."

He stopped walking and put twelve silver dollars into Strawl's hand and closed his stubby fingers over it. "Good luck, son," he said.

The house's door rattled again.

"Come on in," Strawl said.

The draft from the open door snuffled the lantern's flame. Strawl watched his shadow and Dot's on the wall behind the table. She was a square, squat woman, plain as Strawl himself and heir to few of her mother's charms, except astride a horse. There, she transformed into something out of Mallory. Her tiny blue eyes shone like a fury's, and her aquiline nose looked Roman and noble. She sat a horse as if just another one of its graceful parts and rode like an Indian on fire. No man could get more from an animal, Strawl included.

She crossed the room and sat. Her two girls followed, jabbering. They towed the boy, only eight months, in a wagon behind them. They delivered him eggs and sausage on a plate, still warm. Dot removed her scarf and set it in her lap and smoothed a strand of hair that had freed itself during the walk to his house. He watched her lift a bread loaf from her satchel and slice off the end with a kitchen knife. She buttered it and put a piece in the boy's mouth.

"See anyone interesting at your rodeo?"

Strawl chewed a piece of sausage and swallowed. He sipped his coffee.

"Sons of bitches and bastards and a few liars," he said. "I fit in nicely."

"Well, I hope you told them some whoppers."

"Said I was rich." He lifted his plate and shoveled half an egg into his mouth. She stared at him until he swallowed. Strawl mopped the yolk with his bread.

"Esther killed a rabbit," she said.

"Violet jealous?"

"No, though she wanted to shoot at a barn cat to keep square."

"Arlen let her?"

"He told her they were pets."

"Didn't stop her, did it?"

Dot shook her head. "She informed him Sara Rinker had pet rabbits. 'This was a wild rabbit,' Arlen told her, and Violet said, 'All animals are wild till they get tamed.' Then Esther argued the wild rabbits weren't even the same breed as the pet ones, and Violet answered talking about breeding is naughty, and then I put on the potatoes to boil and left it for Arlen to sort out."

"Lawyers, those two," Strawl told her. He finished his coffee. "Officer Dice spent a minute with me."

"Did he mention Elijah?"

"Subject was never broached," Strawl told her. "Them Cache Creek slayings are making noise. He wants some help on it."

"Did he ask you to cease and desist?"

"What?"

"Did he think you were behind them?"

"Do you?"

Dot glanced up from the boy, who was polishing off his bread and butter. Her eyes blinked and the time it took for her to answer offended him as much as the answer. "I've worried over it," Dot said. "You have a reputation, and I don't know you well enough to convince myself otherwise."

"I haven't killed any of them."

"In your experience, isn't that what anyone would say, guilty or not?"

Strawl laughed. "I admire your skepticism."

"I don't," Dot said.

"Well, the powers that be have decided I am on the side of right. At least for now."

"Do they think Elijah is responsible?"

"I told you. They didn't mention your brother."

"You didn't tell me what you think."

"Your brother is a mystery. But I doubt he's a murderer, especially to this degree. Just a thief."

Dot shook her head. "He didn't steal what you gave him."

"I didn't give him half my place to squander."

"I guess you should have put that in the mortgage agreement."

"Maybe so," Strawl said.

"What made Dice think you were back in business?" she asked.

"Heard I was broke."

Dot refilled their cups. "There's no shame in that," she said. Her voice was deep as whiskey and filled with gravel. She sounded like a scold, even when it wasn't her intent. Strawl had always admired her more than enjoyed her. She told the truth no matter the price. It made her noble as a knight, but stern company.

"Wasn't me that split the place," she told him.

When Dot married, she and Arlen took up a house in Chelan where the county employed Arlen to engineer and construct a small dam above the falls. Strawl and Dot wrote only occasional letters to one another, until he was put ass over teakettle by a misbehaving sorrel. The doctor set and cast both his legs and took the horse as payment. Arlen and Dot and the girls returned to tend the animals and plant the fall crop. Arlen left equipment magazines on the kitchen table Sundays when Dot fixed a weekly family dinner large enough for him to cobble the rest into a week of suppers. The literature announced new fertilizers, experiments in weed control, and rod weeders with rotating tines. Arlen had talked Strawl into a fresno to level the uneven knobs Strawl left fallow and spoke longingly of a gas-powered combine that would harvest the place in a few days. He underlined the most compelling points in pen. Strawl had no argument against them except money, which was the only one he required.

Dot's family stayed on, and two years after, Ida—Strawl's second wife and Elijah's mother—drowned alone fishing the river during runoff, as was her wont. Her body never surfaced and it was likely a hundred miles away, twisting in the current toward the ocean. Her passing, of course, stunned the children, and Strawl tried to close the wound by splitting the ranch between them.

He had expected to work Elijah into accountability with his piece and to anchor Dot and Arlen with the other. Neither turned out as he had predicted.

Arlen was smarter than Strawl, but he had little faith in himself. Like a poker player short-stacked, he took outrageous gambles on poor odds and failed to play even money. He had tried to outsmart dirt and moody weather with the wheat hybrid seed fostered in the Palouse, but that country received a half inch of rain Junes and had dirt black enough to grow any seed. The rocky coulee was less generous and by the time Arlen had discovered so, he'd augured his half into a hole so deep, Strawl took it back until he could return it to profit.

After six months of lukewarm effort, Elijah peddled his portion of the ranch to Hemmer, a disagreeable neighbor, which was half of Strawl's worth. The boy lacked the will to finish, and not just his chores. Checkers, he saw moves others missed, but often grew bored and lost or just stopped playing entirely. Strawl had seen him build rolls in a poker game just to drop them betting hands he had no business playing. The boy was not even his blood, but Strawl, too, in his youth, had been hoppy as bacon on the griddle and possessed the attention of a horsefly. He had spoiled the boy. When he and his mother had agreed to live with him, Dot was starting at the high school in town, so, after his chores, the boy was permitted to fish and hunt and wander on his own.

He wondered if Dot knew Elijah's whereabouts. It was unlike her not to share an opinion, but she felt he was her brother, and confidences between siblings were the hardest to pierce. They felt an owing past even husband and wife, whom the joining of loins could undo as easily as it intertwined them. Even parents surrendered their children out of guilt over raising criminals. Childhood was a lonely business, however, and navigating that solitude together seemed to fix siblings fast. Though Dot had been miffed that Elijah received an equal share, when Elijah sold his portion she had been satisfied at Strawl's comeuppance. For her, it was a wash between the two in a strange way. If Dot had apprehended Elijah's whereabouts, she hadn't surrendered them, and likely would not now that he had dealt away his inheritance, and turning her would require Strawl to stoke a wrath in her he doubted he could smother when the issue concluded.

"I was just wanting a little rest," Strawl said.

Dot looked down at her coffee. "I guess he did, too."

"Maybe I should have beat him," Strawl said.

"What he did with his inheritance is your folly and his. You never asked my advice."

"You still mad?" he asked her.

"You were fair." She paused and blinked her eyes. "I was only mad a little and I haven't been for a long while. We've got my wages yet and our half of the ranch. We'll look after you."

"I don't intend to spend my dotage on your porch, useless as a stick, thank you."

"I wouldn't be surprised if you planned it to come to this."

"Wish I was that smart," Strawl said.

Dot sighed and began to collect the children. "A piece of ground is no substitute for love, Father," she said.

"It was never meant to be." Strawl shook his head. "It's got a deed and a price and you can measure it. It's all I had to give. Land."

"I'd swap for more of you and less of it," Dot said.

"No, you would swap for more of someone else standing in my shoes and less of me in them," Strawl told her.

Dot said nothing.

"I don't blame you," Strawl said. "I'd likely trade myself if I thought I'd get a taker. Might be we could swap me for an old brood mare."

Dot chuckled. "Maybe if it only had three legs."

"We'd still be a leg ahead, wouldn't we?" Strawl replied. He walked across the room and examined a worn bookcase Elijah had commandeered as his own many years before.

"I see he got rid of the donkey skull, at least." Elijah had ridden thirty miles to pay a horse doctor for it.

"Except the jaw. He bronzed it with the teeth."

Strawl shook his head.

"Samson," Dot said. "That's how he fought the Philistines."

"Guns are too simple for a true believer, I guess."

"Apparently," Dot said.

"What did he think he needed the money for? Whenever he asked didn't we come up with it?"

"Maybe he needed something he couldn't ask for."

"What would that be?"

"Heaven on Earth. The second coming. Who knows?"

Strawl stood and walked them to the door. Across the pasture and beyond the barn, Arlen had constructed their house. He'd put it at the bottom of Squaw Creek, despite Strawl cautioning him against it, because that's where the elms Dot favored for shade grew. The bottom flooded every thaw, as Strawl had foreseen, and the house might've been ruined if Arlen hadn't carted in river gravel and laid it under the foundation and then run metal culverts both ways. Springs, the floor trembled with the water passing, and the front yard was often a swamp navigable only by a row of two-by-eights he'd cut for the purpose, but not a plank of the house got damp.

"I see Stick is at the ready," Dot observed. The horse was reined to the porch post.

"He's not as hardy as The Governor," Strawl said. "But he'll suffice."

"You could take the truck," she told him.

"Horses don't break down and they don't need gas."

"He's crazy, I hear, your killer," Dot said. "He might want to cut you to pieces and serve you on a bun at the café."

"If the man wanted me, I'd be shepherd's pie or on the coat rack at the livery," Strawl said.

"You agree he's insane."

"It's crazy people that make the most sense."

Dot put her hands on her hips and stared at him.

"Cutting others hither and yon. That's reasonable?"

"Man's got an ordered mind. It's just a sideways order."

"If you're trying to comfort me, you're making a mighty wide circle," Dot said.

Strawl grinned at her. "You don't need comforting. I'm just crossing the river, like I have a hundred times before."

She hugged him anyway, and the rigid awkwardness of their arms and chests turned obvious to both of them.

"Manage to stay miserable, will you?" Dot said. "A person gets your age doesn't want to enjoy anything much. You're old, and pleasure makes the time go too fast."

"True enough," Strawl said. He watched Dot and her family cross the hard dirt path to the barn, then bend through the corral railings.

"You tell your husband he buys that combine he's eyeing, he better just keep going down the road. I won't have it on my place."

Dot turned. "It's not your place, it's mine. Legal as the courthouse."

Strawl pawed a hand her direction. "Doesn't matter. Long as I'm living, it's Strawl Canyon and Strawl Road, and even after. It's my place."

| FIVE |

tick remained in passable shape herding the fifty head of cattle pastured behind the house, but the horse's temperament was the primary reason Strawl favored him. Bullheaded enough to bust a rider's head with a low branch if bored, Stick had some personality, which made him decent company. Moreover, any animal keen enough to catch his rider napping was, in fresh country, all ears, nose, and eyes. As far as covering ground, Stick was not built for eight furlongs but for twenty miles. He could pick his way through a trail like a burglar crossing a squeaky roof, and lope uphill or down from morning till black night if you didn't draw rein.

Strawl scabbarded his .06 and scattergun and holstered a pistol onto his belt. Venison jerky and a tin box of flour, a sackful of coffee and the pot, plus his worn mess kit filled one saddlebag, along with an oilskin satchel full of stick matches, string, a thread and needle, and a burlap sack holding a load of apples to keep Stick through any grassless stretch. Shells for the weapons rattled in the other, and he had a wallet full of expense money the three counties had delivered him in separate envelopes.

Strawl climbed aboard and screwed his black felt Anthony Eden, a piece of haberdashery he'd purchased on pure whim, onto his head. The horse soon broke into a trot and Strawl's eyes teared in the wind. He pulled his hat lower and felt guilty, experiencing such satisfaction leaving his family and heading toward as black a man as he'd encountered.

He boarded the ferry once more, Young Bill puzzled by the horse. On the other side, the sun on the prairie warmed him. A line of mallards sliced the sky, and Strawl watched a red hawk atop a fencepost study a mouse in the grass below. The wind eased as he traveled the road paralleling the river, and he unbuttoned his canvas jacket.

He turned Stick north and east following a game path that paralleled the river opposite Thacker's Ferry, then headed west past the Hopkins Ferry Road, then the mouth of Hopkins Canyon, then the ferry that served it. He passed Clara's gristmill once more, where he had sharpened his saws. The building and machinery had been moved lock, stock, and barrel on a flatboat from the Okanogan country; it was the talk of the county ten years ago.

The road joined the main highway toward town. Cars passed, their horns pressing Stick into the shoulder ditch. Strawl worried he'd spook, but the horse's mind was on his work. In Nespelem, he stopped at the grocery and bought a handful of day-old radishes and fed them to the horse for his troubles.

Strawl took Wack-Wack Road east until he met Joe Bird Creek, which he followed atop the Nespelem Divide until it dwindled to its source. On the other side, he crossed into Ferry County and the San Poil country. He picked through another trail at Peter Dan Creek and meandered with it until the channel and path veered north into a thicket he wasn't inclined to navigate. Instead, he directed Stick to circle through a meadow, where he let the horse eat his fill of bunchgrass and wild oats. Midday, they met Manila Creek. The tribe or county had graded the highway and laid new gravel. Under Johnson Ridge, Strawl rested Stick for half an hour in the shade, then steered north. There was no track, but the country was open. Desert scrub and sagebrush, it was an oven in August, but the dirt was soft and good for horseback travel.

He found a thin path and veered with it west for a flat a smaller stream drained. The morning had become hot and close, like it was preparing for a summer squall. Wildflowers smelled thick and almost sickening in their sweetness. Strawl wove through a thicket of fir and tamarack, then halted at the edge of a rectangular clearing framed by higher, basalt-strewn ground thick with pine and fir and birch that thinned the light and enough low brush to make approach a noisy proposition.

The center was a depression still lush with groundwater. The grassy meadow feathered in the wind, somewhere between green and the yellow it would remain through late summer and autumn. Grasshoppers clicked and floated in the air, good bait for fishing the nearby streams.

Strawl kept in the trees and circled the clearing. On the other side was a well-constructed tongue-and-groove log structure with a tin chimney, and a cord of seasoned wood was stacked against the north wall for insulation. A hundred feet to the south was a wind-driven pump over a well. Beyond that was the peak of the outhouse, built in another hollow to keep the sewage from draining toward the well.

The primary resident was the last living San Poil medicine man. His Salish name meant Raven Flying, but the closest English translation was Marvin.

Strawl avoided the plastic window and banged on the door with his pistol butt.

The door cracked and a watery eye took him in. "No bad men here," the voice said.

"Marvin, I'm not put off that easy."

No one answered.

"I just want to ask you about something."

"Marvin does not know," Marvin said.

"What colored feather is on a starling?"

"Marvin does not know."

"Now you're lying, Marvin. Lying to the law is a serious matter."

"What is a starling?"

"It's a bird, Marvin. That explains the feathers."

"Brown."

"Brown?"

"Brown feathers."

"Jesus." Strawl sighed.

Marvin was quiet behind the door.

"What about these killings?" Strawl asked.

"I do not know of any killings."

"You don't have any idea what I'm speaking of?"

"I do not know about none. No killings. No whiskey for Marvin."

"Marvin, I'm not accusing you." Strawl waited for a minute. He heard whispering. Marvin had a wife, but Strawl couldn't make out if it was her voice or another's. He had seen Marvin's buckskin tied behind the house but no other, and there was no way for a car to get in or out, though that didn't rule out walking.

"That Inez, Marvin?"

"Inez is not here," Marvin answered.

"Then who in hell is it?"

"Marvin."

"That's another lie, Marvin. You lie about Inez, I can put her in the jail."

"Inez is not here," Marvin repeated.

"I'm trying to be civil, Marvin. I know you haven't done nothing wrong; quit behaving like you have. I come here to chew the fat a little is all."

"You are not the law now. They told me."

"Who's they? Those there behind the door with you?"

"Indians. Indians told me."

"Indians behind the door."

"Me behind the door."

Strawl leaned against the wall. He heard stirring inside and looked up at the blue sky. Nostalgia had pressed Strawl to begin here. Back when concerns over an uprising still existed, Strawl had arrested Marvin several times for practicing his medicine. Each time the man was respectful and compliant, but as soon as the judge set him free, he would be back to his powders and singing. Once Strawl hauled him in naked to embarrass him into obedience, but the man simply served his sentence, then left the jail in his prison clothes. Strawl blackened both his eyes and broke his nose before Marvin left the shadow of the jailhouse and then broke two of his ribs, but Marvin did nothing but cover up, then, after the beating, hobble to his home and sing a prayer. Strawl refused to pursue him afterward.

Now Marvin was harmless and too remote to hear anything beyond gossip. At best, Strawl might have been able to rule out the San Poil country, no more. He wanted to see how the years had treated the man, truth be told.

"I can't let you put me off, Marvin. Word would get out I turned soft. Open the door so I can say we talked, then I'll let you alone."

Marvin said nothing. Strawl gave him two minutes by the watch, then drove his shoulder into the worn wood. The chain gave and Strawl pushed into the house. Two doe-eyed grandchildren gazed up at him, then bolted under the table.

"Now, I haven't done a thing to you to imply I'd hurt babies," Strawl said.

Marvin remained quiet. His long hair was tied behind his neck with a scrap of rein and his face was wrinkled but not bloated and gone to seed like so many in town. Inez, his tiny, grey-haired wife, huddled behind him.

"What do you know about these killings?"

Marvin looked down at his shoes. In his early police days, Strawl had equated such gestures with guilt, but he had come to realize that eyeing another man was an insult to the Salish tribes.

"They're bad," he said.

"They are that. An Indian doing them?"

Marvin said nothing.

"I'm not asking for fact. What's your opinion on the matter?" Strawl paused, hunting a word. "Gamble. Would you gamble the killer's Indian?"

"A crazy Indian, maybe."

"A white man. Could he do this? A crazy white man?"

Marvin shook his head.

"Why not, Marvin?"

"No money for him."

Strawl nodded.

"Thank you, Marvin," he said. He looked at the children under the table, all eyes and shaggy black hair, then Inez, cowering behind Marvin. "I apologize for interrupting your day."

Outside was a wooden cable wheel from the dam that locals had scrounged for picnic tables. Strawl untied Stick's saddlebags and left half a sack of flour for Inez upon the wheel and his deck of cards for the grandchildren, along with a handful of sugar cubes meant to treat Stick.

It took him through the heat of the afternoon to retrace his path to the Nespelem road, then ride the six miles to the Indian Agency. Tenement flats that once barracked soldiers lined a grassy field on which they had drilled. Half the place had filled with orphans or widowed or abandoned mothers with their litters. Attached at the far end was a medical center, where a nurse distributed tablets of all sorts to those she could convince to swallow them.

The police department was next to the pole plant, an effort to turn the tribe into capitalists. The best they had managed was to hire white lumbermen to deliver raw logs and employ an Indian crew to pluck them from the rigs with the loader and another to operate the saws. It wasn't that the Indians were lazy so much as they were mystified by the project. The young men would work for a day or a week, then wander off, not seeing how their lives differed at the end of the day from the start.

Their cops, though, were a different matter. They hired the members who had assimilated enough to appreciate a weekly check, and, more significantly, those who saw the job as permission to behave in any manner they saw fit or profitable as long as they kept the Nespelem merchants and the citizens up- and downriver content. As on most reservations, the Bureau of Indian Affairs had undercut the chiefs and medicine men by recruiting the shiftless and mixed breeds to police the reservation. Uniforms turned them into whores and their sidearms into whores with knives.

Strawl tied Stick to the porch rail and opened the station door. The air was heavy with cigarette smoke. Two cops looked up from desks and paperwork and three more from a cribbage board, all in sweat-stained grey uniforms.

The stockiest one, Otis, was in charge, and he recognized Strawl immediately. He set down a deck of cards and stood. "You got no jurisdiction here."

"That's a big word, jurisdiction," Strawl told him.

Otis's oily skin shone in the light of the bare bulb. He'd greased his hair and pulled it to one side. The part was well tended. Strawl unfolded the order granting him police powers over three counties. "Says here different."

Otis walked to him, then looked at the paper. "You got a badge?" Strawl drew it from his pocket.

"This paper don't say we have to help you," Otis told him.

"Then I can't count on your generosity in this matter?"

"No," Otis said.

Strawl nodded. They'd begun to laugh before he closed the door.

Outside, Strawl searched until he discovered a nightstick in one of the squad cars. He lifted it from the seat and put it in his belt. The keys were in the ignition. The same was true for two others.

A mile back, he'd seen a bull pastured and fenced, separated to keep him from brawling with the steers headed to slaughter. When Strawl looped a rope over his big head, the bull was tame enough to be led. Strawl tethered him to Stick and towed him back to the agency. On his way, he found a nettles bush. He gloved his hands and uprooted it, then lay it across the saddle horn, careful to keep the leaves from Stick's hide and his own.

At the police building, he halted the bull, then quietly started two squad cars and backed them against the two side doors leading out. He wound the nettles around the nightstick handle, then secured them with a strap from his saddlebag and led the bull to the only door he'd left unblocked. Strawl worried the bull would collapse the floor, but it held him. He opened the door then led the bull inside, then lifted the animal's tail and thrust the stick and nettles up his ass, then kicked his testicles. The animal screamed and tried to turn, but Strawl fired two pistol shots into the ceiling, which was enough to dissuade him. He splintered two desks in front of him, instead, then bellowed and started toward a pair of the card players, who hurried for the door. Opening it, they discovered their predicament and turned back. The bull broke one's knee and hooked another in the thigh and dragged him into a desk before he could get loose.

Otis stood in the center of the room. The animal stormed toward him, then dropped his head and swept Otis's legs from under him. For a moment he was aboard the bull crosswise. His hands and boots reached for the floor and his head bounced against the bull's thick chest. Then the bull spun and Otis flew from his back into a cabinet. The bull rushed and Otis grunted as he fell under its hooves. Cartilage popped and smacked like chicken gristle. The bull raked Otis's belly with a horn and a bloody line spattered his police shirt. The bull snorted and slobbered over him, then glanced at the two remaining cops, who, upon seeing it do so, hammered a screened window with a chair and leapt out through the glass and wire.

Strawl tried to herd the bull toward the open door, but when he proved too agitated, he shot him twice through the skull. He found the case file in the first cabinet he checked and slipped the contents into a valise left on the desk. He made his way past the men groaning and the bull, careful to avoid the warm blood that pooled on the floor.

There had been some cause to call down hell upon the BIA, but the bull had certainly been a response past reason. He'd supposed the animal would simply chase the cops into a corner so he could collect what he desired, but, once loose, the animal had proven too much like Strawl himself, a bullet from a barrel, hurtling where someone else had aimed it, no more conscious of the damage than lead itself.

His anger renewed, however, when he perused the first page of the file. Stewing, he retraced his morning ride. Arriving at

Marvin's cabin, he did not circle the meadow and outbuildings. One shoulder thrust and the door splintered. The old couple ate bread and sausages at their table. The cards lay near the children's dishes. Strawl lifted Inez by her hair. She yipped and he hauled her over the table, ruining the meal. He shook her until she was upright and showed Marvin his pistol. He nodded toward the kitchen counter. "I see your glasses full of his powders," Strawl shouted. "He practicing medicine again?"

"I am only showing the children," Marvin said.

"That all you showed, Marvin?"

Marvin was silent.

Strawl twisted the old woman by her hair. "I came with questions this morning hoping to be friends. Since, I've been educated. In fact, I'm about as smart as a goddamn lawyer now, and lawyers never ask a question they don't already know the answer to. Now, did someone come for medicine or not?"

"My medicine is old like me."

"Age is not my concern, yours or your powders'." The children had clambered under the table. Strawl released his grasp on the old woman's hair.

"How about it?"

"A man was here."

"For medicine?"

Marvin nodded.

"What did he look like?"

"It did not work."

"The medicine?"

"He wanted ghost medicine. To hide and come back. It did not work."

"He didn't go away."

"No, he remained."

"He local, then?"

Marvin stood, frozen as his Moon of Breaking Trees. His eyes were round like the children's.

"Goddamnit, you'll tell me what he looks like." Strawl dragged Inez out the door. This was not what he had intended, but he was unable to figure a way back from it.

"You seen him," Strawl shouted. Marvin shook his head. Inez said nothing, just breathed and quivered under his hand. Marvin began to hum, then Strawl made out words. "Hell Mary, bless the fruit in the mother. Bless the fruit."

"No Mary here to pray to, Marvin," Strawl said. "Just me. And I'm an angry kind of god."

"He stole from the powder while we went to fish at the river," Marvin said.

"When?"

"Months," Marvin said. "Not a year. Not half. Months."

Strawl twisted Inez's hair.

"He likes the old ways," Marvin said. "But he does not know them."

"What makes you say so?"

"He took from the cornstarch and flour, too."

"You know him, don't you?"

Marvin shrugged.

"You and him are plotting an uprising, are you?"

"No," Marvin said. "No uprising."

"Convince me."

"There is no one to fight that we can whip."

"Except each other."

Marvin nodded.

"That what he's up to? A war? Which tribe is he?"

Marvin shrugged. "His own," he said.

"He's a killer, Marvin. He'll kill these babies and you and Inez because you talked to me. He'll know and he'll cook your grandchildren like Christmas hams. Your only chance to take care of them is to give me what you know, damnit."

"I know nothing more."

"You'd let these babies be cooked?"

"I know nothing. I can lie but you will return like this time, so I am telling the truth."

Strawl cursed Marvin, then set the pistol against the old woman's ear, barrel up, and fired. She cried out. Blood from her eardrum spattered his wrist. Marvin knelt to receive his wife as she collapsed to the ground. Strawl looked at the two of them beneath him.

"You tell me if you hear of him or I'll do her other ear."

| **SIX** |

Strawl rode for Keller Butte to pitch his first camp. The promontory rose out of the long hump that had divided the Nespelem and San Poil tribes for a thousand years, and the rivers bearing the same names even longer. He settled on a ridge that allowed him a view of Marvin's meadow and shack and any avenue leading to it. Behind him was an enormous granite slab that promised to keep him in the shadows in all but the morning hours and kept the lights of the town of Keller a glow beyond another, lower bluff. Underneath a bull pine he found needles in a hollow softened by the deer that had bedded upon it and hatcheted the lowest pine boughs to construct a pallet and laid out his roll and waited for darkness.

A hundred feet below and two hundred yards away, Marvin's grandchildren chased each other, then beat a pan with sticks. The clanks climbed the cliff to him. Marvin's wife lay fetal on a blanket beneath the makeshift table, catching the last of the failing sun. Marvin joined her with a water bucket. He soaked a cloth and bathed her face carefully, then shushed the children in Salish. They quit their noise and curled like pups around her. Strawl could no more imagine their lives together than he could if studying a pile of ants.

Strawl swept clear a hollow, then gathered pine straw into a mound. He added sticks from a downed birch and lit them and nursed the fire until it burned warm, but low enough to escape notice. He poured water from his canteen into the frying pan and made bread to go with his jerked beef.

His adult life, he had watched people turning the same day over and living it again for years at a time, and he thought himself happy it was not his lot. Isolation, Strawl once liked to think, was his penchant, but recently he realized choice had little to do with it. Elijah had made his opinion clear on both farming and Strawl as soon his mother passed and he had a check to cash. Ida, herself, had enjoyed her time alone to his company. And Dot would prefer a book. The grandchildren were hesitant to accept the treats he delivered from town. When he wrestled them, and left an opening to squeeze his nose or box his ears, they used it instead to escape to their mother or father. He was past poor company, it was clear, and the day's events would go far in maintaining that. Twenty years ago, he mistook such a reputation for respect, but as he tracked or camped alone, he discovered even if it played that way in town, it was something else within his own mind. He bent and scooped a handful of earth from the ground. Nothing was more just than dirt. Returning to it squared them all. Two wives, two flower bouquets, two preachers, at least in Ida's case a two-day drunk, all for dirt becoming dirt once more.

Dawn, Strawl woke bent and aching and remained bleary-eyed through his pot of coffee. In the morning light, he sifted through the papers in the valise once more. He sorted interview notes typed on yellow legal paper from the third murder on, likely because Dice and Higgenbothem in Wenatchee had begun to press the tribe's investigation. No person had witnessed a single crime, nor did they recall the victims beyond brief description or any argument of any kind preceding the murders.

The crimes were marked by intricate patterns and the victims by the lack of one, except no struggle. If rancor were at the root, in his man's chest was a heart that beat pure winter and a mind as patient as a buzzard's. Most crimes were born in simple want argued into need. To criminals, the law was an argument, stealing persuasion, and killing misplaced zealotry. It made them self-righteous; a part of them desired capture, saw it as a reckoning. Strawl understood them, even agreed occasionally—most acts a man could perpetrate had been unlawful at one time and legal others. A criminal's birth might be just catastrophic scheduling, the same as a victim's.

The BIA hadn't been completely derelict. Aside from interviewing Marvin, they had spoken with the leaders they could muster from the confederated tribes that resided on the reservation, but many had ceased being Methow, Lakes, Nespelem or Chelan or Palus or Wenatchi. The Nez Perce bore enough physical features that they could be discerned from the other bands and the Bird people kept to themselves, but the others had jumbled into as mixed a soup as the whites disposing them. None knew anything of the crimes, or if so, weren't inclined to share it with the Bureau's police.

Under the crime report was a list of suspects. Rutherford B. Hayes, a six-foot-six Hoosier, had cut a wide enough swath in his thirties to acquire the moniker Pale Horse. Strawl had arrested him three times, the last ending in an eighteen-month stint in Monroe. The time didn't tame him as much as it put him off people. He constructed a commendable house from logs and sod, stealing the shake shingles from the mill yard, only because he didn't have tools to fashion his own. Strawl refused to investigate the matter, citing deficient evidence, though the cedar on Hayes's roof was inarguable.

A thornier issue was the land upon which he built it. The house clung to the lee side of Granite Mountain. At issue was whether Hayes owned the land or not. Actually, there was not much dispute: he had neither deed nor bill of sale. The land was claimed by both the tribe and the forest service, however, and Strawl refused to serve notice without a plaintiff with legal standing. The house stayed. Hayes raised a brood of mastiffs that he managed to keep as owly as himself. Their bays carried miles, and it was rumored they had killed the last brown bear in the country.

Hayes had the capacity to murder, Strawl thought, but the kind of attention these murders drew contradicted the man's last twenty years. Still, without contradictions, no crime would go unsolved.

Next on the list, Jacob Chin, Taker of Sisters, was still in his prime, however. A Chinese Indian, Chin had first earned what money he came by honestly, as a cowhand. But he broke horses in such a brutal manner that they often ended up crippled or so skittish they bolted at the wind shifting. He was better suited for felony. He ran what passed for a black market on the reservation, peddling opium to the coolies and dried coca leaves a cousin mailed to him from Venezuela. He owned two clapboard houses in Inchelium and turned out a spindly Indian woman from each at three bucks a throw. He hadn't built up a head of steam until well after Strawl retired, so all he knew of the man was word of mouth. His crimes intrigued Strawl less than his predisposition toward

Indians. At fourteen, he'd beaten his San Poil uncle to death with a shovel. His record showed eight assaults, all on Indians, and in country where fisticuffs rarely were reported, that was a bevy.

The notes listed one of the Bird boys, as well; they ran in herds and Strawl could not sort this one's name from the others he knew.

The Bird boys, an assortment of uncles, nephews, cousins, and brothers, stuck together and weren't inclined toward town. They raised their share of hell when they visited, and gossip linked them to the death of a Tar Evans, a trapper who didn't know when to stop drinking or talking, but Evans had been running headfirst and downhill toward his grave for twenty years. His death was less a crime than the product of his nature and he'd been felled by a blow to the head with a two-by-four, which made intent unlikely; the man for whom Strawl was searching had more intent than a porcupine had quills.

Strawl himself was part of their list. They'd attributed no opportunity, no weapon, and no motive, other than history and meanness. He was not surprised. It was the reason they'd refused to share the files. If the accusation were true, he'd be tipped off, and if it were false, they would have to contend with his spite. Anyone hunting grizzly faced the fact that the bear was hunting him, too, and was better suited for the endeavor, and so it was with Strawl and their police, and he was armed to boot. The BIA wanted to keep downwind.

There were no interview notes, and Strawl surmised the Indian boys had been disinclined to put their theories to the principals and risk blows or worse, their recent encounter with Strawl proved their caution not unreasonable.

Strawl turned the morning fire's dying coals, then dumped the coffee over them. The day was still cool, but yesterday's closeness had given way to a high pressure and the blue above. He closed his eyes, resting them from the smoke. He recalled with envy the vision his first Indian scouts possessed. They perceived brown and green hues no one other than Indians parsed out, as well as shapes likely to move and the shapes they would move through.

Strawl had enlisted with the army at sixteen. There, he drank whiskey and fought and habituated the Denver guardhouse. What enraged Strawl was everything: all a little and no thing more than another. His belly was constantly filling. The result was one day he'd take what a man shouldn't and an hour past not endure people acting human, then the fisticuffs would commence and cease, and another man would lie in a bleeding heap, and suddenly his living was up to Strawl. Some looked pleading, some looked trustful, and others just waited for him to make up his mind.

Finally, the commandant ordered he either discharge or transfer. He chose the latter and rode mail patrols in Astoria, Oregon, for nine months, fishing and digging clams on the Pacific beach with each pass he earned.

He found the ocean a comfort. The hushing of the constant surf and the wind teeming with the unperfumed odors of all that was alive or dying underneath the swells steadied his heart and quelled his mind like knowledge of the everlasting for believers. From the ocean he drew the only spiritual guidance he could lay claim to, though he could not name it. A stomach ulcer converted him to teetotaler, and, in truth, he was happy for the excuse. Drinking he did not do partway, and drunkenness smothered his memory and conscious self like a blanket over a fire. But his body continued, fanned by winds he did not comprehend though the wreckage and black eyes following were evidence enough of their strength.

Twice during his stint he was accosted by bandits and neither time surrendered his bundle. In the second instance, he pistol-whipped a gold panner and turned him over to the authorities bent in half across his saddle. When the Tonasket colonel needed a policeman, he was promoted sergeant and reassigned.

Strawl watched the dew burn off in the warming morning. He lit a cigarette. The stovepipe over Marvin's cabin issued smoke as either he or his wife kindled the stove for breakfast.

Stick was fresh and Strawl mounted and pointed him north. He rode game trails, letting the horse sort out a direction when they gave way to meadows or bald hills where the deer and elk didn't require paths. Morning's cool graduated into a warmth approaching pleasant, then a heat that put Stick into a lather until Strawl drew rein. The sun disappeared more hastily than it had risen; sunset stretched over the country for a rusty and luminous breath, then darkness stretched back, and with it the sweat ringing his hat and spattering his shirt chilled him. Strawl camped on a ridge beyond Granite Mountain's sightlines and, he hoped, past the scent capacity of mastiff hounds.

The next morning, he rose and circled the mountain until he found an opposite ridge that permitted him a view of Rutherford Hayes's cabin door while keeping him upwind of the dogs. He tied Stick to a tamarack trunk and rested in the tree's thin shade until Hayes opened the door. Strawl put two bullets in the porch's lowest step. The man broke for the house. He emerged with a rifle as thick as a fencepost.

"Put the dogs away, Root," Strawl shouted.

The man's head turned, hunting Strawl's direction.

"If I wanted you shot, you'd be bleeding already. No harm will come to you."

"Who are you?" the man shouted.

"Russell Strawl."

"Sheriff Strawl?"

"I got no paper on you and no inclination to take you past the front porch. I want a word is all."

"Come on, then," Hayes shouted. The man whistled and five dogs each weighing nearly as much as Strawl himself broke the brush from four separate directions. Strawl allowed five minutes more for any stragglers, then hiked from his ridge to the knob that held Hayes's cabin.

Hayes sat on the porch with a broken pocketknife, digging Strawl's bullets from the step. The first lay next to him, a spattering of lead.

Strawl was surprised to see his face shaved clean as if a barber had serviced him and his now grey hair cut in a style that, if not fashionable, was at least a manageable length. His face held the furrows anyone's would after twenty years' passing. Only in his eyes were things amiss; the blue irises were too light, emptied of one thing and filled with another. He squinted at Strawl as if Strawl were a long way off.

"How are you, Rutherford?" Strawl asked.

"I am," Hayes told him. "I am that name."

"Rutherford," Strawl said. "I know you from a long time back. You don't need to introduce yourself."

"You let me keep here," Hayes said. "They wanted to run me off." The man's voice started soft then turned loud, then quieted again, like he was trying to come to the right volume to speak to another.

Strawl said, "I put you in the penitentiary, too, you recall."

Hayes looked at him for a long time, too long, though Strawl garnered nothing rude about his stare.

"I needed jailing," he said.

The dogs scratched and whimpered at the door.

"You care if I let them go?"

"I got no quarrel if they don't try and tree me."

Hayes laughed. "They'll just figure you're one of them or one of me. They don't know much difference." He gave Strawl a handful of jerked deer. When they boiled out the door, Strawl offered each the treat; they did not scrap or fuss or wolf their food like town dogs; in fact, they waited turns until each had a stick of meat. Strawl patted one and the others whimpered so he gave them each their share of affection.

"Seems like good company," Strawl said.

"Safe," Hayes said.

"Safer than people, you mean," Strawl asked him.

It took him ten minutes to collect his thoughts, but Strawl figured he had no need for haste in this place and plenty of time for philosophy.

"Other way around," Hayes said. "They ain't people. It makes them safe from me."

"People can be trying," Strawl agreed.

Hayes shook his head. "I need things plain. It makes me dangerous company." He scratched at a mole under his chin. "Dogs. They're easier to figure, and don't squawk if you guess wrong." Hayes nodded at Stick, who nosed the pine needles under the tree where he was tied. "I miss horses," he said. "I had a ken for them as a boy."

"Come in handy up here," Strawl said. "I'm surprised you didn't add one to your menagerie."

Hayes lifted the spent bullet with his fingers. Strawl watched them shift it in the palm opposite. It balanced there a moment until he shut his fingers over it. "Too easy to travel down there. I might get to liking it," he said. "Or not liking it. Neither one I'm suited to."

Strawl sat and tugged his makings from his trouser pocket. He turned a cigarette and offered it to Hayes, then built another for himself. Hayes drew softly, he coughed, then drew again and let the smoke out, then after considering a full minute, threw the remains of it into the dirt and let it smolder.

Strawl pulled from his own smoke and exhaled. "It's a tedious vice," Strawl said. "You're better off."

Hayes said nothing for an hour. The silence was at first clumsy, then plain, then pleasant. Strawl gazed over the hard-packed yard, watching the dogs wrestle, then hunt the afternoon shade. They dozed happily and he envied them. A few early geese creased the blue sky. Their clatter sounded like laughter, and Strawl watched them for twenty minutes trying to predict in which pothole they might light. He rose and crossed the dirt to Stick, pumped water into a bucket and let the horse drink, then withdrew some coffee and chicory from one saddlebag and his coffeepot from the other. Hayes smiled and took the collection inside his house and lit a Franklin stove and perked the coffee, then returned with two cups filled, a sprig of mint that grew naturally behind the house in each.

"You kill anyone recently?" Strawl asked him.

Hayes took another quarter of an hour to answer. Strawl would have expected some grand prevarication from another man, but Hayes's only intent seemed thoroughness.

"It would have been recent," Strawl told him. "And with a lot of folderol. And more than one."

Hayes looked into his hands. "My mind doesn't work like it used to," he said. "It ain't worn-out like old folks'. It just quit working in words somewhere back. What I recall seems inclined toward more weather and smells and what I remember of them I can't say because the words quit me when the weather does." He looked like a child. He was crying. Not sobbing, just tears welling below his eyes and sliding down his cheeks. "I don't remember people for a long time," he said. "I admit I have had killing in me. Maybe it sneaked back without me knowing."

Strawl finished his cigarette.

"I suppose you'll need me for a trial."

Strawl shook his head. "You didn't do it."

"I don't understand."

"These dead men. Someone would have to thought about it," Strawl told him. "It's more meanness than a man could muster on accident."

Strawl smacked his lips and two of the dogs approached. Strawl patted their heads and listened to them pant in the heat. Another brought him a stick and left it at Strawl's feet. He tossed it and watched all three dogs climb over one another like rough children. One returned the stick and Strawl threw it again, and they all went forth once more, though this time they became so occupied with wrestling one another, the stick slipped their minds.

"That's it, then?" Hayes asked.

"That's it," Strawl said. "Sorry to have intruded. I know people have to be an inconvenience to you." He pumped some water into a cupped hand and washed his face. "Rutherford, you seen anything unusual, at all, come this way?"

Hayes said, "Fire north."

"Forests burning all over this summer."

Hayes said, "Wood smoke, tamarack likely. Nothing pitchy as planks or studs and stringers or hardy as fruit trees. Stove likely or camp."

"How far north?"

Hayes sniffed. "Not to Canada," he said. "But not much short of it."

"Can you catch a whiff now?"

Hayes nodded.

"How come you didn't locate me by scent?"

"You weren't on fire."

Strawl smoked again. Alone, a man's senses honed upon open country like a blade across a whetstone, Strawl knew; his own were sharpened in a similar fashion. He had known those who claimed to navigate by scent, but none whose talents went beyond what seeing and hearing could deliver to an ordinary man paying attention.

Hayes had no reason to lie or gloat, though. Strawl did not doubt his sincerity. But cross a blade against a stone long enough, even the best steel passed its edge and you possessed nothing but a bone handle and filings.

"You seen anything else worth mention?" Strawl asked.

"Well, I did encounter a new trail with a lot of blood in a spot and a dead baby."

"That might qualify, Root."

"The trail I wouldn't think much about. Game track just getting used by people now."

"Blood and the baby on the trail or you find them separate?"

"Half mile or so following it. Not something bleeding out. One big splat and the baby in the middle. Tiny as a new pup. Coyotes hadn't got to the afterbirth, but the magpies scrapped over it until I shooed them off."

"Probably stillborn," Strawl said.

"I figured so."

Strawl extended his hand. "Well I admire your nose," he said. "And I thank you for your trouble."

Hayes said nothing, but, when Strawl rose to go, he commented on the waning day and asked if Strawl would like a bunk on his porch and Strawl agreed. Hayes fed him the remnants of an elk stew, bland without salt or pepper and so thick with gravy and wild vegetables that they consumed it with forks and knives. He had no bread, but Strawl fried his flour and a dappling of starch into a fine flat bread that they used to sop up the remnants of the meal. They fed the rest to the dogs, who waited their turns once more.

he next morning, Strawl rose, surprised Hayes remained asleep in his handmade bed. Strawl guessed even their abbreviated conversation had been, to a man like Hayes, as much effort as 140 miles to the Greek at Marathon. He left some coffee as well as salt and a candle and a matchbook and some tobacco in case Hayes changed his mind on such matters, then bid goodbye to the dogs with another jerky stick.

He rode until early evening, enjoying its cool, when he encountered a boy driving a string of donkeys with a stick. The donkeys packed flannel and wool and other dry goods along with double-sacked flour and grains of all kinds. The boy's hair had been cut with a bowl a long while ago and his bangs hung in his face, which was round and seemed to Strawl angelic. Pudgy, he had yet to gain that wiry length of adolescence, and he waddled when he walked.

Strawl drew Stick to a halt.

"Where you headed?" he asked.

The boy pointed in the direction Strawl had come.

"You bringing those to Hayes?"

The boy shook his head. The donkeys browsed on the wild rye surrounding them. The boy steered one from a thistle. Strawl offered him some jerky and leftover bread. He watched the boy eat them, careful as a coon.

"You know anything about a dead baby?"

The boy shook his head.

"You speak?"

"Yes, sir."

"You done anything wrong?"

"No."

"Quit acting like you have, then," Strawl told him. He dropped another piece of meat at the boy's feet. The dog sniffed it and then looked to the boy, who nodded. The dog's jaws clamped the jerky and he trotted to the shade beneath a pine to take his supper.

"That's a good dog," Strawl said, then nudged Stick onward.

He rode ten miles, considering his choices. Jacob Chin would require a change of direction and more time and energy than he felt compelled to commit to a BIA lead. Instead he determined to take a good meal in Keller and, there, put his ear to the ground. He diverted from the trail leading to Marvin's, instead heading toward the river and town. Keller was situated on the edge of the Swahila Basin, a lowland steppe holding the mouth of the San Poil River. The town had been a quarter mile lower, where the river met the Columbia, but the Bureau of Reclamation had bought it outright, land, buildings, and roads, and burned it in order to clear the reservoir's new banks. West, Strawl could see a few abandoned houses near the river's edge and below, in what had once been a meadow, a cemetery pocked with open graves. A team of three Indians stabbed the ground with shovels. Another transported the bodies higher where a second crew interred them. The Catholic priest mumbled ashes to ashes over those who never knew they were condemned otherwise and added to the pots and beads and headdresses a pewter crucifix. Carpenters beat together planks for caskets, which the church insisted replace the disintegrating blankets and robes wrapping each skeleton. Nobody bothered to seal the emptied sepulchers, and the rising river would rub the graves out.

Of all the towns in this county, Keller was Strawl's favorite. Its tiny houses had followed the riverbank, each with a dock and racks to dry fish and barrels constantly burning, filling the valley with fragrant pine smoke. Small tugs had navigated the channel between the two rivers, towing chained log booms that encircled the raw timber the jacks and skidders had run into the narrower upper river. A small lumber plant cut the pine into planks, and a gristmill turned the spring wheat ranchers harvested atop the canyon. A ferry alternated west and north to transport goods and travelers into the upper half of the Colville Reservation or deliver them to the farms on the far side of the Columbia. The town's major boast was a semi-pro baseball team full of young Jim Thorpes hurling a ball and swinging a bat like they had been at it a thousand years. The town contained only one tavern, but it held a hardware store, which also sold moonshine, and a livery and a dry goods shop where women could purchase gabardine and gingham, as well as two churches, one Catholic and another Methodist, but both took all comers.

Strawl squandered the balance of the day in the only grocery and hardware still operating. He began by perching on the porch chairs where the regulars stopped acquaintances and swapped stories. The patrons, however, gave him a wide berth; as the word passed, the customers simply put off their shopping until finally the store proprietor pleaded with Strawl to leave the premises. Strawl then visited the church, where the new minister, who did not know him, was too flustered by the concerns of his uprooted flock and a church sanctuary that would soon be underwater to offer assistance. When Strawl told him babies were dying, the man looked like he might cry, but he still had no answers.

Next, he considered simply arresting people to frighten them and then peppering his quarry with questions and charges, but if he wanted them frightened of him he'd already managed that, and if they were more frightened of his man, they had more reason to remain silent, not less. Each person Strawl encountered, whether he knew them or not, recognized him and likely had kith or kin who'd suffered a beating or a bullet or a jail sentence at his hand. One farmer, Lori Carlin, sat and talked for a while, though his only news on the murders was that it wasn't Stick Indians, ghosts that both whites and natives attributed to mischief, such as flat tires and fallen women.

"Them ghosts aren't mean," the man said. "Just ornery."

By mid afternoon, he had determined to plan anew. He lunched under a copse of oaks and napped in their shade until twilight, when he mounted again and rode toward the old town site to the one place there might be enough rounders to contribute something beyond gossip.

The first Strawl saw of his son that evening was his feet snubbed to a rope extending from a cottonwood. The town's one remaining streetlight illuminated the rooftop of the tavern but left the tree and Elijah shadows until he'd almost passed them.

Strawl's eyes followed the feet down to pant cuffs and pockets turned out. Elijah's bare arms, bound behind him and fastened to his belt, had goose-pimpled, but his face split with a grin.

"Looks like you're in a spot," Strawl told him.

"I've been worse off." Upside down, his t-shirt had rolled past what little chest he had, his ribs there to count. Otherwise, he appeared unperturbed, his brown skin as smooth as the lacquered walnut of their kitchen table and his eyes darker yet. Pupil and iris seemed one. They reflected what they saw like bottle glass and concealed their contents just the same. His high cheekbones narrowed for his jaw and chin and triangled his wolfish face. He'd cropped his hair short not long after Ida died and now doctored it with oils and combed the part so carefully, Dot claimed he counted the follicles on each side. He was half drunk, and half crazy, but all of himself.

"Been here long?" Strawl asked.

"Long enough to take all the comfort there might be from it," Elijah said. "You wouldn't want to cut me loose I don't guess?"

"Those who put you there went to some trouble."

Elijah laughed. The sound was neither a scream nor chuckle, but it was genuine. Strawl rolled a cigarette, and, after he lit it, bent and pinched it into Elijah's lips and began another. Elijah smacked and puffed until he drew smoke.

Strawl's cigarette ash flickered and greyed. He tugged his pocketknife blade free.

"Won't do to have the poor working against one another, I imagine," he said. He sawed a few strokes on the rawhide and unbound Elijah's hands. His knife hadn't crossed a whetstone in some time, however, and the heavy hemp rope that secured him to the branch was tougher. Strawl halted and contemplated the worn blade's luster. Smoke ascended from Elijah beneath him, his wet breath with it. He grinned and continued hanging. His lollygagging rankled Strawl; he at least could press himself up and slacken the rope.

"You squander my money?" Strawl asked him.

"It's a heap of wampum. I can't spend it that fast. At least on the normal amenities. Maybe I bought stocks and bonds."

"You don't know a stock from a bond."

"Doesn't matter."

"That place is all I had. I halved it for you."

"It's all I had, too, so I sold it. You hadn't ought to be willing things if you're going to keep living. No hard feelings, of course."

"I been talked about dead before," Strawl said.

"How's Hemmer taking care of the place?"

"He's not. I bought it back six weeks ago. Cost me my last dime and a promissory note, to boot."

"That's unfortunate. It'd have been a good joke, you sitting on the porch watching him run things."

"I'm sorry to disappoint you."

Elijah shrugged. "Maybe you'll fall off your horse and get crippled."

"Mornings it feels like I already have," Strawl said.

Elijah spat his cigarette onto the ground. Strawl watched it smolder and die.

"If a son shall ask bread of any of you that is a father, will he give him a stone?"

"You've had plenty to eat."

"And they shall say unto the elders of the city, this our son is stubborn and rebellious, he will not obey our voice; he is a glutton, and a drunkard and all the men of his city shall stone him with stones, so shalt thou put evil away from among you; and all Israel shall hear, and fear."

"Apparently you're deaf, then," Strawl told him.

"Or this isn't Israel."

"It's surely not that," Strawl said. "You going to tell me what you did with the money?"

Elijah, still dangling, shook his head. Strawl folded the blade to sheath it, then built himself another cigarette and one more for Elijah. He struck a match for himself and left the box.

"Suit yourself," Strawl said.

⸻

Rusting automobiles lined the road into the skeleton of the old town. Since the Crash, few could afford gas or oil to move them. Most had resigned themselves to horses once more; they went slower, but on grass, which the bigwigs hadn't devised a way to ration or commandeer.

The town's major lumber mill, now closed in the face of the flood, but a tavern run by a Chinese, which served the best food within a hundred miles, remained. Its owner, Woo, had never considered straying so far north when he was imported to drive rail and later took his chances on mining claims, an endeavor in which success was as dangerous as failure. Those without a strike starved; the few happening onto one fared worse. One winter, a rounder from Lewiston and his partners murdered thirty-six. An early runoff stirred the Snake River bottom enough to loosen the rope anchoring the bodies which passed through the sawmill town of Lewiston, one or two a day. Schoolboys abandoned books and chores altogether for casting lures in the current and the chance of hooking a Chinaman. The murderer was squandering his plunder on gin and whores when word reached him. A day later, he was apprehended lounging in a bubble bath, assuming no one would undertake the nuisance over a gaggle of Buddhists.

Eventually Woo migrated onto the reservation over a period of a year, chefing local spoons and catering hotels, collected enough savings to go halves with a drunken Canadian, who one day went north and didn't return. Strawl had heard Woo was too stubborn to drag up stakes despite the deluge. It was the closest to a useful fact he had acquired all day. Strawl had not put a chair before portions more exotic than chicken pie in years. It was a luxury he'd decided to allow himself.

The tavern had no shingle, but it was not difficult to find, as fewer than twenty people remained where more than a thousand had resided before. A humid odor, more greens than meat, spread itself from the building.

Lanterns provided the only light, one for each table. The nearest still flickered from the breeze he'd let in. Cooking behind a counter were three small Chinese, speaking their bell-like tongue in a kitchen lantern-lit, too, though he'd seen power poles just up the block.

The tavern was one long rectangle, and a smaller one behind it that held the kitchen. A bar reclaimed from one of the Nespelem fires stood in front of the kitchen, with a half dozen rickety stools. The rest of the place held tables with checked linen cloths and, in the back under an overhead lamp, a large card table and a game made up of four white men in clean cotton button-ups, one in store-bought trousers and a shirt too clean for labor, and two Indians wearing checked flannels and canvas trousers.

The room's raw studs held no gypboard, and a warm evening draft fluttered the tablecloths, but the food was highly regarded; people went out of their way for Woo's meals. Three girls tended the dining tables, packing steaming teapots and plates loaded with rice and vegetables. He saw chicken glazed in apricot sauce and thin beef strips cooked with peas and peppers. One plate held an entire duck seared near black with sugar. A woman sipped soup as clear as water; a fried egg was taking up the bottom of the bowl. Girls in dresses and men and women wearing their Sunday clothes dotted the tables.

Strawl tipped his cap to Woo and nodded, though he saw no sign the man recalled him. Strawl was disappointed, as he had

frequented his bar more than others and thought their relation-
ship amicable.

"What you like?" Woo asked. He wore a mustache, though not
one you'd associate with a Chinese. He'd shaved its edges to barely
span the bottom of his nostrils. He shuffled when he walked and
his hand palsied, holding his spatula.

"I'll have green tea," Strawl said, and took a stool at the bar.
"And that sugared duck you cook. And make it peppery. With
sweet and sour gravy and those vegetables."

Woo smiled. "You want soup, too?"

Strawl nodded.

"May be long time," Woo said. "I forgot how to cook real Chinese, I think." He laughed a high-pitched laugh. "I thought you
cop no more."

"I just had a hankering for foreign company," Strawl said.

Woo shook his head. "You just like Woo's duck."

"That's a fact," Strawl said.

The meal arrived family-style. Woo offered a pair of sticks as a
joke.

Strawl piled the food in mounds that he tried to keep separate,
but finally swirled into a tasty mess.

"You chase the bad man?"

"One," Strawl said.

Woo nodded vigorously. "He scare everyone."

"What do you know of Chin's doings?"

"I let you eat free if you kill him."

"I might take you up on that. What do you have against him?"

"He steal my good horse and damned near shoot the bar mirror."
Woo motioned to the bullet holes on the wall.

"He do these other murders?"

Woo wiped a dish and set it on a stack of others. "He might do
them. He is mean."

Strawl sipped the last of his tea. "I'll be looking him up," he said. "How about the Bird tribe?"

"They eat here when they pass. They pay and don't break things. Many of them. I don't know all names."

"Me neither," Strawl said. "They all look alike, too."

Woo nodded. "Big." He thumped his chest.

"Yep. Every one of them could lift a steer and pack it across a creek, women included. You think they're up to killing?"

Woo shrugged. "I ask nothing. I just listen."

Strawl nodded. "What do you hear, then?"

"Same as you. Men killed then torn to be funny. No one knows before. No fighting. Very careful, maybe."

Strawl shook his head. "Too many bodies too fast. Psychopath might kill more, but, you're right, he'd be careful as a cabinetmaker or he'd be caught. This kind of thing takes time and patience and a plan beyond what your common criminal can muster." He sat a minute and sipped his tea, then tapped his finger on the cup's rim. "Killer knew these men, Woo; they trusted him. That's why there's no struggle; they went willing."

"Woo trust no one," Woo said.

"Good policy," Strawl said.

There was a fuss at the back table. One of the poker players had busted. The dealer, young Hollingsworth, stood and grinned, watching him go. Hollingsworth's pants were wide-legged and gaudily striped like the Chicago gangsters', though his western-style boots sported pointed toes and smooth soles. He had bangs like a girl's. Strawl doubted he owned a hat. His father had once tried his hand at politics and campaigned for Strawl's sheriff position. In response, Strawl had revived a rumor Old Man Hollingsworth passed bad paper, and when the man accused him of slander, Strawl produced a copy of a check for the newspaper. It was smudged and would never suffice as evidence in front of a judge, but the public had no legal training and Strawl won the election handily. After, Strawl issued license plate numbers and descriptions of Hollingsworth's three automobiles and ordered his deputies to ticket the cars on sight or be canned. A month and Hollingsworth quit coming to his county at all, circling it for Omak or opting for east and Spokane.

Strawl had arrested the younger Hollingsworth two or three times for general rudeness, once jailing him overnight and feeding him bologna he'd dunked in a piss-filled toilet bowl. The son looked boy; most silverspoons did till the day they died—they had poppas too big to be men ever and wouldn't know a worry from a snipe den.

"Seat right here," the silverspoon said.

"I'm content where I am," Strawl said. Cards never held much interest for him. He saw no sport in throwing away cards just for the prospect of more. Triple the money and it still wasn't worth the time one spent or the company required of him.

Another player circled an arm from the table. He wore striped overalls, the kind the railroad favored; a brakeman, Strawl surmised. His face was red and a pockmarked mess.

"Heard you lost your ranch. Likely too broke for a money game," the brakeman asked.

Strawl smiled and shook his head. "You a real estate maven, are you?"

The brakeman's eyes blazed. "Land isn't the only money."

"It's the only kind that counts, you said so yourself."

"Ignore the old bastard. He's broker than a carousel pony," Hollingsworth said. "I know that for a fact."

"No fighting inside," Woo whispered to Strawl.

Strawl nodded. He pulled ten dollars from his pocket. Hollingsworth was ahead, so he made change. The others at the table slipped back into themselves and waited on cards. A shovel-faced hired hand called Pete partnered with the Hollingsworth boy, it was clear. Two San Poil cowhands held their cards on either side of Pete and the silverspoon. Cloud was their last name; the country held a bevy of them, cousins or brothers. He didn't know which they were, but they recognized him, he could see.

"You know the Bird folks?" Strawl asked one.

They shook their heads and a hand later, swapped their cards for their feed caps and exited through the back door.

"You do that to them?" Powell asked. He was the railroad man. He seemed good-natured enough and offered Strawl a cigarette with his grimy fingers, which Strawl declined.

Strawl said, "I have that effect on some."

All laughed except the dark-complected man across from him. He appeared closer to Strawl's age. Strawl figured him for a black Irish. The man looked too desperate to have a ranch behind him. Strawl guessed he was one the banks undid, and from the looks of his stack, he was getting undone by his cards, too.

The cards passed among the four of them, but Strawl didn't give much heed. He'd ante and cut when the deck was offered and deal his turn. But he rarely opened and never bet past his ante. He was hoping to eavesdrop, but the card players seemed intent on disrupting his peace.

"You ever gonna play a hand?" the dark Irish asked.

Pete, the shovelface, thumbed cards to each player. Hollingsworth nodded, and he flipped Strawl's last card faceup. It was a king.

"Say, a cowboy," he said. "Gotta be some luck in that."

Strawl glanced at the silverspoon, then faced the card down and set it in his hand. He had two more. No one had beaten three kings since he'd taken a hand, but when the bet circled his way, he tabled the cards. When the silverspoon had his turn dealing, he tossed each of Strawl's cards up. There were a pair of twos and a king and two other cards Strawl didn't regard.

"Ain't many card players play faceup," the shovelface said.

"May as well," the Irish said. "He ain't parted with nothing but an ante all night." They dealt him up the next hand and the one that followed, good cards sometimes, a high pair or one shy of a flush.

"Goddamnit, you don't like money much, do you?" the Irish said.

The railroad man took the deal, sliding Strawl three sevens.

Strawl tossed the cards on the deck.

"Why, you old bastard. Who are you to pass that hand?" The Irish stood to circle the table, then thought the better of it. "You're a stupid old goat aren't you? That's what you are. Old goat. Stupid."

"Make up your mind," Strawl said. "Am I an old goat or stupid?"

"Both." He looked at the rest of the table. "Nobody calls him nothing but Stupid. Or Old Goat. Those are his names. You understand that, Stupid?"

Strawl smiled. "Old Goat. I like that better."

"Stupid," the Irish said.

The silverspoon and his partner grinned. Strawl studied them. They plotted like queers. To them it was always a distraction. You had to attend to what you couldn't see. The silverspoon kept a knife. He'd seen him rub the top of his boot to check its place.

A hand later, a clatter rose on the porch. The players glanced up. Elijah opened the door, picked up a whiskey bottle behind the bar, and had himself a belt and then another, then held up the bottle to the light. "Ye have not eaten bread, neither have ye drunk wine or strong drink: that ye might know that I am the Lord your God," he said, pointing the bottle toward the card players, then drank again. "Render unto Caesar what is Caesar's and unto me what is mine."

No one answered him.

"Woo, give to him that asketh thee, and from him that would borrow of thee turn not thou away, or cast ye the unprofitable servant into outer darkness where there shall be weeping and gnashing of teeth." Elijah offered his rifle as collateral and Woo opened the register and separated the bills into ones and fives for forty dollars.

"Goddamn thief," the Irish said.

"Who is that speaking?" Elijah asked. "Is Coyote deceiving me again?"

"Shit," the Irish said.

"It is Coyote," Elijah said. "Coyote it is as the Creator said. All the animals have turned against one another. They have forgotten the Golden Rule."

"Confusing your religions, aren't you?" the silverspoon asked.

"God knows no bounds," Elijah said. He appeared unperturbed. Pete's boot pushed a chair from the table.

"I thank you," Elijah said. "Perhaps you have a many-shots rifle to trade."

"Aren't any Indians talking like that, anymore," Pete said. "You're talking like a used-to-be Indian."

"And now so are you." Elijah laughed. He looked to Strawl.

"Stupid is his name," the Irish told him. "He likes Goat. But Stupid suits him better."

Elijah shook his head. "His name is Death and he rides a pale horse."

"Might be old as death," the railroader said. "We don't have a need for him or his horse. He don't ever bet."

"Might make him good company."

"I don't know why," Powell answered. "He don't never talk, neither."

Elijah said, "I am full of talk and he is full of quiet. We are like the sun and the moon, the Alpha and Omega." He handed the whiskey to the Irish. "Maybe this will at least allow you to live with your small self."

The Irish drank. Elijah went on, "The sun will rise from his lodge in the east, that is sure, though there is no evidence this is so, other than the days. Money will pass hands many times before it finds that person to whom it will remain. This, too, is certain."

Pete the shovelface ignored him, working his stack of ones. The Irish watched Elijah change a dollar bill from the silverspoon's nickels and quarters.

"Andrew," Elijah said to the Irish, "you are poor once more. God has no love for you. You gamble like Sinkalip. You should go to the privy and get some advice from your excrement."

"Goddamn you." Andrew opened his hand to take a swipe at Elijah. Strawl caught his elbow halfway there and shoved the Irish out of his seat.

"I ain't scared of you, Stupid." The man fumbled and righted his chair.

The railroader handed the Irish the bottle. "I'd let it go, Andrew."

Elijah took the deck, rattled the cards awkwardly as he was missing his left pinky finger, then slid them across the table. Strawl was to his right, and Elijah looked to him to open. Strawl examined his hand. He had all diamonds. When he checked closer, he was shocked to see they were straight to the jack. He bet a dollar.

"Well, now maybe we'll get along," the Irish said. He raised, and Powell raised him. It was five more when it returned to Strawl. He looked for anyone to comment, but they were all contemplating their own hands. They bumped again. The bottle went with the betting. The silverspoon and shovelface pooled their funds. Strawl heard them whispering and saw them signal to compare hands. The silverspoon folded his cards on the next pass.

Strawl reached into his wallet for the expense money. Elijah raised five more. Strawl saw it and watched the others do the same. Each was staring into his own hand, certain he had the winner, except Elijah, who was more amused by the seriousness of the game.

Strawl knew putting too much faith in the hand you could see was not good card sense, and it was the good hands that cost money—no one went broke on bad cards—and he saw that each was making the same mistake, courting his own hand rather than guessing against it.

"Cards to draw?" Elijah asked. Not a player took one.

"Shit, oh dear," the railroader said.

The last raise had been Elijah's and he started the betting again with two bills, both twenties. He tossed them toward the middle of the table. The players all watched them flutter, then go still. "One for me," he said. "And one for Jesus Christ, who gave his life so that sinners may live."

The shovelface was short and at a loss.

"I'll put up the Model A," he said finally.

Elijah shook his head. "Money," he told him.

"I ain't got it."

Elijah nodded at the silverspoon. "Ask your near-wife to help you out."

The silverspoon smiled. "Time was, you'd take blankets and beads." He dug into his pocket and sorted for three more fives.

"There was a time as well when Samson slew Philistines with the jawbone of an ass. Then Delilah took his hair. But he learned and prayed to God and was permitted to pull the great house down upon all of them."

"He was just as dead," the silverspoon said.

"But so was everyone else."

The Irishman stared at Strawl. His face had warmed at the turning of each card, but now it had gathered back its gloom.

"You ain't bet all night, why you going all out now?"

"I like my hand," Strawl told him.

"We all like our hands."

Strawl didn't dispute him. Neither did the rest, and the Irish folded.

The railroader followed without checking his wallet. Elijah offered them the bottle and the two sat swapping it.

Strawl raised ten more.

"Petey?" Elijah asked.

"I told you. I ain't got it."

"What about you, dog lover?"

"My last is bet."

Elijah was grinning now. "It's only me and you, it seems," he said to Strawl.

"Whoa now," Pete said. "You can't just shut us out."

"Yes," Elijah said. "I can."

"You know my note's good," Hollingsworth told him.

"I know you say it is," Elijah told him. "But this man may not want to treat with you."

"It's not square to keep Pete out of the game," Hollingsworth said.

"You exiled me like Moses himself."

"You earned it," Pete said. "You wouldn't argue that, would you?"

"I would not. But that's not the point."

"Well we ain't ever had a stake go this high before."

"We may never again if we let you gamble with no folding money."

"I'm not asking to welch," Pete said.

"What are you requesting, then? The only person here who trusts you is Hollingsworth, and nobody trusts him."

"You name it," Pete said. "You and him."

Elijah turned to Strawl. "Would it satisfy you to see this man eat some fresh horseshit?"

Strawl said, "His partner has to settle up, too."

"Agreed?" Elijah asked.

"That's worth double," Hollingsworth said.

Strawl put in another ten, so did Elijah.

Pete showed four kings. Powell sighed.

Elijah shook his head. "All that money before me and bad fortune, too." He threw his cards in the deck without even showing them.

"Well?" Pete asked.

Strawl turned his hand on the wood table.

"Just a flush?" Pete whooped.

The railroader said, "Pete. You better look closer."

The cards were out of order, and the moment it took for Pete to realize he'd been bested felt a little like what hitting him might have. Pete's shovelface turned red. His mouth opened once but only sputtered.

❧

Elijah announced, "My horse is tied to the front rail. There's oats in Woo's stable."

Strawl gathered in the bills, sorting them by denomination, taking his time, but it was Elijah who put them in his pocket.

They took the bottle outside of the tavern. Elijah returned with the feed, and they listened to the horse take it.

"It shouldn't be long," Elijah said. "He is as regular as rent." He lit a lantern from the tavern so he could see their faces. The flame flickered in the wind and their images shuddered. The Irish had kept the whiskey for himself. He was past drunk.

"Should've hung him when we had the chance." He shoved Strawl, though it was the Irish who ended up falling.

"You only lost money," Elijah told him.

The Irish stared at Strawl from the ground. "I ain't no fighter," he said.

"Then don't behave like one," Elijah told him.

"I'd wager Petey could hold his own," the railroader ventured. He lifted the Irish under the arms until he was standing upright.

Neither was a threat except to themselves. The railroader was smart enough to see it, even if the Irish wasn't.

"I'll take that bet," Elijah said.

The silverspoon smiled. "You put a lot of stock in an old man."

Elijah shook his head. "I just have no faith in Pete."

Strawl could see Pete pondering a reply, then, knowing the only response worthy was a blow, choosing to hold off until his odds improved. It was a kind of calculation Strawl despised. It implied he'd weaken.

The silverspoon grinned though his partner was being provoked. It was an alliance shy of square, Strawl could see.

They smoked for twenty minutes until the horse's tail lifted and its bowels flopped shit to the ground. Steam rose with its stink. Elijah had brought a fork from the tavern, and he stabbed a round nugget and put it and the lantern to Pete's face. To Strawl's surprise, Pete immediately grabbed the fork and began chewing. The first bite he vomited, but the second went all the way down. The railroader handed him the whiskey.

"Sweet Jesus, Petey."

Elijah patted his back. "He took to it like a badger to his hole."

Strawl nodded. Pete had taken his medicine without wailing.

Elijah passed the lantern to Hollingsworth's face. He held up the empty fork. "You want to pick for yourself or do you prefer being served?" Elijah asked.

"Neither," Hollingsworth said. "You were cheating, I say."

Elijah laughed. "Why am I not richer, then?"

"You and him are in cahoots. I expect you'll split the money later."

"Show us how I did this thing."

"You're all the proof I need. We ran you out for bilking us before. What's to convince us you're changing your ways now?"

Pete was staring at the fork. "I guess you'll eat if I did," he said.

Partner or not, he didn't want to have it said he ate shit alone. But Hollingsworth was a silverspoon and not accustomed to doing what didn't please him. "You can swallow what you please, but I'm passing."

With that, he thumbed the lantern out and unbooted his knife. Elijah stepped back. He struck a match to the wick. The knife blade in Hollingsworth's hand flickered like water in moonlight.

Elijah's voice was low; he held his hand palm up, like he was settling a colt. "Put the blade away," he said.

The silverspoon laughed. "You think I'm scared?"

"I think you should be," Elijah told him.

The silverspoon passed the weapon from one hand to the other in front of him like it was too hot to hold. He was no knife handler, Strawl could see, and with the next toss, Strawl drove his shoulder and hip between Hollingsworth's wrists and broke three ribs. He heard the blade hit the dirt, then delivered the silverspoon another blow and a kick that broke his shoulder. Hollingsworth crawled for the knife, still on the ground. Strawl ground his wrist like he was killing a snake until Hollingsworth was still except for his labored breaths.

"He ain't gonna be able to eat no horseshit now," Petey groaned.

"No," Elijah told him. "But he would trade a bellyful of shit for his bellyful of blood. You better find Doc Everett."

Pete nodded and Strawl didn't doubt he would obey. He was inclined to follow orders, and Hollingsworth was too busted up to give them.

"They're going to arrest him," Powell said.

"Who's that?"

"The law. Hollingsworth owns half the mountain. They won't ignore him being broken up like old furniture."

Elijah laughed. "This old man is the law."

He and Strawl mounted and loped their horses over the road out. They passed the tree Elijah had hung from and proceeded into the dark of the night. The horses made good time once they hit the valley. After a mile Strawl drew rein and Elijah slowed Baal, his favorite horse, and turned her. Elijah emptied his pocket and handed the bills to Strawl.

"He was right," Elijah patted his mare. "Hollingsworth. I cheated him."

"How did the good hand come to me?" Strawl asked.

"It was the only way I knew to do the trick," Elijah said. "Besides, they would have put me back in the tree if I had dealt myself a straight flush."

Stick nickered. He enjoyed a good run and was impatient to have his head. Elijah gazed into the sky, which had grown clear and cold for late August.

"You got a bunk?" Strawl asked.

Elijah shook his head.

"Well if it don't rain, I got an idea where to sleep comfortably."

Strawl angled his horse west, back toward the divide. In the dark, the planted hills looked like what he recalled of the ocean. He saw Elijah pass and disappear into them. It was a strange sensation, like the country was too tame for a man mounted on a beast. Yet here he was, astride his own.

| EIGHT |

The next morning, Elijah was gone, though his bedroll remained. Strawl filled his coffeepot from a canteen and waited for it to perk under the breakfast fire.

Nine years ago, Strawl had witnessed a line of children in the trading post dressed in starched slacks and white shirts, a deacon minding the brood. An Indian woman buying beans recognized her son and called out a word. A boy, not more than three, turned and bolted, a great crucifix bouncing on his chest, afraid for the strapping the old words brought. It reminded Strawl of Pharaoh rounding up the two-year-olds.

He encountered Elijah a month later, bent in half in front of the church, the priest beating him with a willow switch. The priest reared to strike the boy again, but Strawl bent from his horse and caught the man's wrist with one hand and the boy with the other. He lifted the boy aboard the horse before either could protest. The boy said nothing, just stroked the sorrel's neck in rhythm with its steps. His shirt hung out. The back of it stuck to the places he was bleeding. Strawl dragged from his cigarette, then tapped the ash into his hat brim. The boy snapped it from his fingers when Strawl replaced them on the reins. He lifted his other hand to defend his prize.

"Yours," Strawl said in the Nez Perce tongue.

"You know these words." The boy drew from the cigarette and exhaled through his nose expertly.

"Just the mountain dialect," Strawl replied.

"How come?"

"Because I never did business with the Clearwater side."

"How come you know this language?"

"I used to hunt them."

In Nespelem, Strawl bought some hard candy and bag balm to soothe the boy's wounds. The boy sucked the candy while Strawl doctored him. At Leeland McClune's, Strawl examined the bull he'd come to see and its progeny in the barn. Satisfied, he arranged for a hired man to escort the animal across the river the week following. He paid McClune in cash and returned to the corral where he'd left the boy and the horse tied. Both were nowhere to be seen.

Strawl borrowed McClune's quarter horse and gave chase. The boy had left the road after a hundred yards for turned ground, making him easy to track, until he switched again for a meadow and the brush-choked draw after it. A bald ridge boxed the far end and Strawl made for it. He was waiting behind a tall rock, and when the boy passed on the game path coming out, Strawl grabbed the reins and halted the sorrel.

"It's clear to see how you come to the rod," he told the boy.

Strawl returned McClune's horse and bore north and east for

the Nez Perce plots with the boy. Smoke rose from a few clapboard shacks. Feared by the whites and resented by the Nespelems
and San Poils, the Nez Perce staked tipis or constructed tin hovels
on a few hundred-acre plots the Dawes Act provided them. Their
cattle were often left untended and simply wandered off. The Nez
Perce were not inclined to stitch their god's flesh with fences or
corrals.

Strawl asked the boy for directions and Elijah guided him to
a tipi protected by a tamarack stand. A woman of middling age
emerged at the opening. Elijah grinned at her and slid from the
horse.

"You've raised a fine horse thief," Strawl told her.

She was in a gunnysack dress, but her hands were clean and her
hair pulled back.

"She like living here?"

The boy shrugged. Strawl looked to the woman. "I have work,"
he said. "Your boy here won't have to face the priests and there's
plenty to eat."

He needed a hand with Dot and the cooking, and she and the
boy seemed hard put.

"What do you say?' he asked.

She nodded, finally. He sent a buckboard wagon for them the
next morning.

The boy couldn't even keep to a name. At birth, he was named
Elaskolatat, which meant Animal Running into the Ground in Sa-
haptin, a cousin to the consonant-rich Salish dialects that seem as
many as the trees to those without the tongue to speak them.

Animal Running into the Ground's mother had been his father's youngest wife, and when he had expired in the 1918 influ-
enza outbreak, Animal Running into the Ground had been too
young by years for the night of steam and smoke and fasting when
the appropriate spirits would have visited his sleep and he would

have dreamt his adult name, and that slumber turned impossible for him as he witnessed the incense and Latin incantations and clacking rosaries of his father's Catholic funeral.

At four years, Animal Running into the Ground joined the buckboard wagon loaded with stoic children headed for the church and school. Early on, he did not resist the lessons, especially in language. He understood the power its speakers possessed and was impressed that words could have such might. He was, in fact, deluded in regards to their value, a fiction under which he would labor all his days.

He read voraciously the only text available at his home or the church, the Catholic Bible. He knew it chapter and verse by age eight and grew to believe in the Hebrew God. Animal Running into the Ground was no seer yet, but, in the images that filled his thoughts, he recognized his own face rising. Like taming his reflection in a pond, the harder he looked into the words, the stiller he became, until he felt steadied and right. Then some thought he could not name roughed the picture like a wind or duck landing on the watery mirror of his thoughts, stirring and distorting his likeness.

He devoured his Bible like a fly does his meal, consuming a passage, then vomiting its ideas, then feasting upon his own regurgitation. He stole a Catholic Apocrypha and a copy of the Gnostic Thomas from the priest's library and consumed them likewise. For five months he studied, and when he rose from the books like Rip Van Winkle from twenty years of sleep, the things around him were no longer what they had been, and he insisted upon a new name to fit such a passage. From that moment on, he answered only to Elijah.

His first prophecy was simple enough: a storm. The following day, the church thermometer read a hundred degrees and the air refused even the highest of clouds. Elijah seriously reconsidered both his name and his calling until two days later when thunderheads stacked against the northern horizon and, an hour before dusk, lightning cracked and thunder spooked the herds and a fifty-mile-per-hour wind blew the roofs from several barns and houses and then the clouds collapsed and soaked the whole of the reservation in a gulley washer. It was patience he lacked, and he determined to put no calendar to his divinations. He would announce each season's approach to his mother, and within a few weeks autumn's first freeze would cover the country, and two months after an inch of snow, and, four months following that, buttercups on the bloom. He was chastised by the priest, who told him even the ignorant could foresee the seasons, given three weeks' leeway. However, Elijah knew even then that augury's truths lie less in the specifics than in the audacity necessary for utterance. The point wasn't that the messiah appeared on a Wednesday or Thursday, Elijah replied to the priest, it was that he arrived, and those who foretold of him were proved wise and those who doubted were proved ignorant and faithless. The priest slapped him for insolence, and the boys behind him snickered, for Elijah had predicted just such a response to them only ten minutes before.

Ida sewed moccasin beads and laundered the neighbors' clothes for scraps of meat and flour. She fed the boy and herself pan bread and berries and salmon dried on the racks next to the river's cataracts. Fall, Animal Running into the Ground trapped quail and sage hens with willow snares, and Ida turned them on a spit each evening, frying canned greens in a skillet she set on a flat rock in the fire ring's center. Each winter a neighbor would kill an elk or deer or yearling bear and leave it outside their door and Ida and Animal Running into the Ground would butcher it and set the flesh upon a crosshatch of green branches, then cover the greasy meat in rock salt and let it smoke.

Her emotions Strawl had only been able to guess at; though he married her six months later, she remained but a mirror for his own desires, anticipating what he required and delivering it before he recognized a lack. Even giving her body had nothing to do with herself. He had glanced into her face when they were locked together and recognized in her flat features and dark irises only the husk of a woman waiting for each event in her life to occur and pass so she could be shed of it.

But she had returned life to the house. Though Dot resented the intrusion at first, Ida learned her favorite foods and teased her with such outlandish tales of Magpie and Fox that Dot soon felt compelled to argue. Though Dot was more partial to science than religion, Elijah would study nothing else, so she debated chapter and verse with him until they both spoke the king's English better than a pair of minister's children.

And now they were, for the most part, silent once again, even Elijah who employed conversation much like Strawl himself, to extract intelligence from others, though Elijah's methods were far more generous than Strawl's. No one fussed over others' worries like he, especially if he saw himself the cause. Yet like a drunk on a bender, he'd plunge suddenly into silence as if it were his own country and disappear from his family without warning or apology or explanation.

The sun had mounted the horizon before he heard Elijah clamber up the bank below. He crested the hill with two sage hens he'd captured with a snare and a saddlebag loaded with camas. It had been three months, before the killings filled the papers, since Strawl had seen the boy. He was disappointed he couldn't remain angry with the boy and wondered if he still had enough pluck for hunting killers.

While the coffee perked, Strawl helped Elijah clean the birds, then cut a green oak switch stout enough to bear their weight and turned the portions above the coals. Their grease fell into the fire and spat. Elijah sliced and arranged the onions on the skillet's bottom and set the pan to simmer on a rock. Then he hunted a flat piece of shale and cleaned it, then, with the flat of his knife, pressed the camas root into paste on the flat surface. When finished, he laid several willow switches over the coals and added half the onions, covered it with more of the branches, then moved the fire to one side with a long stick and buried the camas on the other, then returned the fire over it. Uncooked, camas made a person sick as green whiskey, but baked all day, it was a fine squash.

With the birds nearly finished, Strawl slid them from the stick into the skillet and Elijah divided them, thighs and breast, and stirred in a pocketful of huckleberries with the onions and meat, then added water and flour until the gravy thickened. He returned the pan to simmer while Strawl found an aluminum pie plate in his traps to cover it.

The bird basted to their satisfaction, Strawl withdrew it from the fire and forked the meatier back quarters onto Elijah's tin plate, it being his kill, though Elijah split the thighs and legs and returned an even share to Strawl. Their hands and faces shone with grease as they ate. Elijah alternated each bite of meat with one of onion in the careful manner he had always eaten. Strawl rolled them each a cigarette. High clouds ribboned the sky, but the sun was hot and the air dry, and they would burn off before noon. The breeze that rose around dawn had faded to just a breath.

"What were you doing in a card game?" Elijah asked.

Strawl lay back in the yellow grass and watched a raven cross the sky. He let some smoke go and it disappeared above him. "County was in the card game. Seems they got a killer they want shed of. I was just listening like every good citizen should."

"Cain slew Abel."

Strawl let another lungful loose. "The victims aren't kin to one another, and he couldn't be kin to all of them, so I think you got the wrong scripture."

"All men are brothers," Elijah said.

"And every rainbow ends with a pot of gold and a leprechaun."

Elijah lay back and set his coffee cup on his chest. "Did you find anything worth the trip?"

"Just that the youth of today don't know how to gamble or knife-fight."

Elijah finished his coffee, then found his King James in his saddle poke and lay in the grass, tipped on one elbow to study it. Ten minutes later, he closed the cover like he was slamming a door. "I guess I'm the prodigal." He nodded, agreeing with himself. "And Dot, she's the working one. She's got to be mad," Elijah said. "But it's her in the wrong."

"Except she's not."

"Mad or wrong?"

"Neither. Your sister and her husband are tending the ranch that's financing our follies," Strawl said. "I'd speak kindly of her if I were you."

Elijah chewed a piece of grass into threads. "I don't mean any slight. She's keeping to her part of the scripture. I just forgot I was doing the same. It's a relief, I'll tell you."

"Don't get too happy with yourself," Strawl told him. "You keep behaving like a character in that book and you'll find yourself living a story you can't get loose from."

Elijah tapped his good book. "I don't want loose from these stories."

Strawl laughed. "Makes you one up on Christ."

"That's blasphemy."

Strawl shook his head. "Gethsemane. Let this cup pass from me, Lord."

"He wasn't sure yet."

"No wonder the damned Jews never took him serious. He shows up with no gold and no notion of what God thinks, but says he's him. That's a man too broke to drink with and too crazy to pour liquor into even if you had a charitable streak."

Elijah stared at him.

"Seems to me God the father ought to have done a better job informing God the son of his plans."

Strawl watched as Elijah stirred the dirt with a stick, his temper rising. He looked up at Strawl. "Is that what giving away a ranch did? It turn you God?"

"I'm a long way from divine," Strawl told him. "And I had no plan."

Elijah said nothing. His long black hair swooped over his eyes like a bird wing, leaving him looking as delicate as a girl.

"Meek shall inherit the earth," Elijah told him. He walked toward the butte and Strawl closed his eyes and napped. Elijah's shouts stirred him. The boy was on the bluff's edge, pointing. Strawl hiked the hundred yards between them. A gun fired and tin pots clanked below.

"It's Woo banging pans," Elijah said.

Strawl nodded. He heard two more shots.

"Someone's shooting at him," Elijah said.

Strawl put a ryegrass stem between his teeth and chewed it flat. "Someone shooting to be heard."

Strawl turned to mount Stick. Elijah followed. They galloped the four miles to town. Woo stood in the middle of the hard dirt street, whacking a skillet against a soup pot. Pete stood beside him, wielding a 10-gauge. Red casings gathered beneath his boots along with scattered shingles. He'd shot the roof eave. Strawl took the weapon under the barrel with one hand and shoved backwards, bloodying Pete's nose. Unarmed, he quieted.

Woo continued with his hardware. Strawl drew his pistol and put a hole in the pot.

Woo gazed at him, eyes wide. "You kill my pan."

"I'll get you another," Strawl told him. "Now what in hell are you going on over?"

Woo led them behind the tavern to the kitchen door. Hooked on a makeshift clothesline between two poles were the Cloud boys in the same garb from last night's poker game. Their weight sagged the cord and their booted toes tapped the ground when the breeze rose. The piece of ground beneath them Woo kept clean for parked cars. A few drops of blood clotted in the dust. Strawl smelled their body odor; they were not yet spoiling, though they would be soon in the heat. Their heads had been cut off and barbwired into their open palms. His man had taken the time to use a cord and staples to secure them. The lids drooped over their sightless eyes; they appeared embarrassed by their deaths.

"You bunk here," Strawl asked Woo, "or you still with Coretta?"

"Coretta," Woo said. Coretta was a fat Indian woman who told fortunes with a deck of fifty-one cards.

"They this way when you arrived?"

Woo shrugged. "I come in front."

"Well, how'd you discover them, then?"

Woo pointed at Pete. "He drink coffee then go to pisshouse then I hear hollering."

Strawl turned to Pete. "You do this?"

Pete's eyes blinked. "I don't have nothing against those boys."

"Neither did their killer. He just likes to argue using corpses. I kill you now and the town police will cash me out."

"Why'd you want to do that?"

"I like money," Strawl told him.

"And shooting people," Elijah said.

"They were there when I come back," Pete said. "That's all I know about it."

"I shot many with better stories," Strawl told him.

"Holten boys," Woo said. "He kill all three. They rob me."

Pete looked like a steer waiting to be leveled with a sledge. "That so?"

"That's just for openers." Strawl leveled the empty shotgun at him, then lowered it. "You ain't got it in you. How about your partner? He seems to think enough of himself to kill a man."

"He's at the horse doctor," Pete said. "With a cut lung."

"How about them others?" Strawl asked Pete.

"Powell don't have a mean bone in him."

"The Irish?"

"Well, he don't like anybody," Pete said. "If he decided to murder, he could wear himself out, I'll grant that. But he'd still've had to think it."

Strawl set Pete's shotgun against the building, then again examined his man's talents. Flies hovered over blood and bone. Again there was no savagery, just care, and, when he lifted the greasy heads, he saw the same temple wounds. He heard a chick's piping. He thought it might be a killdeer attempting to distract them from its nest, but there was none in sight, and being in sight was the point.

The sound grew louder. The corpses' mouths had been wired shut. Strawl unwound the first, and a sparrow fluttered between the Cloud boy's teeth. It set its wings and flew. Inside the other was a tiny starling. It sat on the dead tongue and cried its birthday cry, then shat.

| NINE |

Strawl cut the cords attaching the heads to the corpses and attempted to undo the staples without tearing the skin. He lifted the bodies from the clothesline. They walloped the ground like sacks of grain. The killer had driven a grappling hook between each boy's ribs to attach them to the line. Elijah and Strawl stood studying the bodies and the heads next to them.

"Jesus Christ," Strawl said. "I can't decide if this man thinks he's doing something ugly or beautiful."

Elijah looked like he would cry. "Maybe both," he said.

Strawl argued to bury them straightaway. Any flat spot where the ground wasn't rocky would do, and they had Woo and Pete to help with the digging.

Elijah shook his head. Petey and Woo kept out of it.

"You're just too lazy to dig."

"Maybe the family has some preparations to make."

Flies hummed over each body's wounds.

"A funeral doesn't require a casket. They hold them for people lost at sea all the time."

"These aren't lost."

Strawl nodded to the boys below him and their heads loose on the hard ground. "Might be better if we told them they were."

Elijah nodded. "We'll need to prepare their parents."

Strawl rolled one of the heads with the toe of his boot. Sand pocked the cheek. A few grains dried in a watery eye. He glared up at Elijah. "How exactly do you prepare a mother for this?"

"The bodies," Elijah said. "Prepare the bodies."

"Suit yourself," Strawl told him.

Pete bent and heaved, but only a line of bile dropped to the floor.

"Put you off your breakfast?" Strawl asked.

Pete said nothing. He opened the back door and joined Woo inside. Through the plastic window covering, Strawl saw the Chinaman's shaky hand pour him some coffee, but Pete made no move toward his eggs and sausage.

Outside, Elijah placed each head atop what he decided was its proper neck. Next, he bored a hole with his pocketknife through the skin under one boy's clavicles. He threaded a cord from Woo's shed through it, then repeated the process on the other side. He disappeared into the shed behind the tavern and returned with a hammer and a handful of galvanized nails. He attempted to pound one into the neck, but the flesh turned greasy and the head rolled away.

Strawl smoked.

"You got any ideas?" Elijah asked.

"You heard my idea."

"Do you want Dot buried someplace without the proper words being said, someplace you don't even know where it is?"

"I don't want her buried at all."

"That is only choosing what isn't," Elijah told him.

Elijah had a point. The boy set his jaw and lifted his hammer and a nail.

"You aren't going to be able to wire their heads to their shoulders," Strawl said.

"Are you going to cite a law that goes against it?"

"Just physics. Skin tears like paper and bone splits, otherwise carpenters would do surgery. Woo got any boards in his shed?"

"Scrap timber," Elijah said.

"If you can find a couple of one-bys long enough and some wood screws, you might be able to bolster their spine and shoulders enough to keep a head to it."

"Like a cross?"

Strawl nodded. He left him to the job. Woo put on some sausage and hotcakes and, at the bar, Strawl washed his hands in a bucket, then watched his second breakfast spit on the griddle. Pete's remained abandoned, though he glugged coffee as fast as Woo could pour it.

Woo soon put Strawl's plate in front of him, then slid the tabasco across the counter. Strawl opened the bottle, turned it over, and hit the bottom until his eggs were spackled orange. He broke a yolk, then dipped a link in the yellow puddle on his plate.

Elijah had managed the boards and the screws and was attempting to find a way to snub the Cloud brothers' foreheads to the top of the board without them slipping through the loops. The heat beaded the perspiration left in their glands and shined the boys' faces and dulled their hair. The cleaved heads were expressionless, as if they found their predicament of little surprise.

A bevy of impatient magpies prattled on Woo's broken eave and Strawl had seen a grey and white dog make the circle around the building twice and then another yellow hound join him. Elijah finally cinched the skulls to their crosses with the boys' pants belts.

This left their heads tipped back and exposed the severed necks. He cut and drove wood wedges between the boards and the back of each skull. Then he drove three wood screws through the boards and into the backs of their heads for insurance. He gazed, satisfied with the results.

Strawl filled a pitcher with water and delivered it to the boy. No one passed, let alone stopped, aside from Woo's few patrons and the boys moving the bodies from the town cemetery to the other above the new waterline.

Woo owned a wagon for supplies, and Strawl yoked Stick and Elijah's mare, Baal, to the T-bar. He and Elijah and Woo lifted the Cloud boys onto the flatbed, then covered them with blankets from Woo's closet.

Elijah drove. The bodies rocked on the planks of the wagon bed. It was midday and hot. Starlings dove at the wagon as it passed a clay bank pocked with their nests. A few larks trilled. Strawl heard the hush of a hawk's wings as it left its perch in a tamarack and weaved across the blue sky. Flies hummed over the wounds, but Woo kept a sack of lime, and they had scattered some across the wounds to subdue the odor.

Strawl's saddle lay behind him in the wagon and he unscabbarded the rifle, opened the bolt, and began to clean the chamber with a fresh handkerchief. He listened to the flowing and the little breeze jangle the drying cheat and foxtail. The road ascended the east side of the crease the San Poil had cut into the country. A trickle next to the Columbia, especially at the close of summer, it still had managed to shape this portion of the county, dividing the rock and pine forests of the Okanogans all the way to Canada. A few of the original San Poil River clans like the Cloud family raised enough cattle to turn a profit. It was as close to the old times as they were likely to find, and Strawl imagined they had counted themselves fortunate.

The prairie in the Swahila Basin was broken with cottonwood and pines and they passed through bladed light and shadows cooling and warming them like they were feverish. In the grass, rodents stirred and chukar clucked among a rock spill and Strawl heard the crickets that Dot's girls worried were rattlesnakes.

"All killings have reasons?" Elijah asked.

Strawl nodded. "Lots and none. Maybe your good book has something to say about it."

Elijah finished his cigarette and licked the end to put out the last of the ember. He clucked at Stick, who was steering for a low limb to clobber them. Elijah tightened the rein until the horse recognized man was ahead of beast on the matter.

He whacked a horsefly, then brushed the remains off his pant leg. "You don't care where we inter those souls behind you," he said. "You just want to avoid dealing with the living over it."

The Cloud ranch buildings at the field's edge had grown long in the shadows. A few ancient elms shaded the house, though they'd lost one recently to disease. Split, quartered, and stacked against the north wall, it would season a year then be priced to warm a winter. The field was irrigated with long pipes extended from a raised water tank fed by a well. At each end rested a giant insect-looking sprinkler. The pastured cattle dotted a sloping hill in the locusts' and bull pines' shade. There was enough grass there to keep them another month, as long as they avoided poisoning themselves with the flowering larkspur and hawksbeard, the only noxious weeds this side of the river.

The road in had been plowed loose, then filled and graded. A black lab yapped and trailed their wagon. The Cloud clan sat in kitchen chairs on the porch, neighbors and shirttail relatives among them. They quieted as the wagon neared. The rate bad news covered country never failed to astonish Strawl. It relieved him, as well. Most of the wailing would be finished.

Elijah drew rein and disembarked from the wagon. Strawl followed. They slapped the dust from their pants, then climbed the porch steps. The men wore denim pants and the bright checked shirts the Indians seemed to find handsome, and the ladies dressed in flowered prints stitched by their own hands.

Strawl lifted his hat. He let Elijah speak.

"I'm sorry," he said. The Cloud boys' mother nodded. Beneath her chair's painted wooden legs lay her leather parfleche, an envelope-shaped satchel the size of an army pack. To stripe it, she'd used vermillion and red ochre and a purple dye concocted from sage buds. A yellow and orange orb painted with birch bark drops and mountain ash looked like an unhinged head over the bright bands. In her hands, she turned a ball of string, knotted and looped to mark the years and good hunts and hard snows and the births and deaths in her family. The string had wrapped around her wrists, but she continued to make loop after loop.

"I have them," Elijah told her.

She looked up at him, and her face twisted.

Strawl spoke up. "The bodies."

"You can see them if you like," Elijah said.

"Here? You brought them?" the Clouds' father asked. He wore a bolo tie stone at his throat and his eyes looked as if he'd just awakened.

"Yes," Elijah said. "Me and him."

"The old sheriff?" he asked. "He is helping you?"

Elijah nodded.

"He didn't do this?"

"No," Elijah said.

The old Indian lifted a pistol from under the blanket in his lap, then opened the cylinder and backed out the shells. He glanced at Strawl. "You hear things," he said.

Strawl nodded.

"You have killed others," he said. The gun was not for evening the score. The San Poil did not believe in revenge very much. For them, time only ran in one direction.

"I understand," Strawl told him.

The man looked at Elijah a moment, blinking his rheumy eyes, then rose and, with his wife, walked to the wagon. Strawl let Elijah take them to the bodies. They stood, gazing upon their boys. The mother rearranged a strand of hair on one. From her dress pocket she withdrew a pair of rosaries and set one on each of their chests. The old man opened one hand of each and deposited a feather, and then they returned to their chairs and misery.

Strawl checked the harnesses on the horses while Elijah spoke to them. He joined Strawl at the wagon finally. "They asked us to take care of them. They don't want the priest finding out and requiring a mass."

Strawl drove the horses. The bodies were close to putrid.

"They bury them in the old days?"

Elijah shrugged. "I've never seen anything but Christian funerals."

"Must be something to it for folks besides exercise digging, I guess, or they wouldn't go to the trouble."

"Ashes to ashes," Elijah said.

"Weren't you arguing for ritual a few hours ago?"

"I was wrong," Elijah said.

They rode awhile in the quiet. The horses' clops ticked at the shortening day. Strawl was thirsty, but the nearest creek was a mile yet and a hundred feet down a steep bank. He didn't know if a drink merited the effort.

He tired suddenly. His legs ached and the place behind his eyes hurt. He handed the reins to Elijah and put his elbows on his knees and set his head into his knobby hands and dug at his temples with his fingers. He could hear himself breathing and his heart rocking in his chest. After a mile, he asked, "Them boys have their guts still?"

Elijah said nothing.

"You wrestled them and that wire. They weigh what a man weighs?"

"More or less," Elijah said.

"Head is ten, twelve pounds tops. Guts twice or more. That'd be near fifty pounds, a third of their body. You'd notice."

"Neck cut would have drained them lickety split," Elijah said. "Just raise their legs and smoke a cigarette and they'd be dry as dust."

"But blood weighs nothing next to flesh," Strawl said. He climbed over the buckboard seat and pulled the covering from the boys. He tugged one shirt open, splitting the buttons, then the others. Finding them unmarked, he examined the neck wounds. Their heads were broken loose with an axe, the flesh hacked and peeled back. Strawl touched their skin. It was toughening, but gave to his fingers. He sifted their greasy hair for the wounds that killed them. They were blunt and deep, likely from the same axe head that had decapitated them.

"He was in a hurry," Strawl said. "He prettied it up, but he didn't gut or drain them and he cut with something other than a razor."

Elijah nodded. "Makes sense. Had to do it between the poker game and breakfast."

"Didn't have to do it at all. He wanted to do it enough to chance it."

By the time they reached the old town site, the day had cooled. Elijah steered them toward the abandoned cemetery.

"You are a lazy son of a bitch," Strawl said.

Elijah grinned. He clucked Stick to an open grave. He took the boy nearest the tailgate by the feet and tumbled him in. The head unloosened and Elijah lifted it in his hands and looked into its face a moment.

"So long partner." He tossed it into the grave, then stood, staring. "I only guessed which head went with which body. Only way to be sure is to bury them together."

Strawl took the ankles of the second boy and Elijah the arms, and they swung his body into the grave. The head, his or not, lolled and the slit throat opened like a meaty, toothless mouth. Strawl and Elijah gazed upon the boys lying back-to-back like two halves finally rejoined.

"Family asked us to stop, coming out," Elijah said.

Strawl didn't reply.

"We'll have to eat."

"Suppose."

"And get drunk, likely."

"Do our manners know no bounds?" Strawl asked.

Elijah climbed aboard the wagon. "I remember when drinking was for pleasure," he said. "Now it's just another goddamned chore."

| TEN |

A dozen cars lined the road into the Cloud house. Elijah lifted a metal loop and dragged a barbwire gate open. They drove through a pasture, then opened a wooden fence to let themselves into the corral and set loose their horses. The animals rolled in the dirt while Elijah deposited an alfalfa bale taken from those that lined the far wall in a manger. Next to it, he added two buckets of oats. Strawl pumped the spigot outside, filling the trough. He and Elijah listened appreciatively to the horses feed and water.

From the house, talk hummed and laughter roughened by liquor. A few stone-faced girls in bright dresses traded a group of boys turns dangling from a rope on an elm branch. Strawl rolled a cigarette and smoked it.

"I'll fetch you a plate of food," Elijah said.

"You hiding me?" Strawl asked. "I've done nothing today but carry home their dead."

"Not many whose memory ends at today," Elijah said.

"I never harmed that family in all my years of work."

"You exist. That's damage enough."

"The Great White Devil."

"Devil doesn't have a color," Elijah said. "How do they know you aren't behind all this murdering, their boys included?"

Strawl pawed the air.

Elijah stayed quiet awhile. "I just thought I'd save you the trouble of a crowd," he said. "You've never been partial to them. No one wants to settle with you."

"That so?"

"You are an IOU nobody can redeem."

"You cashed me out pretty good," Strawl said.

Elijah sat on his haunches and chewed a grass stalk flat. Strawl finished his cigarette. "I'd have a plate," he said finally.

Elijah nodded and Strawl watched him go. In the barn's loft, Strawl constructed a pallet from loose straw and put out his heavy blanket. He brought the saddle from the wagon up the ladder to pillow his head. He wished he'd thought to add a book to his poke, but his bags held only the agency files and he had neither the patience nor light left for that kind of study.

In the late afternoon heat, the crowd milled at the house's near end on a wraparound porch. On a mound in the yard, Cloud stood like a doleful mustang examining his brood. He doffed a genuine Stetson. He'd combed his straight black hair to one side with his hand, though it retained the shape of the hat. His starched canvas slacks would have held their crease in a tornado, and his turquoise shirt buttons matched the stone cinching his bolo tie.

"I want to tell a story," he said. Slowly those around him quieted.

"Seems we were living in the old place on Desautel. A bad wind blew the shingles off the roof, so I sent those two boys up with tar paper to keep the rain out. The roof was steep and they were worried to fall. So they got two lengths from my good hemp rope and tied one end to their belt loops and the opposite to the truck bumper. Then I went to town for shingles."

Someone scuffed his feet in the hard dirt. Two others looked down at their boots.

"They didn't hear the motor go, so the first they knew, they were sliding over the top and down the other side. One fell into an old elm and the other onto the roses.

"When I went back, both were only about half there. One, I don't remember which, cried, 'Don't wake me, I'm dreaming I am a bird.'"

Cloud turned his hat in his knobby hands. He lit a cigarette. "Seemed funny to me," he said finally.

The crowd said nothing until Elijah, who could not purposely abide anyone's embarrassment, shouted, "Well, we were just waiting to hear if the house was one story or two."

The gathering rollicked with laughter, and one of the boys' sisters rose and hugged her father, and his story was rescued as simply as that.

An hour later, Elijah delivered Strawl a plate filled with venison and potatoes and turnips and wild onions, a piece of fried bread atop it all, along with a pitcher of cold tea.

"Thank them," Strawl said.

"I have," he said.

"For me," Strawl said.

"All right," Elijah told him.

He returned to the family, and Strawl ate in the hayloft. Through the open hay door, he watched them pick over their plates stoically, like ants culling their mound. Inside the house, the tables were loaded with casseroles and plates of meat and vegetables. The children ate on the wide windowsills or short parlor tables and the mothers on the floor next to them, while the men bent over porch rails or sat three abreast on the steps. A door shut and, in the backyard, Strawl saw the boys' parents exiting the house. They were silhouetted in the ebbing light, pointed toward the big river and setting sun. They didn't touch, but to Strawl they appeared more attached than if they were stitched together. She bent and lifted a flat board and he turned to face her. She clouted him on the shoulder with the board awkwardly. He bent his legs to maintain his balance. She struck him once more, on the other side, then alternated again. His silhouette shuddered then stilled after each blow, the only sound her labored breath and the board upon his flesh. She went on until she was too tired to lift the wood. He took it from her and placed it next to the back steps, where, Strawl recalled, she had found it. Their behavior had the emotionless trappings of habit and the conviction of a ritual not predicated by the deaths of their sons, but confirming the event nonetheless.

Strawl finished his meal and walked to a mound in the pasture to watch the sun set. He saw Marvin and Inez among the mourners by their voices, as the twilight blanketed the house and its visitors in ashy shadows. Marvin sang a song and the rest put their drinks down until he had finished. Strawl watched a trio of shadows separate from the main group and hurry toward the barn. He lost them in a copse of aspen lining a creek between him and the house. One was Elijah.

Strawl heard two women singing in much the same way Marvin had.

I will never forget you, my people.
I have carved you in the palm of my hand.
I will never forget you, my people.

I will not leave you orphaned.
I will never forget my own.
Does a mother forget her baby?
The child in her womb?
Yet, even if these forget,
I will never forget my own.

Strawl heard Elijah's voice, still in the trees, as the song faded.

"This is our blood, shed for thee," he said. Two female voices repeated the words, then he heard them pause—to drink whiskey, Strawl decided after hearing the women cough.

Elijah announced, "This is our body, broken for thee." Strawl found them on the creek bank. Each pulled at a piece of bread and ate. Their heads bowed as if in prayer. Elijah rose before the women. He stood over them and appeared to bless each with a cross-like gesture. They gazed up at him like animals waiting to be fed. Elijah tugged off his shirt and unbuckled his belt and the women helped each other with their dresses. The sun set on the coulee's lip. A brilliant yellow light lay upon the rock, and the figures were for a moment as precise as drawings. One lay in the cool grass below the trees and Elijah joined her. The woman whined and yipped like a coyote until, finally, Elijah roared as if he were his own peculiar breed of animal; then they stopped and after ten minutes of lying quietly in the grass, the women traded places and Elijah and the other repeated the act and the sounds. After, they rested once more, until the women stirred and dressed Elijah and then themselves. Elijah let them lead him back to the funeral party, as quietly as they had come.

In the stock corral, Strawl rinsed his plate and pitcher under the pump. The dusk had deepened, when he returned to his pallet. He lay and tried to think of nothing. Evenings when they were first married, Dot's mother used to read to him from her Shakespeare volume. *Lear* was his favorite. He enjoyed Edmund, so thoroughly convinced by a philosophy that he behaved as thought itself, hurtling into other people as if they, too, were simply notions and murder just a rhetorical flourish. She favored *Hamlet*. The play disturbed Strawl. Revenge could not have been a motive for such a man. It was simple-minded and bloody and useless against the citadel of time. The man had climbed past the primitive drum of anger but danced to the tune it called anyway.

Strawl regretted the barn roof and beams over him. He'd barter cold against a roof anytime after the snow backed off. Under an open sky, sleep could take a person without his knowing it, but a roof put you straight up against the notion. As a child he'd dreaded his father's last breath upon the lantern. Strawl had woken each morning crying until he was nearly seven, and, though his parents had figured him just a crabby riser, his sobs had been more relief at navigating the night alone. Though his wailing had ended long ago, closing his eyes and abandoning himself to himself still demanded more effort than he was comfortable with.

Elijah woke him past midnight.

"Bless me father for I have sinned."

Strawl blinked his eyes.

"I seen you watching," Elijah said.

The boy handed Strawl a bottle of grape soda. Strawl drank from it. "Isn't much of a transgression," he said.

"It was the boys' wives," Elijah said.

"That is a dicier proposition."

"They wanted me to bring their men back. It was all I knew of to do."

Strawl lay back. He was unwilling to press the boy further. He saw no profit in it.

"I think men have done worse for poorer reasons," Strawl told him.

Elijah lay down in the hay across from Strawl. Soon his breathing turned regular and slow and he was asleep. Strawl sipped the last of the soda and wished he could rise and piss all the venom he possessed into the glass bottle, then replace the cap and bury it someplace he might forget in a day or a month or a year.

Strawl rose and washed his face at the pump. The musty hay filled his nose, and the dew burning off the spring wheat added a doughy dampness. He smelled fresh coffee and could not keep himself from wandering toward the aroma. Cloud sat on the steps smoking from a corncob pipe. He nodded, then invited Strawl to join him. Strawl drew his tobacco from his pocket and started a cigarette. The Cloud woman brought her husband coffee, and upon seeing Strawl, returned with a second cup. Strawl thanked her. He sipped the coffee. It was better than he had hoped, with chicory and a thimble of whiskey enhancing it.

"I thank you for allowing me to bunk in the barn."

Cloud nodded. He sipped at his coffee. His shirt was unbuttoned, and a bruise yellowed his chest.

"I'd like to find who did this to your sons," Strawl told him.

"I thought you would arrest my sons."

"They hadn't done anything," Strawl said.

The old man put a finger over the pipe bowl and drew hard until the ash in it smoked.

"Anyhow, I'm not in the arresting business, anymore. The government is just paying me to find the one doing this killing."

"Killing has not been unusual here," Cloud said. "It is not unlike before, so much."

"It's how the killings occur," Strawl said. "That's what scares them. More than Indians, even."

Cloud smoked. "We scare no one."

Strawl filled his cigarette papers with tobacco, then licked one edge, then rolled it over the other. Cloud struck a match, and Strawl bent toward him and lit his cigarette. He decided to forego technique.

"Your boys know the others that have been killed?"

Cloud said, "The young ones all know each other."

"You have seen those others?" Strawl asked.

"They visited. They slept in the barn, like you."

"All of them?"

"Were there four?"

Strawl nodded.

"They all have been here. The first one baled the last of the fall hay. Another cut wood for meals. He stayed a month. The last two, they were wild. Nowhere was home for them."

"How are they the same? Like your boys?" Strawl asked him.

"They are dead," Cloud said.

Strawl sipped his coffee and smoked. Cloud did the same. A few early risers joined them on the porch. They stretched and yawned and watched the sun pour over the Okanogans.

"Those other boys. They Nez Perce?" Strawl put his finger to his nose.

"I think yes," Cloud said. "Though not from Joseph's band. Maybe Whitebird's."

Strawl thanked the man. They finished their smoke in silence, and when the Cloud woman took his empty cup and returned with it freshened a moment later, he was happy to accept the coffee and remain where he was.

"You will make him stop?" Cloud asked Strawl.

Some argued the Indians' austere intellect, as elemental as hide and skeleton, was what kept this country country, and others declared it a dearth of intelligence at all. If the tribes had managed to equip themselves with concrete and trawlers, perhaps they too would dam a river and fish it into extinction. Strawl only knew that they had not. He had heard it said that when we declaw all nature's monsters, we'll be looking across the table at the genuine article. Whether the speaker meant God or each other, he didn't recall, but now he was chasing the genuine article—and he had come through this ranch and slept in the same barn he himself had a few hours before.

Strawl dumped his coffee dregs on the lawn.

"Yes," he said, finally. "I will make him stop."

| ELEVEN |

Throughout his adolescence, Elijah's reputation swelled, though the locals on both sides of the river were more inclined to describe him as an eccentric than a seer. His makeshift family indulged his whim for wandering as they, themselves, were planets orbiting separate stars, Dot, her husband and first child; Ida, the house duties and her own silent universe; and Strawl, the ennui of ranching.

Elijah soon graduated to predicting car accidents and hospital visits and the occasional arrest, though he still employed time as loosely as a listener would permit. Some would whistle when they discovered yet another prophecy bearing fruit, and others would shake their heads and laugh a little, and some hurrahed him as the Indian soothsayer, though none saw his life's work as anything yet beyond a curiosity. Elijah himself pondered the possibility that he was just observing his surroundings with more vigor than others and that what he saw approaching amounted to a kind of calculation that anyone might exercise given the inclination. He determined to put his shoulder to the wheel. Twice, neighbors reported him for housebreaking, but when they could find nothing missing, Dice refused to press charges. Elijah had admitted to entering the houses; as for stealing, he had no interest. He claimed to simply want to see what living in other houses felt like. Strawl could think of no appropriate punishment, though Dot hid his Bible until he could recite "The Three Bears" to her satisfaction.

Soon locals barely noticed his visits and often felt something close to blessed by his presence rather than victims of a prowling. Like the prophets of yore, however, he suffered from his own darkness. He had gathered enough sense to free himself of witnesses when black moods leaped upon him. He would walk into the woods and fish a creek neck too much trouble for others to frequent and permit his festering mind to race and rid himself of torment, half of himself speaking and the other listening. He'd often shout for hours at nothing but pine needles, sagebrush, or rock, his voice coursing like runoff under a cloudburst. Then the words would trickle to a tolerable quiet.

A month after his seventeenth year, he awakened from an uneasy sleep with a twinge troubling his right arm. His pillow was damp with sweat. Elijah stretched his arm toward the window. His skin silvered in the moonlight. He clenched a fist, and the muscles extending toward it shifted with each finger's shutting, yet the pain remained, not cramp, or rheumatism— which afflicted him when he forecast snow and rain—nor a twisted tendon, which should have slackened when he shifted positions. He located the source, his elbow, and a comparable sensation, a toothache. Nerves strung teeth together, and Elijah concluded that that was what vexed his slumber and, comforted with the knowledge, returned to it.

Two days later on the road out of Nespelem, the malady reappeared as he passed the Catholic church. A week following, he used the road once more and, near the church, the pain nearly knocked him from Baal and his saddle. He stared down at his arm and wondered how it could ache so and remain attached.

That night he retired early and lay in his bed and considered the pain, how it entered him slowly and gathered and then unwound as soon as the church moved from his sight and consciousness. It returned to him that evening when he thought the word "church" and left him when he cleared his mind of it. Another week, on a grocery errand, he saw the bell tower and the pain pressed him. He closed his eyes and let the horses drive themselves past the building. The pain eased, though it would flutter if he even imagined the churchyard's mottled grass or the white pickets surrounding it or the tall double doors at the top of its concrete steps.

He did not pray. If God listened to each of His believers, the Lord would be nothing more than a lackey or at best a gun-for-hire, taking one side over another in exchange for a pile of Hail Marys or Our Fathers. For Elijah, reverence was discovering the sacred within the ordinary. He did, however, double his study of both testaments, adding proverbs and subtracting parables like a bookkeeper squaring his ledger, until he pieced together a sum that kept him out of the red.

A month later, the new priest encountered Elijah at the bottom of the church steps, warning the arriving parishioners.

"When?" a child asked.

"Soon," Elijah said.

"What is this?" the priest asked.

"Fire," the little girl said. "In the church."

Elijah offered the man his prophecy. The priest listened, his clean-shaven, fair face brightening in the warmth of morning, and cocked his head.

"Why would this church be burned?" the priest asked.

A crowd had gathered, white merchants in tan jackets and Indians wearing thin pale shirts buttoned to their throats. The white women moved past into the church, but the Indian women remained. The priest was a polite man, shy except perhaps at the pulpit, where he could read scripture at the tops of the parish's bowed heads and offer short sermons all would find agreeable.

"The Lord sends fire when he wants cleansing. He tried the water, but it was a mess, if you recall."

"What here is unclean?" the priest asked.

Elijah said that the reason belonged to God, and that they would have to take him at his word.

"We can't do that, I am afraid," the priest told Elijah.

"That is why it will burn, then."

The priest moved him off the property, but Elijah remained outside the church fence through both services, politely repeating his prophecy. It was early winter and fire was the least of the parishioners' concerns, but each following Sunday, after taking his breakfast with Ida and Strawl at sunup, Elijah met them with the same warning, as devout in his way as the most pious of their flock. The children brought him gifts, hard candy, a biscuit with butter and honey, unfinished cigarettes they collected from ashtrays. Elijah took his gloves from his hands and blessed each of them by making a cross on their foreheads with his finger. This scandalized the members and they insisted the police expel Elijah from town, but the BIA had no interest in crossing Strawl or working Sundays.

Winter relented, but spring delivered only dry, warm winds from cloudless skies. The snowmelt filled the creeks, then they ebbed to late summer's trickle. Disced fields raised dust enough for the fire department to mistake it for smoke at least twice. The locals had heard of the Dust Bowl and successfully avoided that catastrophe, but soon the strands of grain whiskering the field ruts drooped and yellowed. Cattle turned unruly for lack of drink.

Spring gave way to summer and the adults in the church's flock began to ridicule the prophet. Their sarcasm and mockery combined to turn the children from him, as well. Instead of gifts, they pelted him with pebbles and chanted, "Fire, Fire, put him out."

Patience had become second nature to Elijah, but the public was another matter. It wasn't the ridicule that troubled him; it was that his prophecy was turning the parishioners from the Word rather than delivering them to it. June continued hot and the forests caught fire in the dry lightning, putting all the able-bodied Indians on crews with a pick and an axe, and the lawns died and the alfalfa refused to sprout because the irrigation pipes could pump no water and the buildings dried like kindling. Elijah realized it was his prophecy at the root of this strangeness. God was bound by it and would withhold the rain until Elijah's fire turned truth. Providence sweltered in the sun.

The last week of the month, the parish came and went on Sunday, fanning themselves with bonnets and hymnals. The mercury climbed to 95 degrees, and later the priest harnessed the team the livery provided him to visit the shut-ins. Elijah struck a match to the woodpile stacked on the sanctuary wall. The sulfur flared yellow and smelled acrid until the wood above it caught and the seasoned pine crackled and wood smoke replaced it.

"Lord, I release you from this promise," Elijah said, and walked away while the flames climbed the porch railings.

The police visited the ranch the next morning. Dice and a BIA Indian questioned Elijah at his kitchen table. Ida, too frightened to face the police, paced in front of the corral. The parishioners were strangers. He had no motive to wish them harm. The new priest had always been kind to him, and, if Elijah were a heathen, he'd not waste seven months on believers or risk an arson charge for a building they would replace with another within the year, anyhow. The experience would bind the flock rather than scatter them.

When he'd finished, Dice said, "I can't argue with any of it."

The BIA cop rose with him, and Elijah watched them walk to the Studebaker patrol car and leave, dust rising in the already hot air. Strawl stood awhile, too, until the car broke over the coulee's lip and its dust thinned to a haze.

"Dodge a bullet?" Strawl asked.

Elijah said nothing.

"Well, how do you want your eggs?"

Elijah chose scrambled and walked into the root cellar in the dirt bank behind the house for a rope of German sausage, and together they peeled potatoes and fried them in grease and boiled coffee and stirred up enough breakfast to treat Arlen and Dot and the girls, who had risen early and were presently teasing their yellow dog with a sock-covered pinecone to keep his mouth soft to retrieve birds.

The next Sunday, Elijah put out a coffee table across from the church ruins, where he lined bread squares and several shot glasses he'd filled with grape juice.

The Christ Elijah knew was an offering to redeem the sins of the Father, not those of Man. The Lord was a mean and selfish parent, and he was heartbroken over it. The crucifixion was a self-inflicted wound intended to square him with his flock. But He had not counted on the son's travails and the sympathy others would attach to them, and resurrection became the only way to escape another instance of ogre-like behavior.

The following Sunday, the churchless congregation had pitched a tent borrowed from the army. A low sky lay over them, bruised and drizzling. Tendrils of fog and mist clung in the draws and stretched in a patched and lacy streak above the river's course. When the parishioners passed Elijah, the men nodded and a few tipped their hats, and the women averted their eyes, but the children stared at him with unabated awe. The priest glanced at his face a moment before he moved on. Elijah had expected worse, but he now found himself wishing for more, that they would understand that the fire was not the point, or what sparked it. Some Great Will was pressing at them, but they had abandoned their lives to circumstance, making miracles as mundane as weather, bearing each like animals scurrying for shelter from a sky full of rain or snow or heat and emerging afterwards as if nothing at all had occurred.

Children surrounded his table, snacking on the bread and sipping the juice, trying to avoid wrecking their best clothes.

"But this is not really your body," a child said. "How do you make it your body?"

Several children agreed and the parents smiled, amused at the stumped prophet. Elijah raised his hand. "You're right," he said. "This won't do. Fortunately, there is the old way."

Elijah drew something that shined silver as water from his satchel—a hatchet honed hours upon a whetstone, they would later discover—which, after he placed his hand upon the table, he employed to amputate his left pinkie finger in a single blow.

"Now," he said, as it skipped across the dirt toward the children. "It is my body."

| **TWELVE** |

Inchelium in the mid-thirties was little more than a scattering of hovels and a post office at one end of Gifford Ferry, which still traverses the Columbia from dawn to midnight each night of the week. The side opposite the Colville Reservation belongs to the Spokanes. In the old days, a blonde-haired Indian named Barney Whitehead ran a honky-tonk with a dirt floor and a canvas roof just past the ferry site. The place sold bathtub gin for a nickel a throw and beer three times what it cost at the market.

Once, when Strawl happened to travel by, the regulars had carted chairs into the parking lot where they sat, beer bottles between their knees and shotguns set to fire at any goose unlucky enough to pass.

Strawl did not expect to find Jacob Chin in Inchelium any more than anyplace else on this side of the state, but for reasons as varied as their fortunes, many of his ex-wives, concubines, and conspirators resided in the town along with a sister, who most agreed was the most beautiful woman they had ever encountered. She never ventured from Inchelium, where it was rumored she rode horses through the forested trails in the nude. It appeared to Strawl as good a beginning point as any on the man.

When Strawl had mounted to leave two evenings before, Elijah had Baal saddled, as well, and there was nothing more said. They approached Inchelium from the Colvilles' side after traveling Sherman Pass through several thousand fire-strafed acres. The grasses and wildflowers had commandeered the flats, the ruined trees compost feeding them. The field parted and waved in the wind.

The early afternoon sun lifted the dew from the ground and rock and trees' needles, and the air was hazy and damp. Strawl tipped his hat back and wiped his brow. He drew rein and allowed Stick to drink at a public trough on the town's edge. Elijah did the same with Baal.

"You know your way around here?" Strawl asked him.

"Does the Lord know his sheep?"

"We're about to find out," Strawl said.

They rode on until they reached a blue house with a tar paper roof. There was no lawn other than weeds, though someone had planted a thin rosebush next to the wooden steps.

Strawl dismounted. He wound Stick's reins to a wire fence that lined the property.

"Have at it," Strawl said.

Elijah glanced at him, then swung his right leg over the back of Baal, rode a few steps, then walked to the door and knocked.

"You seen Jake?" Elijah asked.

The woman who'd answered the door was in her forties; she looked past Elijah to Strawl behind him.

"Don't know him," she said.

"Martha, you were married to him," Elijah said.

"Was," she said. "Now I don't know him so well." She shut the door.

Elijah put his hands on his hips, then lifted one arm. He spun his finger. Strawl tried to steal behind a shed to find the back door, but someone had stacked a cord of wood between the house and a high fence. Strawl stepped on the sticks, but the pile shifted. He lost his balance. A quartered round banged his bad knee and another clobbered him in the ear. In addition, the ruckus stirred a litter of woodpile cats. Following a chorus of yowling and hissing, three sprang upon him, each digging into his hide when he pulled it off. Next door, a dog barked.

Strawl retreated to the street. Elijah surrendered without knocking again and was aboard Baal when Strawl returned. They rode two more blocks to a dwelling across from the cinderblock school and firehouse.

"Better clean yourself up," Elijah said.

Strawl pulled his handkerchief from his shirt pocket and dabbed the blood from his forearms and the backs of his hands. Elijah had dismounted, and he watched Strawl from the ground, shaking his head.

"You'd do well not to mock me," Strawl said.

"Big talk from a man that gets whipped by cats." Elijah turned for the door while Strawl walked Stick to where they couldn't be seen. He rolled a cigarette. A light wind from the river pressed at an oak's green leaves, and a swing set chain creaked in the schoolyard. The grass surrounding the school shone where the kids had beat a path from the dirt street to the play toys.

The house's door shut, and Elijah walked dejectedly back to his horse. The muscles behind his jaw knotted. He rode to the next house and rapped on the door. When no one answered, he didn't bother to get aboard Baal, and instead walked her the few feet to the next house and secured her rein to a tree limb. A wooly white man answered, his grey hair askew like a badly fitted halo.

He shoved Elijah off the step. He wore no shirt, just suspenders, and his skin pinked in the doorway. Elijah stared at the man, who blinked. He eyed Strawl, then turned his attention back to Elijah.

"I don't know you," he said.

"That's right," Elijah said.

The man closed the door.

At the next house, an old Indian woman nodded and offered him a pastry, which he fed to Baal, but had no information on Jacob Chin. Elijah inquired at every house on the block, then crossed the street and repeated his work on the other side.

"You know any of these people?" Strawl asked.

Elijah shrugged. "Some."

"You don't act it."

Elijah wagged his chin at a house up the street. "Warren there. I helped him and his brother butcher an elk this past winter."

"You didn't attempt much conversation."

"I'm looking for a killer," Elijah said.

Strawl laughed. "What did you say to him?"

"Told them I was hunting for Jake."

"Never said hello?"

"No, just inquired about Jake."

"Another time, you'd have chewed the fat a little, wouldn't you?"

Strawl lit a cigarette and let Elijah lead him past the school toward the only cross street of notice, where a service station and a grocery took up two kitty corners. A shut tavern and the town livery were on the other two.

"Asking straight out isn't natural," Strawl said.

"Neither is pretending I'm not looking for someone I am."

Strawl sighed. "You married to the truth?"

"Truth is natural," Elijah said.

Strawl shook his head. "Getting what you want is natural."

They were quiet awhile. The wind was cooling. Summer was losing its traction.

Elijah pointed toward the Columbia. "Its fish suit me when I am hungry and its water if I have a thirst, but if it's between me and those places I want to go, then I find a ferry or a bridge. And those are the lies."

"Could be they're just truth told in a different way."

"What kind of way?"

"Way that will get you across the river."

Elijah was quiet awhile.

"What's a dam, then?" he said finally.

Strawl considered for a minute, but he saw no way the metaphor could go further.

"It's a big piece of concrete that stops up rivers, you goofy bastard," Strawl said.

Elijah laughed. Strawl felt a little defeated and was sullen as they rode out the north portion of the town up a dirt road that led to another one, which finally ended at the foot of a shale escarpment beneath the ridges the river had cut. Strawl heard a spring. He and Elijah stopped to let the horses slake their thirst.

A home lay in an elm copse; it was not board and nail but granite rounded by a thousand years of river current pressing against it. The stones were stacked edge-wise and mortared with concrete troweled with a care unusual for these parts. The roof was shingled in green shakes to repel fire. Genuine glass windows fit into the careful gaps left for them, which held no caulk to square their sills or frames. There was no reason for the structure not to stand into the next millennium. A smattering of lawn surrounded the place, and a gate with no fence attached stood poor sentry against thieves or visitors. No dog sounded. The place had no outbuildings or corral. Smoke rose from the stovepipe. Those inside were afoot.

Elijah tied Baal near the concrete porch steps and opened the door. A lantern's light drifted through the doorway. A few minutes later, Elijah's arm beckoned. Strawl snubbed Stick to one of the elms near a patch of wild oats.

Inside, the lantern lit a low table next to a bench sofa, which held Chin's sister. Her beauty had instigated a multitude of broken noses and twice that many arrests. Though its height was some years behind her, she remained as exotic and beautiful and was now handsome, as well, with high cheekbones and skin the color of well-finished wood. Her nose was tiny and her eyes large and full of something that Strawl could see even now might turn a wise man idiot. She'd stayed thin in the places it suited a woman and broad in the places that it suited one, too. The cards before her on the table lay in rows, and each flip was accompanied by a toss of her plaited black hair, the snap and whoosh the only noises in the room aside from the lantern burning its kerosene reservoir. An older man, not quite Marvin's vintage but at least Strawl's, smoked and drank tea. Once, he corrected the woman's play, and she exchanged the cards as he advised without a word. No one spoke until she had sorted through her discards twice for a play she might have overlooked. Strawl watched her gather the cards and shuffle them, her fingers not blunt, meaty male digits, intent on bending the deck from shape, but the flutter of bird wings, mixing the cards in a synchronized rhythm—feathers in air.

Instead of dealing out another hand, she squared the deck and set it aside.

"Please," she nodded toward a chair in the kitchen. "Sit. Excuse my manners."

"Obliged," Strawl said. Elijah, too, fetched a chair and nodded his thanks.

"Are you hungry?" the woman asked. Then she waved away the question. "You are hungry," she said. "Who is not hungry this time of evening?"

In the kitchen, she cut some tortillas from a roll of flat bread and stoked the stove, then began to warm the hard beans she had soaked. When they were near soft enough to refry, she lifted a door in the kitchen floor and disappeared into the cellar to return with a venison back strap that she shredded with a hand-grinder. She set the meat to simmer and added a half dozen spices.

Strawl examined the room for any indication Jacob might be on the premises or that he'd been a recent visitor. He found nothing. His sister kept an immaculate house, though it appeared to be her nature, rather than a ploy. He watched her carefully for nerves while she continued to circle from pot to skillet to the cutting board, and, when she thought he and Elijah and the silent man on the sofa had hit the dregs of their drinks, she widened her orbit to refill each cup.

She fed them on porcelain plates, and the fork and spoon were genuine silver, though the knives were stainless steel for practical reasons. She filled five cordial glasses with brandy and set one next to each plate. The silent man unscrewed a quart jar of green chilies and peppers. Strawl sniffed the lid, then spooned the concoction onto his plate. He dipped a forkful of beans into it and, pleased with the result, tipped the jar and shoveled more over his meal. Elijah opted for no garnish, but ate as if he had a bet on it, and the woman rose to refill his plate before she had taken a bite from her own meal. Strawl crossed his eyes at him and the boy looked hangdogged until the woman returned with his food and bent and kissed his forehead. He glanced up and she remained a moment to let his blinking eyes look into hers. She smiled and, in that moment, Strawl felt a thread of envy for the boy.

They drank their brandy and tea and finished their meal in silence aside from the silver's clack against the porcelain. As the woman cleared the plates, the old man filled a hooked pipe with tobacco. He nodded and Elijah and Strawl built two cigarettes and followed the man to the porch.

Each lit a match and pulled in smoke until there were two embers lighting the evening and another shadowy, sinister glow. The man was grey at the temples, though for the most part, his hair remained black. He'd cut it like a helmet around his face. His slanted eyes looked less so because of the weather his face had seen. One might have mistaken him for just another farmer.

The woman joined them, gathering her skirt and upon a step below, gazing as the trees stirred in what was left of the river's breeze and glancing at the men only occasionally through smoke.

"You are hunting Jacob Chin," said the man.

Strawl nodded.

"My brother-in-law. My woman's brother. You come here to this home."

"Yep," Strawl said.

The man sighed and considered his situation. "Do you think," the man said, "that it is wrong to call your sister a whore?"

Strawl remained quiet; the man tipped his face toward Elijah.

"Seems a little hard," Elijah answered.

The woman ducked her face into her brandy and drank.

"What if she was? I mean if she was a prostitute by definition. She accepted money or gratuity for the favors of her sex."

Elijah remained silent.

"Would it be unlike stating she was brown-haired or tall or short?"

"It would be mean," Elijah decided.

"Would it?" the man asked. "If you spoke it lovingly, like a mother who told people my son is a congressman or a doctor. He helps people. Does not a prostitute heal us?"

Elijah looked stumped. Strawl turned toward the door to avoid staring at the back of the woman's head.

"It's her brother saying it," he said finally.

"Jacob?"

The man nodded. "Who is her brother to lie?" He shifted in the chair he had brought from the kitchen so he could see Elijah and the woman. She stared into the yard, leaving a man's workshirt she was wearing and her plaited hair to answer for her.

He turned his attention to Elijah. "If he said she had a pleasant ass, well, that would be wrong. But it might be as true as saying she was a whore. If he liked skinny buttocks, with only a little curve where the hamstring thinned and the flesh turned meaty and then a smooth, graceful rise like the arc of the horizon, then a steep drop like a teamster with no brakes barreling off the hills to a spine flat as Nebraska. And if instead of packing around a caboose as broad as Mae West's half moons, two muscled crescents as small as a boy's pressed her legs forward, and those paired muscles were just about as beautiful to him as the sound of dogs on the scent or a blue sky in the morning, well, wouldn't that be as worthy a truth as there is?"

Elijah drank from his brandy and then his tea. He looked disappointed. Both had cooled. The woman's fingers threaded a strand of grass. She put it to her lips and whistled through it.

"Would this man not be lying if he claimed she did not possess a backside of the same proportions that he found most pleasing? What path is there for such a person?"

"Ignorance," Strawl said.

The old man smiled. "For you and I, yes. We have enough

winters behind us to think practically. We know spring is always coming."

"And then another winter," Strawl said.

The man rapped his pipe against the porch railing. "Hope and despair, they chase one another like children, and time is only the gods at play. We know plenty."

"Like any backside is only as good as the front side."

"Well said," the old man replied. "But our friend. He doesn't have enough seasons to be certain. He thinks spring might someday remain, despite the winters he has seen."

"A romantic," Strawl said.

"Would this observation be such a sin in, as you say, a romantic?" He relit his pipe and pulled from it, then unloosed a cloud of pungent smoke. "Would not such a man be tortured? Would not he have to be crazy to be sane?"

"I don't know," Strawl said.

"And remember, this sister, with this anatomical wonder, was selling it, or renting it—that is a much more accurate manner to think of this thing—so she and he would have food enough. Would it not be impossible for him to separate her ass from the sister who possessed it, just as it would be impossible to separate the voice that moaned and gasped under those tenants from the one that called him to meals or that had cooed to him through childhood fevers and injuries?"

Elijah rolled a second cigarette.

"It would be a relief to blame the girl, but then she would blame her parents, who abandoned the two of them to St. Rose of Lima Catholic Church in Bellingham, and then they would cite their own starvation, and who can find a rationale to condemn a person for existing and wanting to continue? Who is responsible for so many unfortunate pregnancies gestating to fruition? Lust, you may argue, was their weakness, but they acted upon it in the only manner the good book prescribes. That is a ridiculous argument, I think you would agree. A god who claims our heat for one another is sinful and then requires it to make families. Well, he makes more difficulty than is reasonable. God cannot be so unfeeling or impractical."

"Unless he has a sense of humor," Strawl said. He looked at Elijah. "You going to let him talk down the almighty?"

Elijah said, "It's not my God that he's talking about. It's the Catholics'."

"Hairsplitting," Strawl said.

The man stared into his open hands, then at Strawl. "Do you believe such cruelty comes from above?"

"It doesn't matter what I think."

"But it does. You are an orphan."

"That's no secret."

"So you have no sympathy?"

"Like I told you, doesn't matter what I think."

"Do you have a sister?"

Strawl shook his head.

"Ah. Perhaps if you did. And if she were beautiful."

The evening was cooling. Elijah put his jacket over the woman's bare legs. Strawl listened for the horses until he was certain both were where they had been left.

"So that is the end of blame," the man said.

"All right," Strawl said. "I absolve our friend of any indiscretions with his sister. He has earned a reprieve."

The man nodded. "And you would agree, then, that he must be forgiven for resenting his sister's patrons. Because he now has twice the reason to be offended: that of a brother and that of a lover. So it is natural he would hate them."

Strawl nodded.

"And not unnatural that those whose spite includes a discourteous comment directed toward him or his sister would leave him especially angry. It would be no shock, then, that he would decapitate three or four in those years and tie them by their hair or their beards to streetlights, where they would be discovered the next morning by the priests and nuns engaging in their constitutionals following morning prayers. In fact, you might admire his restraint. And forgive him, even, for murdering the grocer and his wife, who had neither touched his sister nor spoken to him, but was nevertheless engaged in a great conspiracy to kill them, by eating when he and his sister had no food and sleeping when they were tired and having a house when it rained. Who can say, without any consideration, that he, himself, would not have done the same?"

Strawl smiled. "Not me," he said.

"Would you arrest such a man?" the old fellow asked.

Strawl shook his head. "I'd kill him."

"You would feel no pity?"

"What worse punishment is there for that man than breathing another breath?"

"But he is guilty of nothing."

"That's not true."

"Well, then he's no more guilty than the rest of us."

Strawl nodded. "Rabid dog, he isn't sick on purpose, and prophets, they never set out to hear God in their heads, yet that doesn't stop us from putting a bullet into their brain buckets or nailing them to a pair of perpendicular beams. And it doesn't make me or the Romans anything but right for doing it. According to your theory, Judas was as innocent as the virgin. Nobody's guilty, but people still need killing, for their own sake or others'. It doesn't matter to me except when the pay comes through."

Suddenly the woman began to laugh and she continued for

a long enough time to hush them. She looked at the old man through the smoke. "Maybe now you can put that story away for good, Howard. I'm damned tired of us all being saints."

She rose and stepped past them, dropping Elijah's jacket in his lap before disappearing into the house, where she lit a lantern and carried it to her room, then drew the curtain. The light floated beneath as she discarded one garment and donned another, and that was enough to hold their attention even after she turned the lamp down and the room was nothing but dark.

"You know why I'm here," Strawl said.

The old man nodded.

"She does, too?"

"Yes."

"This Jacob, what is he to you?"

"It's what he is to her."

"I just heard a story about all that. What is he to you?"

"It's what she is to me."

"Your wife, then. Seems you'd both be glad to see the back of him."

"That may be true," the man said.

"But it can't be your idea?"

The man nodded.

"Just tell me where to find him. I'll think the rest myself."

"How do you know he is the killer you seek?"

"I know he's murdered and that he's twisted as a top. That moves him to the front of the class."

"He will not go to prison."

"You'd be surprised what people will do once their alternatives dwindle. I expect he'll hang, anyway."

"He won't allow it."

"Then I'll kill him. I get paid and you get shed of his shadow betwixt you and her."

"No," he said. "That is not something you can kill."

Strawl snuffed the last of his cigarette against his boot heel. "We'll sleep on it," he said. He walked behind the house and loosed his bedroll from Stick, and Elijah did the same with Baal. It was cold and they built a fire to keep the morning frost from them. The man invited them inside, but Strawl preferred a cold sky to a warm bed, especially in a house with so many different versions of the same people residing in it. Elijah said nothing. His quiet was not sad, but measured like he was waiting for the scales to quit rocking and level. They both slept easily until after midnight, when they were awakened by the woman's howls and the old man trying to settle her. It took a half hour and Strawl listened to her quiet, then catch herself on a sob and cry some more. Elijah rose and entered the house and then her bedroom.

"I am an incestuous whore," she said.

"You are not either," Elijah told her.

"I am," she said.

"There is no glass in nature," Elijah said. "Did you know that? The alchemists hunted the philosopher's stone to conjure two things: gold and glass. One for obvious reasons, the other for miracles, because what would be more of a miracle than a stone one couldn't see, but could see anything through? Your beauty is glass, and it reflects the beauty of others like a mirror. You are a miracle. But you do not know it. You possess a soul that lights the glass. And if you recognized your own light, you could expect love, and return it.

"But then a man tells you a hard truth, one you don't want to hear, one he doesn't want to speak: there is no God, or the poor don't inherit the earth, or your beauty is not timeless. And you shout at him, 'Why are you telling me this?'

"It is only later, you realize he does not see through you like glass and does not want to. He instead longed to open his skin with the shard that is you, to bleed upon you and make you visible."

"Who is this man?" she asked.

"He is any one of us. The man isn't the point."

"Did you burn the church?"

Elijah laughed. "Lots of things burned that summer," he said.

"Is my brother the killer?"

"No."

"How do you know?"

"Because I don't want him to be."

When she was silent half an hour, Elijah returned to his sleeping bag. He and Strawl lay and listened to the crickets a long while.

"Miss that pinky finger?" Strawl asked.

"Just counting ten," Elijah said.

They were quiet awhile.

"I never saw anyone as pretty," Elijah said.

"Me neither," Strawl said. "Though she'd have had better luck plain as a sack of barley."

Elijah didn't reply.

"You might have lied to her," Strawl said. "The brother looks good for it."

"But you're not sure, so it's the truth until another truth takes its place."

Strawl said nothing, but he considered the circle of damage Jacob Chin and his sister had wrought until he dropped off.

When they woke, she fed them a breakfast of venison sausage and biscuits and gravy, and they ate past their fill. Neither offered a word toward Jacob's whereabouts, though Strawl discovered a cash receipt drawn on a Wilbur bank and, reflected in a bedroom mirror, a buffalohide cape of the type the Montana Crow constructed, too large for the man or the sister, separate or together, but the kind of garment a man like Jacob, Taker of Sisters, would hang on to out of vanity. If it was here, he was south, where the towns and murders were and where the autumn had not yet reached.

| THIRTEEN |

When the horses returned them over the ridge lining the San Poil, Strawl directed Elijah to inquire at the houses and line shacks in the valley. Strawl took the ridgeline and looked for smoke. Late afternoon, he saw Elijah ascending once more. Jacob, Taker of Sisters, had a woman in the Swahila Basin. She took in his laundry and cooked for him several times a month. He'd been there two mornings before, then boarded the Wilbur Ferry. Apparently he had some history with the Cloud boys. One of them had insulted him.

"He might've went to old Canada."

"What makes you think so?"

"No reason."

"Exactly," said Strawl.

Jacob would be carousing in the towns across the big river, where the wheat had been cut and the farmhands were flush and whiskey-inclined following a month of seven-day weeks and fourteen-hour days. Cards and dice made them easy marks.

"It's supposed to be harder," Elijah said.

"What's that?"

"Finding them."

"What makes you say so?"

"Books."

"Books don't know," Strawl said.

At the Keller store, Strawl purchased flour and dried beef enough for a week of camps and Elijah a whole cake in a box, which he tied carefully to his saddleback, employing three ropes to anchor it against the horse's bouncing back quarters. The old Keller Road wound them through the north and eastern portions of the Swahila Basin, the best farming country on the entire reservation. Yellow wheat bent, then relaxed under the evening wind, the bearded stalks bouncing like froth upon a flaxen sea.

Across the river, the only true palisades north of the Big Bend bordered the water for three miles, leaving no beach or bank. The granite glittered silver and green and red, depending on the light. The two-hundred-foot cliff threw a shadow over the hastening river and the opposite bank, where Strawl and Elijah rested and watered the horses. The two of them collected wheat stalks and rubbed the kernels from the hairy seed heads and fed them to the horses. They continued until dark, meandering toward the ferry until the horses were well fed. Twilight, they shared the flat ferry's deck with three Fords and a Chrysler. Their drivers sat sullenly at their steering wheels or fooled with their radios, though no station transmitted past a hum in this low country. The ferryman pitched his bow into the wind to bisect the river's waves. The spray spattered the cars' window glass and wet Strawl's face. He lifted his hat and let the top of his head cool, then wiped his hand across his damp hair and his hooded brow and the orbs of his eyeballs and his abrupt triangle of a nose and then the thin lips and worn teeth beneath them. They felt like corpses might to the mortician who prepared them.

The horses tipped their faces into the air and enjoyed the wet breeze. Elijah chewed a jerky strip in silence. The pilot swung the bow opposite the lined pilings, then gunned the throttle a moment and cut the engine. He scrambled to the bow, gaffing the first hoop in the concrete dock; he pushed off once to brake, at the same time threading a rusty chain with links as large as fists through the hoop, then snubbing it with a heavy lock, then he was on to the next hoop, stopping the ferry entirely with such precision the boat didn't rock, nor did the bow chain grow taut. He unhinged a metal ramp, spat a stream of tobacco into the water, lynched the bolt securing the plates to the landing, and waved at the first car, which turned on its lights and exited, as did the others, stitching a yellow and red lit chain on the switchbacked grade rising from the river.

The weather was mild. Strawl and Elijah allowed the horses a leisurely pace. In the fields above the breaks, threshing machines hummed in the darkness along with the voices of the men who sewed the grain sacks shut and others who threw them into long horse-drawn wagons. Implements crawled, stirring the dust and chaff, while the scarlet moon poured light onto the skyline. The cool, settling air smelled rich as a baking oven.

They both lit cigarettes when they climbed past the canyon rim, then glanced at one another.

Elijah gazed into the night, now fully dark aside from the starlight and the red moon.

"He isn't any more likely to murder tonight than last night," Strawl said.

Elijah said, "No less, either."

"He might kill some gossip or blowhard, though."

Elijah smoked a minute, then spit on his thumb and forefinger and snuffed out the ash. "He done the world little good as it is. Sinful to halt him if he's balancing the ledger."

Strawl nudged Stick and he made for a dirt road off the gravel, then another that had dwindled to a set of weedy tire tracks. A mile following it put them at an ancient line shack. The walls were not going to keep much out, but the weather was calm, and inside were a metal stove and enough wood to cook a decent breakfast. They hobbled the horses in a grassy eyebrow to let them feed and doze. Both put out their bedrolls and lay atop them. Elijah drank water from a canteen and then rinsed his face over a tin. He dropped his eyes and doused the rest of his head. Satisfied he was clean, he bent over the tin and raked his scalp as dry as he could, then let the remaining water tick from his hair into the tin. Finally, when it had quit, he combed it back and pillowed his head with his saddle and dropped to the quick and ghostless sleep of the young.

Strawl, himself, could not. He lay and listened through the glassless windows at the wind move, then quit, then begin again, until his ears climbed under that sound and found the horses, Stick alternating his weight from one side to the other and Baal tugging shoots from the ground and turning them to paste with her mouth. A truck pulled the hill, motor whining until the driver clutched and shifted down.

He would like to have been able to say he lay until dawn recounting his sins, or pondering the physics of a planet that spun so plumb it held all the creatures upon it upright, yet kept such poor time the calendar required an extra day one year in four to make sense. He was the kind to ponder in such terms, but a manhunt pressed those high thoughts into hibernation. He slept through their inevitable questions intent to awaken with the sense of the puzzle maker rather than another witless piece. Knowledge was just the jug a man drank from, anyway. Arithmetic might fill one and words another, and a man could swap bottles and drink his fill of both yet understand nothing because most men's minds are sieves, not cisterns.

In the predawn blue, Strawl watched a paint labor on a game trail. Its rider, an immense man, was hunched over the saddlehorn, asleep. Jacob, the Taker of Sisters, was nearly too much weight for his mount. He required a quarter horse or maybe an Arabian cross if he were to cover any ground at all, not the skinny paint he was aboard.

The Lord had constructed Jacob for the Iliad: loose-jointed as a cat and thick in the chest and the ass; he had thin legs and arms thick as tree roots and greased hair pulled back that shone purple in the low light—power you could not write away for in a magazine or curry with dumbbells. God's intent resides in such men's bodies, more so even than it inhabits a priest's soul or a lover's heat or a surgeon's blade. Just breathing, such a man was prophet and prophecy, an act before thought, as quick as the almighty's mind and as inculpable. Whatever made him was before sin or forgiveness or the guilt in between.

Strawl watched man and horse descend the road into the river bottom, then choose a fence-line trail and negotiate it in the predawn gloaming. Cattle lowed as they passed, and the wheat stirred in the wind that pushed through this country every morning, whether it was ninety above or ten below. Jacob dismounted to open a barbwire gate, then shut it behind him. Strawl heard a truck engine turn and then catch. The horse and Jacob glanced in the sound's direction. Sparrows cheeped. Bobwhites bobwhited. A great horned owl whooed and went silent, and the gulls over the river cawed and fussed and circled the ferry landing and the garbage containers. Killdeer scolded and the chukar in the shale falls clacked as horse and rider passed, just threads of shadow in the thin, coming light, blessed horse and sacred man, just tracks and light diverted a moment, then not.

A year before Strawl retired, a Lincoln County deputy called Lucky—who was anything but; Jacob had put his eye out rather than be arrested—had told him about the dilapidated ranch building where Jacob was bound. The deputy had done some homework and discovered the place was neither abandoned nor inhabited. The Chin sister had purchased it and ten useless acres from a bachelor rancher for a paltry sum and services rendered, then signed the deed over to Jacob. The deputy had no interest in walking into a hornet's nest, but he told anyone who would listen in hopes another might be game for the risk.

Strawl had at first figured Jacob's direction to be north—Loomis and Palmer Lake, where he might drink and fish and lie low. It's what a guilty man would do. Instead, Jacob parked himself in the wheat ranches and farm towns where the locals would not likely miss his coming or going. He could hold out against a single man there, but a group could take him without much trouble. The move troubled Strawl.

Elijah's joining the hunt troubled him, too. Strawl could see no reason for it and wasn't inclined toward company, though Elijah would be handy if they crossed swords with a man as formidable as Jacob. Still, it remained another thing he didn't understand in a business where blind spots had killed better men than himself.

FOURTEEN

Strawl rose and lit a fire in the stove. He set coffee to perk and then fell into a silent, dreamless sleep and awakened only when he heard a cured bacon side popping in a pan. A circle of hard biscuits rose in another and Elijah, bent, guarded them from burning.

Strawl ate his breakfast and glanced at Elijah, who was mopping up bacon grease with a biscuit.

"He's down Spiegel Canyon," Strawl said.

Elijah sipped at his coffee and watched the black surface rock in the cup. He lifted his eyes and blinked.

"Dropped in the west break and an hour later out the east."

"Then he isn't in the Spiegel Canyon."

"The road," Strawl said. "They call it Spiegel Canyon Road all the way to the river."

"Well, you should have said it was the road you meant."

"I never said it wasn't." Strawl lay against his bedroll and closed his eyes.

"You aren't in any hurry, are you?" Elijah said.

"Neither is he. Careful man never is."

"He doesn't know we're trailing him?"

"He's been chased his whole life," Strawl said. He sipped at the coffee, but it had cooled.

"The river is at his back and cliffs on both sides. One road in and out."

"He knows what he's doing."

Elijah remained quiet awhile. He refilled Strawl's coffee.

"You ask a lot of damned questions," Strawl said.

"I haven't asked a one."

"No, but there you sit, waiting to be answered all the same."

Elijah looped and cinched the strap securing his bedroll.

"You don't sound smart enough to make a study, anyway."

"Smart person keeps it to himself."

"Well, don't let me make you a moron. Silence appeals to me as much as the next person."

Strawl waved a hand to dismiss him. "You'd talk the bark off a tree."

"But I don't require the tree to say much."

Strawl drifted back toward sleep; his hat, smelling like hair and sweat and living, shaded the light. Twilight offered their best odds. The light turned tricky at the end of the day, and the birds' chirping would provide cover. They might even catch Chin drunk. Strawl tried to sleep, but the rheumatism in his hip and knees moved him to shift positions, and his rest was fitful at best. He finally quit on it altogether and propped himself against his saddle. He drank a cup of lukewarm coffee, his face blank of emotion.

Elijah struck a match head against the floorboards. An acrid sulfur smell reached Strawl as it caught, and then the tobacco burning.

"You never liked ranching much."

Strawl shook his head. "Can't all be as fortunate as you. Selling a place you never owned and buying rounds at the inn."

"I've been blessed, I admit," Elijah said. He drew on his cigarette, then exhaled. "But you enjoy this. You got the bit between your teeth and are near a gallop."

"Trouble you keeping up?"

"My horse is complaining," Elijah told him.

"Might need you a bicycle."

"What I can't figure is why you quit. I'd say maybe you were slipping, if three counties weren't paying you for the same job because they can't manage."

"I was getting old."

Elijah pawed that answer away. "Ranch was making you old. That's why you wanted rid of it."

A cigarette batted Strawl's hat followed by a book of matches. Strawl set the hat on his chest. "I killed a man." He lit the cigarette.

"You killed more than one."

"Guess I finally limited," Strawl said.

"That's no answer."

"One time, not long after I started copping, I ended up chasing a big cat. He'd killed a child and scarred another. We used to get called out on those cases, like the bears and wildcats were criminals. Well, I treed the thing, and it crouched on a high elm branch, one hundred and seventy pounds of muscle and claws and teeth. Its ears pinned against its skull. It batted the air and roared, spooking The Governor. I put my eye into the peep site and waited for it to leap to another branch or uncoil for the ground. When I pulled the trigger, I still thought that cat would fly or turn smoke or just disappear. Do some kind of miracle. It didn't seem possible he would die, but the cat just shook when the bullet hit him, then lost his footing and fell on the ground. He breathed a minute, then died. That was that."

"That must've been a lot of years before you quit."

"Thirty, maybe."

"Damned old reason."

"I'm a slow learner," Strawl said.

They dozed the rest of the day. Evening, Strawl collected his traps and saddled and Elijah did likewise. The ride into the canyon, Strawl said nothing. Elijah did not press him. You could creep up on a man like Jacob Chin, but it was impossible to surprise him because he expected nothing but what happened next and was only unnerved by waiting for it.

Spiegel's Canyon doglegged. The Spiegel Ranch peered over the lip, a two-story plantation building with a columned porch and a swing creaking in the evening wind. The barn and shop lay a hundred yards behind it, a corral between, but the ranch had outgrown horses and cattle. A stand of barley awaited cutting and a DC crawler waited to turn the earth and start again.

They followed a seasonal creek bed. The sandy inclines remained inhospitable for vegetation. They proceeded cautiously, Strawl on the draw's edge, Elijah navigating beneath him at the bottom.

Where the canyon bent to gather the runoff from a neighboring draw, Elijah raised his hand and Strawl drew Stick's rein. An engine coughed and fired, but it was west and only audible because the wind had switched direction. The canyon ended abruptly where the prehistoric floods had slashed a mile-wide chasm of scattered basalt and silty loam, remaking its path into a dozen dry channels.

The bottom country beneath had little worth. The bottom country turned too steep and strewn with rocks for cash crops. The wider tracks were green with alfalfa or orderly canopies of scraggly peach or apple orchards. A few listless heifers and their calves gazed up at the men, then continued browsing the hillside. Strawl could see no fence keeping them, just a coursing river and a steep climb and a bovine lack of ambition.

Across from Strawl, Elijah let Baal sort her descent through a shale slide and later a birch copse where the ground held water. Coyote willow and rabbitbrush grew in the shadows, complicating Baal's work. Beyond, Strawl heard a horse whinny and a goat bleat and, after a moment of working through the country with his eyes, located a small house, a patched corral and a sagging barn. The seasons had worn the sideboards paintless and the winds had separated a third of the shingles from the roof. The most recent remnants were scattered upon an uneven stand of green grass between the house and corral.

The wind was up, but he heard the horse step hard, then crow-hop and land. The goat bleated again. Strawl untied a saddlebag and lifted a glass to his eye. The horse was rolling in the grey dirt and the goat looped circles around it until the horse stopped and the goat butted its neck, which prompted the horse to return to all fours and make its own loops, with the goat at the center this time spinning like a top. Then the horse tired and walked to the high point in the corral and gazed regally at the barn and corral and the house, and the goat slept in the shade the horse made.

Men were killed in such pacific environs as often as in barroom riots, Strawl knew, but he wasn't clear if Elijah did. Strawl swung his leg from the right stirrup and dismounted. He walked Stick partway down a gravel slide until they encountered a tiny hollow and dipped a neckerchief in his canteen, squeezed the excess water into a puddle from which Stick could drink, then tied it to his forehead and returned his hat to shade himself from the sun. Elijah climbed the grade. Crickets buzzed and ticked. A cat investigated the brush adjacent to the house until a rooster pheasant exploded in flight, throwing it backward in surprise.

A quarter hour later, Elijah led Baal to his position. Strawl offered him the field glasses, and Elijah examined the cabin, then returned them to Strawl and drank from his own canteen.

The sun descended the sky and they sat swapping the glasses. The horses grew bored and slept upright. Strawl and Elijah dozed as well, until Strawl heard the door's creak below them. Jacob, Taker of Sisters, filled the opening, then circled the house and stared into the pinking west. Clouds feathered in the heat, blue and violet, too thin to bear anything other than dew. Jacob leaned upon a rifle and studied the horizon until dusk purpled the night. He turned toward the canyon and waved his rifle at them.

They watched him feed the horse and goat and speak to them as if they were human. Another cat trailed him silently, sniffing the horseshit next to the halved oil drum, which was his manger, when suddenly Strawl heard wings beat the air and saw an owl rise with a third mewing kitten in its talons. It climbed toward the moonlight until a rifle sounded and the bird pinwheeled and released the kitten. Beneath, Jacob, Taker of Sisters, leaped the corral rail, parallel to the ground, then hit the hard-packed dirt and rose, kitten in hand.

"Could you do that?" Elijah asked.

Strawl shook his head. "Not even in my prime."

They were both silent awhile, then Strawl fired a shot into the night. Jacob answered it, like a knight from Malory crossing sabers.

"We'll arrest him another time," Strawl said.

"I thought we were going to kill him."

"Then we'll kill him another time," Strawl said. "He'll be just as dead."

Strawl stood and clucked. Stick, still bridled, approached, and Strawl took his reins and began to weave down the hill for the house at the bottom. He glanced at Elijah. "Not like you to avoid an interesting conversation."

⁕

Strawl halted a hundred yards from the house with Elijah behind and still far up the hill. He whistled and it was returned twice. Strawl walked Stick toward the goat and the horse. Both lifted their heads and stared as he passed. The kitten scrambled to the brush and made a frantic circle that ended behind a crude kitchen chair where Jacob reclined, his back against the house. A pipe between his teeth glowed. He looked like a photograph of Roosevelt pinching his cigarette holder and selling the NRA. The kitten climbed into Jacob's lap, and he worked his hands behind its ears.

He nodded to a log split lengthwise. Strawl looped Stick to a tree and sat. Elijah was not long following. Inside the house, Jacob filled a pair of pails with oats and rice. He set them beneath the horses and fed each a handful of sugar cubes. The men listened to the horses' noses bang the buckets, and, when they were finished, Jacob led both to the barrel trough to drink.

"Hello Elijah," Jacob said. "Sorry to hear about Ida."

"Appreciate that," Elijah said.

"You, too, I suppose."

Strawl nodded.

Jacob fetched two tin plates and, from a cauldron in the fire, deposited a scoop of sugared beans and ham on each and culled from a bucket limp radishes and carrots picked from a garden somewhere behind the house.

"You don't look so frightening," Jacob said to Strawl.

"Age and sentimentality turned him infirm. He's only a shade of what he once was," Elijah said.

"That's lucky for me," Jacob said.

"I'm not anyone's horseshoe, yet," Strawl told him.

The crickets sawed at the night. A kitten stirred the grass followed by another. They circled Strawl and Elijah, then reappeared at Jacob's shins. His hand dangled over one knee and when one of their tails batted it, he gently tugged until the kitten mewed, then released it, and the cat reversed itself for more of the same pleasant torture. Elijah bent and lifted the other and stroked its head, but it struggled and he released it. The kitten hurried beneath Jacob's chair, then stared back at him.

"Funny as people, aren't they?" Jacob said. "Killers, too. Used to be lizards and gophers and mice and chipmunks plenty. Their mama went on a murder spree likes of Bonnie without Clyde. Only thing lives within a hundred yards is a badger and when these two come of age they'll likely harass him to distraction."

He turned his finger and the two of them batted it.

"They bring me their kills," Jacob said. "Drop them half eaten on the step. Rabbits and snakes, even. They're not hungry. I feed them meat and gravy and biscuits and they take to it like trout do a stream." The cat, tired of play, curled into a ball under him. "Practicing for when I'm gone and they have to fend for themselves," Jacob said. "You know, they torture mice. They'll keep them alive an hour just for entertainment."

"I guess they can't get into the picture shows."

"Probably attack the light on the screen. This one would." He rubbed the cat's back once.

"That the one you killed the owl over?"

"Saw that, did you?"

Strawl nodded. "Owl was just killing, too. Same as cats. Doesn't seem he deserved to die."

"Killing is nature," Jacob said. "I'm as animal as these two. As that owl, too. And I never planned a killing, not even hunting.

I just sit someplace until I get hungry and something that needs killing always come by."

"Men, too," Strawl said.

"I don't eat men."

"But you killed some."

"I get crossways of others occasionally."

"You seem to come out living each time."

"So do you," Jacob said. "Maybe we just got more practice than most."

"Killing's not something to be done half-assed, I suppose."

"Not if you want to stay off the killed side," Jacob said. He leaned back, stretched against the chair, and crossed his palms behind his head. His thick arms swelled. "Stealing's wrong and I won't do it no more," he said. "But killing? You can't live a day without being part of murder or manslaughter or armies lining up on one another. Babies killing their mommas being born or us eating biscuits and jerked beef while a thousand Chinamen die for lack of a bowl of rice." He turned a log in the fire and let the coals spit while he stared at it. "But you decide," Jacob said. "How do you think people dead?"

"No conscience, I guess."

Jacob nodded in agreement. "Books and laws are just words and sounds and not a shade, not the scrawniest shadow, compared to killing." He dropped the stick into the flames and shook his wooly head. "Dying should be like bad weather; if you're not where there's a roof, then you're going to get wet, and sooner or later we all get rained on." Jacob shook his head. "I spent too much time alone. Makes me talk in wide circles."

Strawl nodded. "Better than being a duck in a pen."

"Not if you're the pen builder," Jacob said.

Strawl laughed and Jacob did, too. Their laughter tore at the night, while Elijah watched their contorted faces in the firelight.

A pair of swallows swerved into a gnat cloud just out of the light, then wheeled and dove again.

Elijah lay against his saddle, pistol still within reach, studying Strawl's strange interrogation of Jacob. Neither was afraid of the other, nor was either sure he had the upper hand. Elijah realized Strawl had wanted the circumstances such.

Jacob rose and went into the house.

"We had the high ground," Elijah said to Strawl.

"He knew we were coming," Strawl said.

Jacob returned with a coffeepot and two tin mugs. He handed Strawl one and set the other on a grate to warm.

"Heard you in the wolfweed over the hill. Then a lark quit singing."

"But you kept here," Elijah said. "Your sister send word?"

"She'd be the last one to."

"It did strike me six feet of dirt covering you wouldn't ruin her day," Strawl said.

"She don't want me dead. She wants me to not've been."

"That's a cold trail, I'd say."

Jacob said, "I'd likely follow it, though, right back to where me and her are unbuttoning each other the first time. Doubt I'd go further. I'm a sinner, but an honest one."

Strawl smoked. "I got to say, I don't understand it completely. Them that diddle their mothers; they're just trying to backtrack to the womb." He tapped his ash on a flat stone, then set the cigarette down. "But a sister. Sort of like diddling yourself, isn't it."

"You're a crude-talking bastard," Jacob said.

"Interesting, seeing as what you did to her."

Elijah eyed his gun and Strawl shifted his weight to his haunches, but Jacob hunched his back and stared into the fire.

"No one did her worse than I did, it's true." Jacob looked up.

"Well, she is a looker," Elijah said.

"She is perfect," Jacob said.

Strawl shook his head. "She's not without sin. Not unless you forced yourself on her."

"I never forced her."

"There's lots of ways to coerce a person," Strawl said.

"True enough," said Jacob.

"Lots of ways to surrender, too. You went at her more than once, that right?"

Jacob stirred the fire.

"See, once I'd understand. Well, at least I'd see excusing it. No accounting for the random. But twice, you can't claim ignorance or a bad drunk. So how'd you go about it? You could have held a gun to her, but that would probably make balance a problem. Maybe you went at her from behind like a bull. Wouldn't have to see her face that way. She'd likely be crying and hurt. But you'd want to watch that most of all. You'd need to trap her hands and feel her resisting. You'd want your face over hers so you'd be so close on her, that's all she can see. You'd want to see her give up. You'd need that."

Jacob looked at him closely. "I never forced her. We thought we were taking care of each other."

Strawl went on. "Were you reshuffling the deck? Figure a little you gets into her and a little her into you and you can play a fresh hand? And now you're attached to the memory like a pining schoolgirl. Good thing you didn't have a brother's all I can say." Elijah's gun was in his hand.

"You're as black as they say."

Strawl nodded. "I am. But I had two sisters and never even seen them naked and never wanted to. Where's that put you?"

"You're a murderer," Jacob told him.

"So are you," Strawl said. "A twisted, insane sore on the ass of the world. And I'm here to lance the boil."

Jacob stood, muscle and bone and meat blocking the sky. "Kill me, you man-killing son of a bitch. I'm right here and I don't move for man nor beast nor bullet." He clouted Strawl's shoulder with a roundhouse blow that knocked him from his seat to the ground, then stood and straddled his waist. "Kill me."

Strawl rolled toward a quartered round and busted it across Jacob's kneecap. Jacob howled and, from all fours, Strawl drove his shoulder into the big man's testicles. Jacob grunted, then landed a blow on Strawl's ear that clanged his skull and blurred his eyes and dropped him back to his knees. Jacob vomited silver bile into the fire. It hissed, and the alarmed cats watched from the light's edge. Jacob spat. "I ain't running and I ain't scared." He limped to Strawl's saddlebag and unscabbarded his rifle, then breached a shell into the chamber. He skidded it across the grass between them, but the rifle bounced and the trigger caught a stone, sending a round into the house and cats scurrying every direction. Even the goat and the horse sought cover in the hay shed.

"Your gun hunts on its own," Jacob said.

"Habit," Strawl told him.

"It's well trained," Jacob said.

Strawl touched the lump behind his ear gingerly. "Can do everything but aim. But that would be a lot to ask."

Elijah propped himself on one elbow. A cat curled with him and yawned. "Who's getting the best of it?"

"The rifle," Jacob said.

"Well, if you're past killing one another, go fight yourselves bloody, just as long as you don't wake me and don't plan on me digging your graves." He turned his back to them and settled his head against his blanket.

"You still want killed?" Strawl asked.

"I could take it or leave it," Jacob replied.

"Well, I can't promise nothing for the long term. But I've expended all the energy I care to this evening."

Jacob nodded. The coffee perked and he poured a cup for himself and Strawl.

"Dice's been out here," Strawl said.

"He told me you were on a killing spree," Jacob said. "Said I should expect you."

"And here we are."

"You don't strike me as an artist," Jacob said.

Strawl chuckled.

"Imagine he told you it was me doing the murders," Jacob said.

"Not in so many words," Strawl replied.

The fire burned and they watched it.

"Dice doesn't care who it is," Strawl said. "He figures one of us will kill the other and he'll argue whoever is dead is his man."

Jacob pondered this awhile. "If it's me, I'd have to be drunk," he said. "I'd kill sober, but not make a riddle out of it. That's not practical. But drunk I am anything but practical. I go dark pretty quick and then the horse has the reins." He sipped his coffee. "We'll need some evidence, I suppose."

"You carrying some around with you?"

"Just a bad reputation." He nodded at the door. "You're free to search, though."

Strawl passed the coffee cup from one hand to the other. "You drink often?"

"Once or twice a month, depending on when I come into money and how much. If it's a fistful, I hide it from myself."

Strawl set his cup on the ground and pulled his cigarette workings from his shirt pocket. "You smoke?"

"Just the pipe."

"Suit yourself." Strawl folded the papers, then opened the tobacco pouch with his free hand and sprinkled the paper gutter with tobacco. Jacob rose and disappeared into the house. Strawl licked the papers, then turned them until they were tight. He struck a match and put the cigarette in his mouth in time to see Jacob reemerge from the doorway with a jar of corn whiskey. He tipped the jar at Strawl.

"If I get drunk, then who will interrogate you?"

Jacob thought a minute, then poured a little shine in the remains of Strawl's coffee. "That's all you get. Then you'll remember and I won't have to say I drank alone."

Jacob filled his own cup and drank. His sigh was deep and certain as a dog's going down for the night. Strawl envied it. He sipped at his cup. His scalp tingled. He closed his eyes and his lids peppered with reddish light, like his blood was the firmament and the alcohol beat the constellations beyond it.

Jacob drank deeply while Strawl continued to dawdle over his cup, disappointed and relieved he was limited to the contents within the coffee. Jacob refueled, adding the last of the coffee to cut the sting. He squinted and blinked, then pursed his lips and made a humming sound. He found two kittens rubbing his chair legs and lifted one in each hand as if he were balancing them on a scale. They squirmed lazily. One bit his thumb and he tossed it toward the fire. It lit on a hot stone, mewed, and bounced into the darkness.

"I'm sorry, cat. No hard feelings." He put another stick on the fire. "Forgiveness is hard-won," he said.

"What do you need to be forgiven for?" Strawl asked him.

"Every moment I breathe air," Jacob said. He took a long drink, then spat into the fire.

"Living is no sin."

"It's the worst sin," Jacob said. "It's the only thing that makes no sense. World is easy arithmetic if you subtract life."

"But there'd be no one to calculate the numbers."

"All the better," Jacob said. "You know they are making national parks? No one can hunt or fish them. You can catch a trout on this side of the boundary line, but you can't on the other, but the line is invisible except in an office. Does a trout know what a line is, even?"

Strawl tapped his cup with his forefinger. "Hard to speak for a fish."

"You think I killed them others?" Jacob asked.

"I believe you have concerns beyond the ordinary," Strawl told him, "and they were killed beyond the ordinary."

Jacob nodded and drank. "I get carried away. You going to arrest me?"

"Not with that posse of cats watching over you."

"They are small but mighty."

Strawl nodded.

"So why'd I kill them?"

"You tell me."

"Because I'm not Indian, maybe."

"You're half. We're all half of something. Or quarters or worse."

"I'd kill over that. Being half of something. It's awful."

Strawl's cup was empty of shine and coffee. He reached for the pot but it was empty too. He found his canteen and drank. Jacob offered him the moonshine.

"Still on duty," Strawl replied.

Jacob tipped his cup. "Here's to idle hands," he said. By the sky it was nearly first light. Strawl stirred the fire, but Jacob stood and walked toward the river. Strawl watched him disappear.

"You better follow me," Jacob said. "No telling what I'll do."

Strawl rose despite the ache in his knees and lumbar and followed Jacob's drunken path by sound. Soon he could hear the river passing. They both stopped and threw a few rocks and listened to them plop into the water.

"Here," Jacob said. Strawl followed his voice to a towering pine a hundred and fifty feet high and half a thousand years old. Jacob was already ten feet above him in the tree. Strawl pulled himself up by a sturdy bough, then, balancing his weight, found a branch a few feet higher. Above it was a step hacked into the trunk, then a trimmed limb for a foothold. Jacob led him. Through the pine aroma, Strawl navigated the snubbed branches Jacob had cut for steps. In other places he had nailed scrap lumber for rungs, and a hemp rope dangled from above if they should slip. Strawl's hands stung. Pitch and sap clung to them. Above, he could hear Jacob ascend, and to the east sunlight swelled on the coulee lip. Half an hour later, the country went grey, then brown, then golden with light. He was near the top of the tree. Beneath him, the river winked and sparkled like a handful of quarters on a sidewalk. The water's sound never ended. Even from a hundred and fifty feet above, it beat like a pulse pressed by a heart made of something he could not conceive.

Jacob waved at him, a kidney-shaped shadow with an arm. He sat perched on a bench he'd constructed. He slid to accommodate Strawl. The seat was long and the branches above it pruned to the trunk.

Somehow Jacob had managed to bring the shine jar, as well. He drank and sighed, then offered the jar to Strawl, who still demurred.

"You are fatherless?" Jacob asked.

"I guess that is no secret."

"Fathers are just stories." Jacob spat. "I hate stories, and I'm not fooling. You should arrest anyone telling a story."

"Then you'd need arresting."

Jacob shook his head and drank the last of his cup. He let it go and they watched it tumble from limb to limb until it clacked on the ground. "I'm fighting words with words. It's why people think I'm crazy."

"Here I thought it was because you ran whores and killed those that vexed you."

"And slept with my sister."

"And had a yen for postmortem art."

"Buffaloed them all, ain't I?" Jacob drank again.

He set the jar next to him. "A thousand years ago, a smell or a taste did not need a word to be. Days without hours—no six o'clock, causing seven o'clock."

"They'd still be days," Strawl said.

Jacob shook his head. "Dawn don't follow hours and neither does dusk. I'm sitting next to you; last time it was sunup, I was miles away, but that doesn't make it a day."

"You got a good point," Strawl said. "Time had better lay low."

Jacob shook his head. "Stories are a prison," he said.

Strawl nodded. He'd read light could travel 186,000 miles per second, but darkness was even faster, because it never left. Narrative was such a constant. You could not recall its taste or its scent or its syrupy weight in your consciousness, but then you didn't recall the smell of rain until it was upon you. If knowledge was the apple the serpent proffered Eve, then story was the next fruit she plucked, memory and story, and in the Tree of Life, the angels guard forever the sweet fruit of amnesia.

"You're just old enough to be senile," Jacob told him. "But God hates you."

"If he's anything like the preachers say, that's likely," Strawl told him.

Yet with the sky so deep and blue in the dawning, he felt anchored securely for the first time in many years. He sensed the earth moving beneath, inventing time and memory and the stories Jacob so despised. A stillness enveloped the houses and the barns on the skyline, the thirst-strained fields. It enveloped even the river, and Strawl felt as if he were in huge, comforting hands. Together he and Jacob watched the sun climb the horizon and the blue sky. The birds sang and then sang louder, then quieted. A hawk circled beneath them, hunting. Magpies chattered and flitted from branch to branch. Larks trilled and a raven answered with a caw. A breeze whisked the needles, then stilled as the temperature rose.

Strawl thought about a life spent tracking those like Jacob, wise fools who still preferred their crimes illegal and unencumbered. They asked no redemption, simply witnesses.

"I could have done it," Jacob said. "It's not unlikely."

Strawl nodded. "A man who builds a chair this high in a tree, you can't put anything past him."

Jacob smiled. He seemed pleased to know he had the murders in him and that they might have originated from the same place in him that climbed a tree. They both fired their pistols in the air to celebrate the new day.

They dozed in the warm sunshine and the first blow from the axe did not rouse them. The shudders felt akin to sleep, and Jacob dreamed a frozen lake and a doe bounding a few graceful leaps, then falling, its feet kicking the air. Strawl dreamed too—of white smoke so thick he couldn't see, yet could breathe like air—until the clang of metal tearing wood woke him.

Elijah looked up. "I told you not to bother my sleep."

"Man takes his rest earnestly," Jacob said.

"Rest is about the limit what he's earnest concerning."

With each blow, the tree shimmied. Strawl glanced at Jacob, who blinked his eyes in the light.

"You want me to shoot him?" Strawl asked.

Jacob shook his head. "Axes are made for trees and trees are made for axes."

It took a half hour of hard blows to topple the pine. Elijah possessed a rudimentary understanding of physics and more than a few years' experience felling timber. As a result, the tree quaked upon the point of pulp holding it upright, then, after a final blow, tipped toward the water like a falling arm, turning at the last moment to spill Strawl and Jacob to the downriver side of it, where they would not be trapped or swept under.

Both slapped against the water, then, stunned and cold, kicked a few yards until they found grips on a stone rising some ten feet beyond the bank, where Elijah offered them a rope and fished them out.

FIFTEEN

To Jacob, stories were the accidental or arbitrary colli-sion of events with whatever fortunate or unfortunate soul happened to be in their paths, but people starved for meaning knitted luck and gossip into matters of myth.

Perhaps, Elijah pondered, memory will fall from men's minds like primordial tails from their asses when they were monkeys no more. The next thing you know we'll emerge into a paradise once more, pure and storyless. But until then, stories, tired as they are, would have to suffice, and prophets will be pewter jugs that pour themselves out in water and blood as the new story, as rivers remain both ancient and new when they pass.

Elijah drifted as they rode, thinking these things as if he were in a far-off galaxy, observing the elliptical orbits of the planets and implosion of stars and collision of asteroids into moons that would carry their wounds a hundred thousand years, and in such a state he was not afraid of the moments in the lives of any one man, himself included, though, like gravity, he felt compelled to yield to such forces.

Strawl halted them at a Keller grocery and replenished their food stock. Outside he saw Elijah speaking to a cousin of the Clouds, who was wearing a backward cap.

"What did he want?" Strawl asked.

"Peace of mind."

"He ask for that, did he?"

"No, he asked if we'd found the bad man."

Strawl continued loading their grub.

"What did you tell him?" Strawl asked.

"Judge not lest ye be judged, seven times over."

"Criminal must have said that."

"We found one?" Elijah asked.

"Not likely," Strawl said. "Not unlikely either."

"Why not arrest him, then?"

"You watched us scrap. Tough to arrest someone whipping you."

"You might have just shot him, then."

"If I shoot him and another Indian gets carved up like Thanksgiving, then where would I be? Unlike you may have heard, I shoot people for a reason."

"Mad a reason?"

"The only reason, sometimes, but I am not mad enough to kill the man and am not certain enough he needs killing. He should have went north if he was on the run. Or east. Even west, he could hide in the foothills. But he headed the only direction he shouldn't have gone. How come you're so interested, anyway? This is more work than you do in a year."

"I'm not getting paid, so I count it as pleasure."

Strawl said nothing.

"If I whet my glittering sword and my hand takes hold on judgment, I will render vengeance to my enemies and will reward them that hate me with arrows drunk with blood."

"Doesn't sound like the fisher of men," Strawl said.

"Nope, but sounds like you and me."

"Speak for yourself," Strawl said.

"Let tongues not wag against me."

"If you're going to keep spouting scripture, I wish you would do it out of my earshot."

"I believe I'll oblige you. Marvin has a kind ear. And he has made Ida's medicine bag."

"What will you do with it?"

Elijah shrugged. "Throw it in the river. It's as close to a grave as I've got."

Strawl nodded and watched Elijah lope Baal among the houses along the San Poil, pausing to visit anywhere a lantern remained lit.

Strawl took the ridgeline looking for camp smoke. He made his bed once more above the shaman's cabin. He dug the camas from beneath the firepit's dead coals and cut it into thin slices and put them in the skillet. He started a low fire and let the camas soften with a slice of jerky while he plucked and dressed two quail and a grouse he groundslew that afternoon. He added them in portions to the skillet along with a fennel and wild oregano, then opened a bottle of beer and poured half into the stew, then stirred in enough flour to thicken the concoction and finally garnished it with chives plucked from Jacob's garden. He kept the fire low and finished the warm beer and let the pan and its contents simmer until Orion sparkled above him in the clear night.

Even this far off, Strawl clearly heard Marvin and his grandchildren and Elijah at the makeshift table in front of the house while they ate frybread and a stew Inez had prepared. The children prattled for stories and Elijah encouraged them until Marvin took a seat on an apple crate and pitched his voice at the sky. He spoke in English because it was the only language his grandchildren understood past the smattering of Salish they spoke for secrets.

"In this country, you complain the sun is too hot, but it is summer, Coyote, heat is necessary. But you don't like it.

"So a cloud passes and makes some shade for you, yet you are not satisfied.

"More clouds come, enough to darken the sky. But even this does not please you. The clouds begin to drop rain.

"'More rain,' you demand. The rain is a downpour. Beaver's pond fills and he stirs from his dam to play. Deer bed in a serviceberry thicket to hide. A creek appears beside your path, and you step in, but it is not enough for you to bathe, and you are on a gambler's roll. 'It should be deeper,' you say.

"The creek swells until it is a big river. The water boils across rock. Coyote, are you not afraid? You are a fool. You are swept over by the current. You roll like a stone down a grade. It is a storm without air. You are drowning in your wishes. You gasp and vomit on the river's bank. The buzzards circle over you. You convince the buzzards to hunt farther for their meal, or is it your shadow that argues because it wants to remain? This is the reason Big River washes against its banks and the salmon swim in its current, because you will not find shade to get out of the sun."

Marvin stopped and drank from a tin cup.

"Later, you teach the salmon to follow the river. When you encounter the human beings, you command a salmon to leap from the water into your arms and invite the people to feast. You offer the biggest portions to the villages that give you the most beautiful maidens. An Okanogan maiden refuses you and you stop the river with a rocky falls the salmon cannot climb. You make more rock falls at the Kettle and Spokane Rivers because in these places, too, the maidens refuse you. You are selfish. That is your way."

The fire burned and the children shifted places around it. Elijah remained quiet. The light drained from the sky before he began once more. "Coyote taught the people that Caluk cured horses and Oregon grape leaves made a tea that did the same for children. Vanilla mended blindness and mosses eased arthritis."

"Cusick's Sunflower wakes an ailing organ," Elijah added.

"Yes," said Marvin. "These are all good things, but Coyote also made jimsonweed and nightshade and belladonna. And they are not unlike their edible cousins. This was to rub out those who refused to hear the Animal People or to relieve the villages of those who had leaky minds and could not recall one flower's color over another—so the children must listen to their elders. This, too, is because of Coyote. It is also his way."

Marvin finished with something that could have come from Elijah's Old Testament. "When the Animal People return, Sinkalip will bring all the spirits of the dead with him. There will be no more other-side camp. All the people will live together. There will be no difference between the living and the dead. Then things will be once again right," Marvin said. "And now we wait."

Finally, Marvin turned the porch lamps down and Strawl heard them retire, including Elijah, who was likely sleeping in a nest of blankets somewhere in the kitchen.

Strawl realized he was hungry. He rolled two cigarettes and set them aside for later, then he hunted a flat rock and washed it with his canteen, and, when it suited him, drew the grouse from the skillet and spread its breast and wing upon the stone along with the sauce. He divided the meat with his buck knife and ladled the gravy into his mouth with a flat stick. His teeth tore the gristle and blood dripped onto his chin. He was glad for it, as he had not taken a meal by himself in a long while, and it was alone that eating turned pure philosophy, stripped of nuance. What was flitting and thinking a bird's thoughts now fed him.

An hour later, the dry wolfweed rattled, then a rock shifted, and Strawl heard a man's breath as he regained his footing. Crickets halted, then after a minute passed, renewed their hum. A rabbit or badger broke its cover. A pair of owls stopped calling and Strawl heard the branch beneath them when they shifted their weight and set themselves for flight. There were two men, single file, at least ten yards between them. The insect sounds and pauses scattered before and behind them. Marvin's house was unlit, but Strawl had ruled out any of those below when he heard the awkward noises. A serious man would be harder to detect, or if not, would simply wait him out. No one of consequence moved with so little grace.

Strawl lit a cigarette and cupped the end to hide the ember, though he doubted those passing had enough sense to discern it as separate from the fire. They halted to rest near the crest of the butte, their lungs panting enough to hush the insects and alarm a scolding chipmunk.

The interlopers approached his camp from upwind, and Stick nickered. Strawl kneeled outside of the firelight, opposite them, behind a bull pine and a thicket of gumweed. The silverspoon's arm was in a sling and he leaned upon a crutch. Strawl watched him in the fire's glow as he kicked the blankets covering his saddle.

"He's been here," he said.

"But he's not here at present," Dice said.

"We've got him penned up."

Dice examined the fire and Strawl's trappings. "Or he us," he said.

The silverspoon's breath faltered under his damaged ribs. "You said it yourself. He's a criminal."

"It's him you need to convince, not me." Dice turned a stick in the fire. "The old man who built this fire taught me a rattlesnake doesn't think he's wrong and fangs don't require your agreement to put their poison in you." He looked up at the silverspoon. "Do you really want to traipse into the darkness after someone whose mind works that way after your recent encounter?"

The fire ignited a pitchy branch and snapped, and the two of them deliberated for a while.

"You took a beating and you want to square it, I know," Dice told him. "But maybe now's the time to go home and heal a little."

The silverspoon nodded, and Dice led him away the direction that they had come, just as noisy but less foolish.

Strawl dismissed the silverspoon out of hand—he was attempting to save his face, if not to others' opinions then for his own vanity. Strawl considered more carefully Dice's part in the exercise, however. He wondered if he knew the situation straight off and purposefully clattered up the butte like a billy goat banging a tin can to keep Strawl clear of them. Dice had proved hard to predict. He'd crossed Strawl twice, though with enough subtlety that the true number was likely higher. Still, his motive remained clear, and Hollingsworth, silverspoon or not, was not likely to serve the purpose. Assault was difficult to prove, especially when the accused was working on the dime of three county police departments. The silverspoon may have money, but he had the same witnesses Strawl did, and Strawl was certain they feared him enough to report honestly, and that would be the end of it.

Marvin's house below was still, aside from the small plume of smoke rising from the stovepipe, the fire ebbing to coal but keeping the house warm against the coolness of even August's early mornings. The horses below neighed and Stick answered them, though his interest was clearly flagging. Strawl added one more branch to the fire, then transferred his saddle from the light's reach, mostly out of habit. A killer remained at large. Yet Strawl feared nothing in this country and was certain that those threats his skills could not fend off, his reputation would, even while he slept.

day and a night later, Strawl woke handcuffed to a Grand Coulee hospital bed. An intravenous tube dripped saline from a bottle above him. One eye wouldn't open. He blinked with the other until he could make out walls and a window. His chest ached. He raised his hands until the chains stopped him. His knuckles were skinned and bloody. The ring finger on his left hand looked broken.

After they had beaten him nearly senseless, the BIA lackeys still ambulatory, with Hollingsworth and Pete leading them, dragged Strawl into a birch copse fed by the creek. Hollingsworth shackled his wrists, then his ankles. The others had three longer chains. They bound Strawl to a tree that they had pruned carefully to the height of his head, then undid his shackled wrists and chained each to opposite branches. Hollingsworth stood him on a rock and cinched the chains and clasped the lock securing them. He employed another chain to hold his ankles, then another his waist. The others leveled guns at Strawl. Hollingsworth, with the help of two tribal cops, knocked the rock free using another as a hammer, and Strawl was draped upon the tree.

"They say Christ, he died of suffocation, actually. The diaphragm, it just wears out under the weight and can't pull in any breath," Hollingsworth said. He and his cohorts collected their tools and left the same way they'd come. Strawl watched the dust rise all along their path out until it settled again in the darkness.

Strawl could not keep from making water and stayed wet through the night. His weight tore at his shoulders and bent his back. He slept in fits and woke dew-covered. The first full day he fought any way he could, shaking the tree until the branches chattered and leaves and aphids drifted from above on the warm air. The weather turned hot and he burned in blotches where the sun slanted through the tree's thinned canopy. He twisted himself to relieve the pains one place but the effort ended with just another burned spot and he surrendered. Ants worked near his ankles and when his bowels pressed loose late in the day, they fell upon his excrement and began to pack it away. A few ventured farther into his ass to finish the job.

A bit of wind at sundown eased him into night, which he spent sleepless. His urine quit. He could smell the pain, a tang like metal, but unsharp, and smoky. By the end of the following day, he was not sure what might be beneath or above him. Both directions glimmered like the sky or water or sun-baked fields. He listened to his own breathing, the sound of his pulse. He knew a person didn't have to attend to his body's workings, that the mind could keep the parts together without thoughts, but he feared losing his grip on the gears altogether.

All his life, he'd clung to solitude. Now, like the pain, it shook him with a trembling that neared joy but was not. Aloneness was impossible and inescapable, and evading it was what directed him toward it, and he recognized his mind circling madly like a calf with the turning sickness, remembering what it knew, then just remembering the remembering.

When he awoke the third morning, Dice was stirring a fire and boiling coffee. Once he'd had a cup, he sawed the branches and unlooped the chains and Strawl unfolded against the tree. Dice poured fresh water from a canteen into his coffee cup and held it while Strawl bent his head to drink. His face was a shadow in the sun, but it quaked and shuddered with his breaths. Strawl's dried lips bent and bled, and he drank until his thirst was slaked.

"You're a kitten now, aren't you?" Dice said.

Strawl was silent.

"I'm looking for a killer," Dice said. "Are you?"

Strawl remained too weak to respond.

"I didn't think so. Maybe because you found one in the mirror."

Dice arrested him, and he slept for two days. When he awakened, the nurse was changing his feed bag. She hurried out, then returned with Dice, who sat himself in a chair across the room, smoothing his thin mustache.

Strawl rattled the handcuffs.

Dice nodded. "You recall you are under arrest."

Strawl reached his free hand for a cup filled with lukewarm water. He drank.

"Hollingsworth make a hefty campaign donation?" Strawl asked.

"His father did, actually."

"You've done their bidding so I guess you've earned it. Am I going to be arraigned here or at the courthouse?"

"Courthouse, when you're able."

"I'm able now," Strawl said.

Dice stood and lifted the chart from the foot of Strawl's bed. "You have three cracked ribs and a concussion and a bruised lung along with a fractured finger, a dislocated shoulder, and various contusions and abrasions. You're a beat-up old man."

"I suppose you've put those BIA boys that jumped me behind bars, as well."

"You didn't have to set that bull loose on them."

Strawl's head hurt him and he closed his eyes for a long moment. "I didn't figure you'd approve of me shooting them. It seemed the more measured response."

The room was quiet awhile, Strawl's labored breathing the only sound.

"Can't solve a murder without a case file, Dice."

"But you didn't solve a murder. Instead two more followed. All with you in the vicinity."

"I might've done better if you weren't playing both sides against the middle. You sic everyone on everyone else and figure you'd arrest the last of one standing?" Strawl drank from the cup once more. He sighed and rubbed his bad side. "It won't make an indictment."

Dice shook his head. "Don't need one. Banged up as you are, you can't appear for arraignment for a good month. That's September, and Judge Higgenbothem will be out of the county for a wedding back east, then October his honor's absent again two weeks for hunting season. And then it's November and elections."

"You send them breeds up the butte?"

"I didn't discourage them."

"After you lulled me with the silverspoon." Strawl tried to laugh, but wound up hacking. "Guess I overestimated your ethics and undershot your guile," he said, when he could speak. "You might make it in politics, after all."

"I intend to," Dice said.

"In that business, it's always November," Strawl said. "You'd do good to remember that." Strawl considered throwing something at him, but nothing was within reach that would leave a proper dent.

"I'm not quitting."

"I hired you. I'm firing you. This case is over. You are all I need."

Strawl shook his head. "You're a damned fool. I got your money and I got a gun and a saddlebag full of bullets. I'll look until I'm satisfied and I am not as of yet. And you will be damaged, my friend. I will go out of my way."

Dice chuckled. "The handcuffs and guard at your door say different."

⁂

The guard at Strawl's door delivered the weekly papers to him and a magazine or two. Strawl saw an archived photograph of himself captioned "The Accused." The article read as if Dice had written it, offering just enough detail to ease people, though not any claims he couldn't back away from later.

A week into Strawl's detention, he ordered cookies that Elijah bribed the hospital kitchen to pepper with laxative. Strawl offered them to the deputy minding his door. Three hours later, the guard grew uncomfortable and excused himself. Strawl blinked a flashlight through his room glass and Elijah climbed the fire escape and broke the glass and applied a pair of metal-cutting crimps to the handcuffs. Strawl, still looped with opiates, took a good while negotiating the swinging steps to the parking lot below.

Elijah delivered him to the ranch in the flatbed. Dot met them on the porch and helped Arlen and Elijah pack Strawl to the sofa.

"You're being charged with murder," Dot told him.

"Yep."

"Do the police think you did it?"

"No."

"Why did they arrest you, then?"

"Because I could have done it," Strawl said.

Dot blinked her eyes. "Do you have an alibi?"

Strawl shook his head. "I'm not even sure which days I need one."

Strawl's legs shuddered and he held on to a chair.

Dot stepped toward him. "You can say, 'I would never do something like that. I would have no reason. I am not that kind of person.'"

"Is that true?" Strawl asked.

"No," Dot said. "But I'd like to hear it."

Elijah rolled Strawl a smoke and drew it lit. "You have no alibi, then."

Strawl inhaled a lungful of smoke.

"They don't care about my alibi. What did you do with my ranch money?" Strawl said.

Elijah didn't reply.

Strawl set his cigarette on the edge of a saucer Arlen had fetched for the ashes. "I need to sleep now," he said.

He slept a thick, dreamless sleep and woke with the light, missing the pain medicine from the hospital. Once upright, he hobbled to the kitchen and put on some coffee and ate three brownies from a covered plate. The caffeine and sugar steadied him. Walking was easier, though his ribs ached like a bad tooth.

Arlen lay under the crawler chassis, greasing the U-joints, his wiry arms wrestling a clutch casing. He scooted from underneath the rig. Strawl nodded at him. Arlen took his glasses from his nose and wiped them on his shirttail. His newsboy cap hooded his narrow face, which looked as if the bulk of it had pulled toward his nose like a gopher Strawl recalled from the funnies. The result left him appearing tipped forward and eager sometimes and at others as if he were fighting a headwind. Arlen stared a moment, watery-eyed through his glasses, then knocked his hands together and returned to his chore.

Strawl changed the oil in the trap wagon, his injuries turning a half-hour job into one that required triple the time. Dot brought them their breakfast. After his first wife's demise and before Ida arrived, Strawl had returned from manhunts to visit Dot and she would take his hand and walk him to the river, and there they would toss stones and branches into the current. He would smoke and she would chew Jujubes from the Omak five-and-dime. She had quit speaking in school, as well as to the Cunninghams, who boarded her. He never asked her why.

He and Arlen pulled themselves from under the machines. They washed their hands and forearms with an oily goop that cut grease, then rinsed under a well spigot outside. Dot set their plates on cinderblocks and put a bottle in the boy's mouth.

Dot waved her hand at them. "Eat," she said.

They made short work of their eggs and ham and fried potatoes. Arlen was soon under the tractor again, the girls offering him tools he didn't need but accepted all the same. Inside the barn were the plow, the cultivator, and rod weeder and seed drills, all scrubbed clean and folded upon themselves like grasshoppers. Strawl had been content to keep them in the weed patch by the creek year-round, but Arlen had even filed the rust that ate at the drill wheels. Strawl spied six or seven one-gallon paint cans stored under the bench, all International Harvester red.

"You went hunting bad men when Mother died, too," Dot said.

"You remember anything of your mother?" Strawl asked.

"No," she said. "She's just gone."

"You know how?"

"She cracked her head on something."

Strawl nodded.

"You think I'd kill and dress out Indians. I kill her, too, you figure?"

"God no," Dot told him. "Her death broke you worse than me."

"I was broken already," Strawl said. "And Ida?"

"The river," Dot said. "Not even you can whip a river."

Strawl tipped his coffee cup to his mouth, then set it down. "You know, there's no predicting what the worst criminals will do because they don't know, themselves. The ones who make a career of it, they'll weigh the odds and do their time when they're caught. But these others, they're another matter. They've probably been committing little crimes all along and not even calling them such and then the moon changes and they're holding a gun on someone and wondering why the rest of us are so wound up."

"Doesn't sound like it takes much wit to be a detective."

"They might be no trouble to find, but they'll kill you quicker than Wyatt Earp. They've been desperados from the crib. They don't need motive to murder, just inclination."

"You pity them?"

Strawl looked at Dot. "You're smart, but you don't know it all," he told her. "Goose flies south in fall, but it ain't conscience directing him. It's just he knows that's where all the other geese are headed."

He looked over the girls and the baby. He had nothing to say to them, he realized, and that was as significant a sin as his others. He returned to the trap wagon, cranking at the filter with a tool Arlen had constructed to make it easier. He watched their feet from beneath, until they opened the squeaky door and were out of sight.

The evening following, Strawl sent Elijah to Keller Ferry to put his ear to the ground concerning Pete and the silverspoon. Jacob would be no trouble to apprehend if evidence made him a more likely suspect, but Elijah was better suited to keep the reapers cutting than to sort the chaff from the grain. A murderer was about, and employed or not, Strawl had determined to take the man himself. First, though, he had decided to clear a few debts from his ledger.

| SEVENTEEN |

After he had heard Baal's footfalls disappear into the distance and watched Elijah's lantern come on, then go out again in the darkness, Strawl limped to the trap wagon and turned the ignition key. He drove the highway to Coulee Dam. His hands on the steering wheel glowed in the green dash light. The speedometer floated near fifty miles an hour and the truck wandered like a gin mill drunk. Any higher and it would spill him off the pavement.

Past Buffalo Lake, the light ahead nearly blinded him. Bureau contractors had gone to double shifts and the electricians had strung chains of high-powered electric lamps over the worksite. Others lit the tent city, more the cofferdam. The longest were looped to the lower bank on the other side of the river, abutting the west end of the project. There, a portion of the construction had settled and labor had commenced on the powerhouse structure. Generators larger than houses lay on their sides, the metal glinting. The turbine wheels that would fit within them were finned with twisted iron plates two tons each. The riprap upon the banks glittered as if a thousand fallen stars were holding the water in place, and the galaxy itself fueled the work.

In a metal box welded to the cab of the trap wagon were Strawl's tools. He cut his lights a block before the police station and left the rig to idle, then filled his pocket with three wrenches and a flathead and a Phillips screwdriver along with wire snippers. In the parking lot, he found a cruiser with a broken axle and withdrew the call box. He wired the leads into the trap wagon's cigarette lighter, then drove to Dice's home address. The lights in the house were out, but an unfamiliar sedan had parked across the street. From the microphone, Strawl reported a prowler to the dispatcher and stammered the address as if he were reading it from a piece of paper. Then he parked himself at a high spot, which allowed him a view of the house.

Strawl rolled a cigarette, then lit it and watched the smoke break in the cool dark air. He recalled learning to hunt on his own after he'd squandered the few dollars his father offered as severance. He remembered being alone and starving and standing over the first rabbit he'd ever snared. He enjoyed its dying like a job well done. It puzzled him and he killed three more that same way. He listened to them squeal in the traps and later studied their peeled carcasses on a makeshift spit over his fire, each fitting against the other like tongues into grooves.

Strawl sipped a cup of coffee from a thermos he had thought to bring. He could not see the dam or even the black river from his vista, but the light boiled out of the work below like bitter bile from the world's pierced entrails. Strawl had heard Arlen say that all we had once thought sturdy ground was not. Country floated like pieces of eggshell on an ocean over a yolk so elemental and hot that it melted rock into an angry, smoldering glue. Strawl knew nothing of the world that inclined him to argue.

Blue and red lights flashed in the distance against the cloud cover. Dice had been farther to the west than he ought to. Probably in Coulee City. A rodeo cowboy had opened a tavern there a few years ago. He had built a stage for bands. People traveled miles to eat and dance and drink and fight.

The car was covering the miles. Strawl bent and stared into the black coffee, letting the heat bathe his face. Dice had married his wife too young. He treated her to dinner out once a week, and last year had bought her a bracelet with diamonds, but money didn't matter to most women. It was love they wanted, same as men, it turned out.

The squad car made the turn to Dice's house, tires spitting gravel against the metal fender. He did not cut the blues or the siren, likely hoping the commotion would hurry the principals from their adulterous joining so he could continue to convince himself his suspicions were just a cop's natural inclination.

Strawl sipped his coffee. It was bitter and hot and hurt his throat going down, then lit in his stomach like a stone. He heard the car door slam, then the house open under Dice's key. He dumped the coffee dregs on the gravel outside the window and tipped his seat back and fell asleep.

Morning, Strawl entered the police station from the back door.

"Dice beat up his wife," Barnes said, upon seeing him. Barnes was from the South and he always sounded mid-song, and thought as slow as he talked. Strawl had kept him on because his simple mind allowed him to carry out any order without questioning it and that was the closest thing to loyalty he'd encountered.

"She's in the hospital." Barnes nodded at the pistol in Strawl's belt. "You don't need that. None of us took it too serious, you being arrested."

Strawl nodded. "Never can be too careful, it seems. You seen her?"

"No. Just him."

"Dice?"

"Yes, sir. He's in the jail cell. He just locked himself in and tossed the keys to me. I don't know what in hell for. She had it coming."

Barnes was leading up to something, but he was too much a lackey to offer an opinion until he was asked. Strawl let him stew a full minute.

"What is it?" Strawl said finally.

"What should I do with him? He hasn't done anything," Barnes said. "Not really."

"He's surrendered his gun?"

Barnes nodded.

"I'll take care of him," Strawl said.

He found Dice's hat and his tobacco and pipe on the desk, then delivered them to Dice, who was huddled in his cell. It was mid-shift and he was the only captive the jail held. Strawl sorted Barnes's keys until he found the right one and let himself in. Dice wouldn't meet his eye until Strawl ordered him to.

Strawl took the pipe from his pocket, filled and lit it. Dice looked up through his messed hair, then accepted the pipe. Strawl opened the cell door. "Come on if you want to fix it."

Dice rose. Strawl led Dice to the squad car. Strawl stopped at the flower shop and bought a bouquet and handed the flowers to Dice. Dice stared at them. "You're a rotten man. Not any better than the rest of us. It's time to show you, you hypocritical bastard," Strawl whispered.

Strawl parked at the hospital and they crossed the gravel lot.

"His wife," Strawl said.

The receptionist was a God-fearing woman and had never thought much of Strawl until it had come time to vote. She gave him the room number. Strawl passed the nurses' station on the second floor. Two of them were nodding in their chairs at a radio show. A monitor blipped. He found the room himself.

"Look at the havoc you have wreaked, Sheriff. How will you live with yourself now?" Strawl said. "You can't."

Karen Dice lay on a hospital bed, a tube sputtering in her throat. Strawl looked at her chart but could make nothing of the doctor's squiggles. Her cheek looked like it held half an apple. On her brow, a line of sutures oozed with the swelling. Her ear was blue and dotted with blood.

Dice sat in the chair next to the bed. He scooted himself forward and put her hand in his. She squeezed back, though she was still unconscious with the morphine. When the doctor made his rounds, he looked at Dice over his wire-rimmed glasses. Dice released his wife's hand as if he'd lost a husband's privileges. Her hand dangled over the metal bed rail, her fingers spread like she was reaching out or just trying to mount enough strength to return it to the warm place next to her.

The doctor bent and opened one of her eyes with his thumb and flashed a penlight in it. The whites were shot with blood and the pupil dilated with narcotic. Dice returned her hand to her side. He patted it and the muscles in her forearms fluttered. Strawl realized the man was responding in a manner he never could, one beyond guilt and shame. The demon for which she had yearned had been aroused. Strawl shook his head. Dice had been too impatient. Revenge, they said, was best served cold.

He glanced into a mirror on the door. He was unshaven and tired-looking and his own eyes were purpled from his own beating. He listened to the machines working. The doctor set the stethoscope on her breast and listened. Strawl thought it strange, all those men wanting just to touch that same spot, their hands trembling, and her trembling, too. The doctor, though, let the disc lie and counted to himself, like touching there was the same as anyplace else. He wrote another number on the chart, then hooked it to the bed foot.

Dice found an empty water pitcher. He ran the faucet, then set the flowers in it. He put the arrangement on the nightstand. Outside the room, the doctor met Strawl. He was an old man who had come through the Great War.

"Sheriff," he said. "Did you put him up to this?"

"The Lord works in mysterious ways," Strawl said.

"There's nothing mysterious about you," the doctor said.

| EIGHTEEN |

Four days later, Dot opened Strawl's front door to find Elijah on the step. She and Arlen had brought the children and a plate of supper each evening since Strawl's return, and while her family ate, Dot changed Strawl's various dressings and applied his ointments, then rubbed liniment into his lower legs to stave off atrophy.

"Look what the cat dragged in," Dot said. She opened the door and allowed Elijah to enter the room.

"You want a bite to eat?" Strawl asked.

"Loaves and fishes?" Elijah asked.

Strawl shook his head. "Beef and taters."

Dot placed the child in Arlen's arms and prepared Elijah's meal.

Elijah winked at the boy. "Against any of the children of Israel shall not a dog move his tongue," he declared.

"Don't preach to him," Dot said from the kitchen.

"You want heathen children?"

"No, I want them to consider the source."

"Bible's words, not mine."

"You're the one saying them." Dot set his plate in front of him, but Elijah didn't eat. He sat silent, chastised.

"For whosoever shall do the will of my Father which is in heaven, the same is my brother, and sister. Are we not brother and sister?" he asked.

Dot sighed. "Brothers and sisters trust one another. They don't shirk."

"Quit squabbling and tell me what's the news," Strawl said.

"Well, Hollingsworth is in high spirits," Elijah said. "Carrying around the newspaper with your mug shot and reading the article out loud."

"Them BIA boys gloating, too?" Strawl asked.

"They figure they're in charge again."

Strawl mopped a spot of gravy with his buttered bread. "Chickens will cluck," he said, "but it takes a rooster to crow."

"And an ass to bray," Dot said.

Strawl clacked his fork on his plate. "You are ruining my digestion."

"Maybe you could digest better in jail," Dot said.

"Jail wouldn't have him," Elijah told her.

Arlen leaned forward. "Come to think of it, why haven't the police visited? This is the most likely spot for you to land."

Strawl shrugged. "I left them the address to forward my belongings. They confiscated my buck knife and I owe a debt or two to that blade."

Dot said, "That's no answer."

"Bringing men out here to arrest me would require Dice to admit I escaped. He'd rather avoid that."

"That's not the reason," Elijah said. "You hear about the Dice woman? She's been in the hospital ten days and will likely see that much more."

"You wouldn't beat a woman?" Dot asked Strawl.

"He didn't need to. Dice did it."

"He beat up his wife?"

"Nearly killed her."

"That doesn't sound like him," Dot said.

"No it doesn't," Elijah replied. "Kind of makes you wonder what would light that kind of fire in a man." He looked up from his meal at Strawl, then scooped a bit of potatoes. Dot stared at him, too.

"Man puts a key into the ignition, doesn't mean he built the motor, doesn't mean he owns the car. Just means he knows where the key goes."

"Did you make the sheriff harm that woman?" Dot asked.

"I was asleep," Strawl said. "And it's God in charge of creation, ask the prophet."

Elijah smiled. "It's quite an alibi. Even Dice wouldn't argue. And I know he won't pick up the wrong end of a rattlesnake again."

"As it should be," Strawl said.

Dot put her head in her hands. "You coaxed him into assaulting his wife. My God, wouldn't you think my mother would have finished you for hurting women?"

The room grew quiet.

"What do you think you know?"

"I was four years old, not four months."

Strawl nodded.

"You were my favorite," Dot said. "I used to sit on the window ledge for hours, loyal as a dog, watching for you to come up the walk." She glanced up at Arlen. "I see the girls behave the same with him. I envy that. She did, too. I could tell, even then." She pulled Esther, the serious one, next to her by a loose dress tie. The child stood dutifully while Dot stroked her hair. "You were my favorite," she said again.

"Lord knows why," Strawl said.

"She knew why. She encouraged it. For you, not for me. And surely not for her."

"You can't remember that kind of thing."

"I do," Dot said. "Because I catch myself doing the same."

"Why's that?" Strawl asked.

Dot shrugged. "Love," she said. "And a normal life. There's some comfort in the routine and something pleasant about having a minor celebration every evening when your husband comes up the walk."

Strawl was quiet. He could hear his own ragged breaths. "I ever tell you about your grandparents?"

Dot shook her head.

"There's a reason for that," Strawl said.

"You didn't mean it," Dot told him. "I remember you didn't mean it."

"Well, I wish my memory was as generous as yours," Strawl said. "Too many things I meant to do get in the way of believing you."

"It was a long time ago," Dot said.

"It was," Strawl agreed. He rose and lumbered into the kitchen for more of his meal.

"What was that all about?" Elijah whispered.

"It's none of your affair," Dot snapped.

"I sold the property," Elijah whispered. "Is that why you're so wound up at me? He bought it back. You'll get it all. I did you a favor."

"Property doesn't have anything to do with it, though good manners might have led you to inform us. We had a bargain. I took care of my end. You were supposed to watch him. Instead, you sold your inheritance and squandered it on who knows what."

"He doesn't seem looked after?"

"No, he looks beat-up. And there were two other killings."

"I don't know he did them or the others," Elijah said.

"Do you know he didn't?" Dot whispered.

Strawl hobbled back into the room with his second helping. Elijah turned his attention to the baby. "He called his servant that ministered unto him, and said, put now this woman out from me."

Dot stared at him. "And your children shall wander in the wilderness forty years, and bear your whoredoms, until your carcasses be wasted in the wilderness," she said.

Elijah ignored her. "You girls sass your mom often as you can?" He poked Violet's ribs and she giggled.

"They're intolerable as always," Dot said.

"And this baby's well?"

"Yes."

He looked to Arlen. "You in good health?"

"We're all fine," Dot told him.

"Good," Elijah said. "Now, I have presents, if anybody is inclined."

The girls squealed and trailed him through the door to Baal and the saddlebags. Dot waited a moment, then scooped up the baby and followed.

Strawl gazed out the window. The maple remained filled out with summer, the leaves green and slick in the slanting light. Elijah treated the girls to rock candy and ribbon and offered a ball to the baby, who immediately put it in his mouth.

"I see the big hill's been disked. You thinking about planting winter crop there?"

Arlen nodded.

"Makes sense," Strawl told him. "That dirt holds water better than the rest, though it shouldn't, being on an incline."

"Ground there is soft," Arlen said. "Snowpack can sink instead of run off."

"I knew there was a likely reason. Just didn't know what it was." Strawl pointed his chin toward the door. "Tell her it's all right," he said. "Tell her I told you so and you believe me."

"Except I don't."

"You can swear it off in a prayer if you can't bear the lie."

Strawl stood. He ached everywhere but was as mended as time would allow. He made his way to the door.

"I'll start morning," he said to Elijah. "You'd be better served to stay. There will be a shit storm and you don't appear to own the clothes for that kind of weather." He looked at Dot. "Don't say a word. You know I'm not listening."

"I got two boxes of bullets, yet," Elijah said.

"You'll need them."

"You figure I squandered your money," Elijah said.

"Nope," Strawl told him. "You got more imagination than that."

"Then why do you think I took it?"

"I have no idea," Strawl said.

"What if I told you?"

"Then I'd still have no idea," Strawl said.

First, Strawl felt compelled to square the rest of his more recent disputes. He and Elijah cornered the remaining Bureau of Indian Affairs policemen at their office as they arrived for their morning shift. Most limped and two still wrapped their skulls in gauze, following their encounter with the bull. Strawl handcuffed the six of them to one another, then herded the group to the truck bed and

latched the odd cuffs to the low end of the stack muffler pipes to
keep them there. Strawl directed Elijah north and east toward a
copse of hardwoods and huckleberries above Owhi Lake rife with
bear droppings and matted hair. He ordered the deputies to strip,
then organized them in a ring around the tallest tree and cuffed
the ends to close the circle. Ten pounds of pork from the grocery
were stowed in the cab along with a few jars of honey. Strawl
poured honey over their heads and torsos and legs, then strung a
pork chop or ham around each's neck, then scattered scraps in the
surrounding brush.

Each breath was a difficulty, but he ordered Elijah next to drive
to Hollingsworth's ranch, where Strawl splintered the door with
an axe and took both the silverspoon and his father from a fine
lunch served by their wives and attended by the children. Strawl
cuffed them together as well. When the old man, whose face was
red with spidery blood vessels, began to bluster about law and due
process and friends in advantageous positions, Strawl broke his
nose with his pistol butt.

Elijah drove silently and said nothing when the silverspoon attempted to negotiate with him, though it was clear from his expression that such grisly work had not gone easily on him. Strawl
considered how to dispatch the two. Killing them crossed his mind,
but even he would have difficulty arguing his innocence when he
had taken them in front of a houseful of witnesses.

Elijah persuaded him to dump them in the middle of nowhere
and gamble on how they'd manage their return. Strawl chose the
west end of Omak Lake where there was no road, and the few
Indians who inhabited the area were far enough into the past to
think a pair of white men were devils. To add to their difficulties,
he sliced off the soles of their feet, poured gasoline on the wounds,
and lit them afire.

That evening Strawl reclined on a saddlebag while Elijah made camp and cooked three trout from Friedlander Creek.

"Who is this killer, if not Jacob Chin?" Elijah asked.

"Someone with enough sense and patience and money to keep clear of witnesses," Strawl said. He pointed his finger and banged it against the palm of the other hand. "Most crimes, one person and another disagree on what belongs to who, and they don't have the smarts to connive it from the other nor the patience or faith to wait for it to fall to them. So they rob or kill."

"Or both."

Strawl nodded. "Then the one who committed the crime runs. If he's really mean at heart, he might leave clues that lead the people to think some other poor lout did the thing, though that happens so rarely and usually is planned so sloppily it's not worth mention. Mostly it's the first. A person behaves without courtesy or decency and only later grasps he's perpetrated a crime to boot."

The fish had finished cooking and Elijah slipped one onto a bed of leaves for Strawl. Strawl opened his pocketknife and sliced a piece loose. The golden skin tasted of salt and the one eye looked up at him. Elijah remained quiet. He separated the fine bones from the flesh and carefully drew the skin back.

"You didn't like cutting those boys' feet, did you?" Strawl said. "Or making the BIA boys bear food."

"I didn't do any of it."

Smoke curled from the fire. Strawl added a stick and watched the flame take it, flipping images as if they were moving pictures without the screen, raw light and perfect black and the shadows alternating between.

"You permitted it," Strawl said.

Elijah nodded. "Do not allow what you consider good to be spoken of as evil."

"Or the other way around."

"Yep." Elijah sheathed his knife and set the fish beside him on its leaves. "What if I didn't allow it?"

"Read some more. You'd be dead. Or I'd be. Or one of us would have converted the other, which is what happened."

Elijah's eyes gazed into the fire. He blinked once, then again. Otherwise his face was calm as a lake. "I can't see it that way," he said.

The flames burned and smoked. It was a good fire, bedded now with a floor of coals that would keep through morning and banked by rocks and a bough green enough not to spark with a delinquent ember. Strawl prepared his bedroll and pillowed his head with his saddle. He closed his eyes.

"Maybe he can't help himself," Elijah said. "He enjoys murder and intends to keep at it, wrong be damned. Plenty of enjoying what you're not supposed to in that good book, too. Look at David with Bathsheba."

"Or Samson and Delilah."

"Solomon."

"Solomon and who?"

"Song of Songs. Whoever."

"Sodom and Gomorrah."

"They're towns, old man, like Nespelem and Keller, not people."

"Lot and his salt shaker, then," Strawl said.

Elijah chuckled. "Adam and Eve."

Strawl waved his hand. "Cain and Abel."

"Changing subjects."

"Subject is murder."

"Well, you can hardly turn a page without a killing in the Old Testament."

"Moses killed his share with all those plagues, didn't he?" Strawl said.

"God sent those. Moses never shed blood once he started as God's prophet."

"Well he's just a damned politician, then," Strawl said.

Elijah stepped out of the firelight and pulled a blanket from his horse's saddlebags, then bedded down across from Strawl. He padded his head with his saddle and made certain his rifle scabbard remained within his reach.

Strawl tried to sleep as well, though the talk troubled him. He rolled his blanket away from Elijah. "Old days, I had a name and a description and a gun, and the criminals were scared and I wasn't. Deer or pheasant will lie in a thicket until you practically stomp on them, yet a man bolts first he hears you no matter how good he's covered."

"This one's wiping his tracks."

Strawl shook his head. "This one doesn't leave tracks."

Elijah smoked awhile. Strawl waited for sleep.

"Then what is it we're doing looking for him?" Elijah asked.

"Pretending," Strawl told him.

"Pretending what?"

"We know."

"And the BIA and the Hollingsworths?"

"They were pretending, too."

"Pretending what?"

Strawl shrugged. "Whatever lets them sleep eight hours. We're no different than them."

"Then how did they come to their hard roads and we didn't?"

Strawl turned and faced Elijah. He patted the firm earth with his hand, flattening a spot. He drew a stick man with his forefinger. "They can invent themselves any way they want. I have no qualms with that. Their pretending got in the way of mine, though. So I pretended something past what they could."

Strawl was quiet. He closed his eyes and studied the bloody red of their lids in the light from the fire. His blood beat through him. His heart opened and clamped shut, pressed his lungs like a bellows; his breathing was as constant as the starlight falling over him and still it moved; moving was its constancy. The earth spun and circled on its tether of gravity, making day and night and spring and fall, but for the sun it was always day and for the moon night, without letup or meaning or hope. They were as gods, and Strawl realized this was peace.

The boy read from his good book in the waning light. His lips muttered and his body rocked with the language in his head. Strawl wondered at the boy's love of such stories, then did not. His own time had produced nothing to rival such epics, just dime novels invented to sell. Stories of Billy the Kid and Bat Masterson had little truth and less art. Like Jacob preached, they weren't story, just things that someone said happened, sense and moral applied to them after the fact. What was unsaid and undone would chronicle Strawl and his ilk.

Yet a sweet-voiced cowhand with a guitar singing "Utah Carol" could move him to tears when his own offspring could not, and "The Strawberry Roan" drew laughter from him that ought to belong to his grandchildren.

He recognized the rituals people built from their lives and knew others expected he possessed his own code and they treated his actions as if they belonged to a larger whole, and he'd responded as fittingly as he could manage, and turned story himself for a time, and violence only multiplied the community's admiration of him. But self-annihilation is the end of every myth. Men don't worship a god; they grieve at his murder and their complicity in the crime. Gods are less entities than faulty compass points the world uses to guide itself, anyway—at least until it becomes lost enough to seek out another tale promising true north.

Strawl realized he had done his work too well and, in keeping alive, had managed to outlive any story that put him on the side of right, and he realized, too, he had no inclination to change it.

NINETEEN

They rode to Swahila Basin, idling through the morning until they reached the Cloud ranch once more, where they were fed and then informed that a bored fisherman with a weakness for berries had freed the BIA cops. They were beset by fire ants but had made enough noise to encourage anything larger to keep its distance. The silverspoon and his old man crawled upon a logging path and, finally, a skidder who clothed them with gunnysacks and drove them in a wagon to the Omak hospital, where they were bandaged and released.

"The Lord works in mysterious ways," Elijah said.

"Still protecting fools."

"Then why'd you get beat up?"

Strawl ignored him.

"You think God is in this, James?" Elijah asked.

Cloud nodded and said it might be so, but his eyes were tired and it was clear to Strawl he humored the boy like he might have his own a month before.

"Jacob Chin rustled a calf but wasn't cited," Cloud said.

"Cops that side of the river in league with Dice?" Elijah asked.

Cloud said, "Farmer never swore out a complaint. He just mentioned it at coffee."

"Maybe we ought to go see about him."

"You have a hankering for veal?" Strawl said.

"Thought you wanted to find this killer."

"I've ruled Chin out," Strawl said.

"Who have you ruled in?" Elijah asked him.

Strawl plucked some tobacco from his saddle's satchel and turned a cigarette.

"Thought you were a cop," Elijah told him. "You spent a lot of time on squaring yourself with other cops, lately, with no killer in sight."

"I'm a man staying level with any who want to tip the scales otherwise before I'm a cop or a citizen or any other damned thing."

"Level means even."

"No, level means upright," Strawl said.

He smoked and Stick pawed the earth and switched his tail at a fly.

"He is like you," Cloud said.

Strawl pointed his chin at Elijah. "Him?"

"Yes. Him. And Jacob Chin," Cloud said.

"I'll agree on the latter." Strawl nodded. "That's why he needs a visit, I suppose."

It took them most of the day to cover the ground and catch the ferry once more, and they didn't sight Chin's cabin until dusk. No smoke rose from the stove and the corral was ungated and empty of the goat and the horse. Strawl fired a shot, but no rifle replied, though birds cackled and flew. Strawl and Elijah dismounted and called but received no answer, so they opened the knobless door, hinged with leather boot heels and secured with a strap threaded through holes on both sides of the jamb. The single room was surprisingly well kept. Plates and tins were stacked on a shelf next to a skillet and two pots, one inside the other. A lantern rested next to a pallet and a couple of books, one about history, the other without a cover. On a makeshift scrap two-by-four table lay a bar of soap and a washing bucket still half full and, in one corner, a straw broom.

Elijah glanced at Strawl, who only shrugged.

Outside, he roused Stick and Elijah Baal. They rode a hundred yards toward the river until Stick wheeled the direction they'd arrived. Strawl sawed his rein. Stick fought, then relented and, with his head aimed at the ground, began again toward the river.

"What's the matter?" Elijah asked.

"Blood," Strawl said. "He smells blood. Goddamnit."

They rode the game trail toward the big river. Two of the kittens skittered in the long grass, paralleling them. Strawl ducked for a low branch, then so did Elijah. Yellow pollen clung to their clothes and hair.

The last of the light draped the river ocher and shadow, along with the coulee's basalt, the turned earth and post-harvest stubble, the dark pine and birch silhouettes picketed against the corduroy sky. The light dwindled further and its long threads seemed to stretch across the horizon like waning amber echoes distorting whatever voice color possessed.

Soon they heard the insects' hum, then the squabble of magpies; then they caught the sweet reek of meat in decay. Jacob's armless body hung upside down from a pine bough ten feet in the air. A breeze following the river rocked it. The body was held fast with a metal rod driven through the ankles at the Achilles' heel, then snubbed tight to the branch with a chain. Beneath the body, a fire had been reduced to coals and their pink light pulsed eerily, flashing upon Jacob's head. A dollop of melted fat slipped from his flesh, then hissed and smoked upon the coals.

Strawl approached and bent to examine the dangling head. The scleral orb had shriveled to half its original circumference. The heat had oranged the eyewhite without opening the vessels. Each pupil had expanded to eclipse all but a narrow rim of iris, which had itself darkened sufficiently to be barely discernible. The eyes resembled a child's marbles more than anything else, each loosely secured in their too-large sockets by a string of optic nerve.

Above, his lips had thinned and the taut muscles maintained their awful grimace, as if he were still partly present to witness his predicament. The skin of his cheeks, pulled by gravity, bloated his face, the flesh not blackened or scorched but cooked—smoked meat as sure as an elk's hindquarter.

The flames had baked his hair to a fine dust that floated from his scalp whenever the air around him was disturbed.

The odor swung with the breeze but there was no respite from it, no matter where a person stood. The kittens mewed and sniffed and then began tussling over an errant sinew. The magpies ventured a return, and Strawl shot three in succession before the others retreated into the lengthening shadows.

"The coyotes must have taken the arms," Strawl said. But five minutes later Elijah discovered them drooped in a neighboring tree, chained at the wrists. Dangling, they looked like some ancient, brutal cuneiform.

Strawl examined the head more closely. He found no sign of the weapon his man preferred, no sign of a weapon at all. He pulled the arms from the tree. The killer had hacked them from the shoulders with an axe, and the sockets were bruised with poorly delivered blows.

"He was alive for this." Strawl shook the pair of joined arms and their manacled hands waved. "Jacob, you put up a fight. I'll give you that. The bastard had to have at you alive and you made work for him. And look." He motioned to Elijah. "This fire's built low and the bastard dug a ditch to put it in. You see this bark in the sand? He set the fresh wood against the burning just right so it would roll into the coal bed as the old burned out. This is a slow-cooking fire."

Strawl hunted until he found a stray branch. He poked the ash beneath the coals. "It's been baking him for days," he said. "And he was alive for it. He'd have bled out eventually, but that would take hours." Strawl shook his head. "How long did he cook and know he was cooking?"

Elijah said nothing. He had dismounted and kept both Baal's and Stick's reins. The horses cropped the grass and Strawl listened to their jaws work. Elijah gazed at the coals as if hypnotized, the rosy light playing on his smooth face.

"He suffered, then," Elijah said.

The emptied sockets would have ached brutally, though blindness would have enraged a man like Jacob more than any pain might. Dying would have bothered him less. But he was bound to endure both all the same, the second slowly, without illusion or hope or faith. Blood would first have left the branched veins and arteries piping the chest cavity, but femoral arteries would feed the heart and maintain its rhythm, and the brain, suddenly served by gravity rather than drawing against it, would become more aware than it had ever been. He would have heard his blood tick on the sand and hiss in the fire beneath him; he would have known the sickening loss of buoyancy as if he were in an emptying bathtub, and smelled his singed hair—an offensive odor even when it was not your own. He would have felt it disappearing into his scalp. Past the torn and chopped flesh and muscle and ligament he'd borne, his fat cells would've slowly liquefied and he would, finally, understand that his skin, as it shifted and peeled from its muscled mooring like wet cloth, was abandoning him.

Strawl bent to one knee. His head seemed light, as if it had received a blow. It floated upon his neck and above his body like a child's balloon batted to and fro with the wind. He shook it slowly, to remind himself a string still attached his consciousness to his physical self. He opened his mouth, made an oval with it, inhaled a breath; the air cooled his lips and made his teeth like wet rocks. He spoke a small sound, a vowel alone, the guts of a word without its consonant skeleton. His gaze shifted down into the sand beneath him, a grey stone almost too small to perceive yet a hundred million times repeated on this beach until it was all that remained on the band between the flora and the river, except what washed against it, which would eventually disintegrate into more of the same. His hands shuddered as he raked his fingers into the earthly shingle, which left jagged, digit-sized marks. He breathed to calm his hands, but they declined to obey. They floated, like his head, barely tethered to the rest of him.

He tipped his head toward the night above and the darkness was like the sand, the constellations only worth mention because of the vast blackness between the flecks of light, a blackness that would devour them as the sand swallowed the driftwood and dying insect and the flesh of fish and men. His hands quivered. He slapped them together, thinking one's quaking would equal the other's and together they would be still. Instead the spasms multiplied and he appeared to his own floating consciousness a repenting sinner shivering in the face of his angry Lord. He broke them apart and drove each into the cool sand. Their vibrations climbed his arms into his shoulders and chest and he heaved as if he were sobbing though he was neither sad nor hurt nor tearful. Blood sounds beat in his ears and when he closed his eyes he could see the sound drumming through his lids, its rhythm grey, then black. The river itself coursed like a vein obeying a similar symmetry, one it knew nothing of, yet it knew nothing else. The black water was as dark as the sky, black as the blackening coulee around them, black as the trees' forms, black as the rock, black as the birds flitting across their tiny portions of the sky. It was only the temporality of light that made them appear any other shade. But under, under remained the darkness and an order that required no policing, a government without need of law, a religion without dogma or theology—one that required no prayer or even faith, such was its undeniability, though it was absent of light and warmth and no longer even possessed a name because politeness and fear had erased the word but not the thing itself.

To believe in craziness was once sacred: seeing the face of God, how could a man remain sane? Why would he desire to? Strawl breathed again, a short, wracked breath between the seizing of his trembling diaphragm. Most would find horror in this moment and the rest sadness or tragic order. Strawl felt none of these. The air in his head grew heavy and clouded; his chest heaved for another breath and he realized he was in danger of passing out. The muscles in his face opened and he felt the skin stretching in a manner he couldn't recall. The other portions, reacting through habit, attempted to flatten his expression, but the inclination this time was too powerful. His face split open like a jack-o-lantern and smiled.

Strawl laughed. It was the first instance he had done so in earnest in forty years. The sound echoed in the coulee.

"I thought you had half a fond spot for the Taker of Sisters."

"I admired the man," Strawl said.

Elijah shook his head. "So why are you so amused by his demise?"

"Demise?" Strawl asked. Jacob's blood smelled to Strawl like welded iron, what was beneath the burning, the loosening metal bead crawling back toward rock. He recalled Jacob asserting his claim to his sin with his sister and the certainty and vehemence of a man standing on his own property with a notarized paper to prove it, and, in the doing, he seemed to draw up the one moment with which he refused to part no matter the damage, and in that instant resided all the pleasure and tragedy a life contained. And it was as if the event devoured his heart every day and each day he ate it right back into himself.

Strawl had no such reminiscences. His memory was an animal's, containing no room for sentiment. Any emotion he'd encountered was grounded in anger or fear—same as the great cats and bears, the same as their fodder, too—or duty, which was a poor guess built upon witnessing others he figured knew better and followed with an awkward imitation.

"This man didn't rot from the inside and fall in the forest like a dying pine. What kind of a man dies like this?" Strawl asked. He threw Jacob's chained arms at Elijah. They skittered into the darkness. But Strawl could still smell them, still feel them in his hands. "They had to drill and shoot and dynamite him from this world like those breaking rock for the dam. The riprap is spread up and down the river for miles each way, the rock was so gigantic and stubborn. That's what kind of man this is. Fondness. Hell, I love this man, now." He paused. "What is the line? What a work man is? That's Shakespeare, not your goddamned Bible with its prophets and messiah. What a work *man* is!" Strawl said.

"And what of the man who did this?" Elijah asked him.

"Him, too. They bestride this narrow world like a colossus."

"More Shakespeare."

"Yep."

Elijah shook his head sadly. "Man is like to vanity: his days are as a shadow that passes away." He nodded at Jacob Chin, Taker of Sisters. "Ask him."

Strawl backhanded Elijah into the sand.

"I did," Strawl said, standing over the boy. "And he answered."

| TWENTY |

In Nespelem, Truax reported nothing from the surrounding counties of which Strawl wasn't aware. Strawl ordered ten pounds of jerked beef, two peppered with cayenne. He paid with cash.

"You don't want me to just put it on your bill?" Truax asked him.

"Nope," Strawl said. "In fact, what is the balance?"

Truax told him and Strawl peeled enough money from the expense roll to cover it. "We square?"

Truax nodded and dug in a drawer for his pipe, then packed and lit it. "You all there, Strawl?"

"I am not," Strawl said.

They were quiet a moment. Outside the window, Strawl noticed the sky turn grey while a cloud blocked the sun, then a moment later, return to its midday hue.

"I was just thinking," he said. "Wasn't six weeks ago when you had the body back there that clanged the bell to start this race, and now here I am again ready to finish it. I guess I'm just an old paint circling a track."

"Seems shorter than that," Truax said.

"Or longer," Strawl remarked. "Depends on which end of the scope you're looking through."

"I never knew you to cavort with the bottle. You take a fall or get clobbered again?"

Strawl shook his head. "You asked if I was all here. I'm about half here and half there, but I am fit as a fiddle and here to dance to any tune the fiddler plays."

"Well I hope you're not letting those BIA boys and Dice make the music."

Strawl shook his head. "All they can make is noise, and I can hear noise twenty miles off. I'm talking about music, not clatter."

"Well, watch your topknot," Truax said.

"Do the same," Strawl told him.

Strawl then took his leave. The doorbell clanked on the lock stile when it shut behind him. The day was warm but crisp with fall. The military contractors had sawed circles every six feet of the boardwalk, and centered in each hole was a spindly white oak, new enough the branches and leaves cast shadows thin as fishing nets over the streets, in an order that contradicted the scattering of pitched and flat-roofed buildings and their gutterless eaves.

Strawl stopped to make a cigarette, then walked through that flickering of shadow and light, his boots thumping each step in a slow, rhythmic beat, more than the random rattle most men made. His legs moved with their own purpose, sure of what he was not

but making him more certain every time they clacked the grey
pine boards under him, half a foot across broken by a quarter inch
of gap, then another, and his shadow floated between the order
and chaos of the others. He smoked and stepped through the
smoke, smelling its burning, different than the stink in his lungs
and on his clothes. Fourteen horses were tied to the fence at Hurd's
Tavern along with a four-door Buick sedan and a rusted 1923 Ford
grain truck with enough space in the bed to haul ten men. The
weather had relented enough to keep the dust down, and the sun
shone in the blue sky cleanly, and Strawl could see past the end of
town to the varying greens of the pine and fir and birch scattering
the nearest ridge and the grey and rusty rock where nothing grew,
and the blue-grey sagebrush that pocked the grade below, all that
took in the thin soil there.

The boy he had seen six weeks ago, then a week after that, hurried the other direction upon recognizing Strawl. Strawl watched
him disappear in an alley, his dog nodding and loping after him. A
doorless Model A clanked past in the other direction, then a pair of
bays with Indian riders followed. Strawl could smell the animals
and the men damp with their own perspiration. A mile east, he
heard a woman speak to a child, and closer, but south, a straw boss
directing an Indian to take the tractor and turn the summer fallow.
There was no entrance in the rear of the tavern, just the one on the
street and another opening into an alley. He could sit at a table between the two and see both with no trouble. Elijah had tied Stick
and Baal to the livery for feed and a good watering, where he'd
also borrowed a single-wheeled cart and drove it to the trading
post for their necessities.

Strawl approached the tavern and with each step, he grew more
assured and less dubious about his endeavor.

He opened the tavern door and stepped inside.

The place was owned by Garfield Hurd, an ex-army sergeant

who had earned a fortune bootlegging to the Indians and now was slowly losing it serving them legally. The building, like every other in Nespelem, was thin-walled and shingled with shakes that in summers left it a tinderbox. Fires had already gutted the town twice, though it was less than thirty years old.

Strawl stood in the doorway a moment and allowed his eyes to correct for the darkness. Inside were twelve men who ranged from seventeen to forty-eight. All had received a letter by post a week earlier. Hurd raised a hand, and Strawl returned the greeting. Hurd poured a schooner of beer. Strawl took it and drank. He looked to the three back tables seating the Bird clan. "I'll need six buckets and the bourbon," Strawl said.

Hurd hunted the whiskey under the till, then, finding it, glanced up at Strawl to make certain of his intent. Strawl wagged his finger and Hurd set the bottle on the bar. He commenced to fill the wooden buckets with beer. Strawl took three, then returned for the rest and the bottle, eschewing a shot glass, knowing the Birds were not inclined to measure their whiskey.

Strawl purchased two dozen cigars, as well. He lit one for each and offered the beer until the clan was all smoking and drinking. Strawl sipped his beer and dawdled over his own cigar for half an hour. The veins of the leaf wrapper burned hotter: they pinked and glowed before the ash like bloody rivers crossing a dark topography, the light not unlike the coals baking the Taker of Sisters.

Strawl unbreeched his revolver and tumbled the cylinder, listening to each chamber click until the wheel slowed to a stop. He set five bullets into the chamber and spun the cylinder once more, then replaced the works and pressed the pin centering it and fired a shot into the wall above the clan. The report hushed the din. The Birds stared at Strawl.

"Boys," Strawl said. "Don't let me interrupt your revelry. Please. It does my heart good to see men at ease."

The room remained quiet.

"I said drink," Strawl shouted. He put a round a little lower on the wall. One of the Birds lifted the whiskey from the table and took a tug, then handed it to the next who did the same, while the others lifted their beer glasses, still eyeing him.

Strawl ordered six more buckets of beer. Smoke rose from their cigars to the ceiling, where it collected, then descended back upon them in silver fog. In it, Strawl could smell Jacob's fat dripping on the fire. He recalled his mind floating in that scene and felt it again unloose and hover outside his head. He fired his pistol into the floor to direct his thoughts, but though the shot rang in his ears, and the powder's stench crowded his nose, and the hole in the floorboards was enough to put his thumb through, his thoughts remained apart from him.

"Yesterday, I saw a man. Someone cooked him. Slow. While he was still living."

The Birds quieted.

"He was a criminal, I guess. There's paper on him in two counties, though neither describes his crime. They just tell of some things he did. Stealing and fighting. Those aren't crimes unless someone else decides they are. The damned bigwigs steal every day. It's why we're in the fix we are, isn't it? And fighting? Taking every breath is a fight, isn't it boys? Can you recall one moment that wasn't a fight? Guns and fists are what the law doesn't like, but for some, all they have is guns and fists, and some, they're fighting things guns and fists can't even crease."

He paused and looked at the silent group. Some cradled their beer glasses and others sat with their hands in their laps, gazing down.

"That man, he took it. His arms were hacked from his shoulders, then he was strung up like a beef and cooked and he kept alive. He could've picked dying. I've seen plenty do it when they recognize their clock leaking time. But he didn't do that; he kept alive.

Knowing nothing was left but cooking and dying anyway." Strawl fired into the ceiling and a bolt of light shot through. He squeezed the trigger and let off another round and another luminous cord bisected the room. Strawl stood and the two rays crossed his torso.

The oldest Bird rose. He had greyed at the temples, though he was as smooth-skinned as a child and the only wrinkles he possessed, cornering each eye, made him appear wise and alert. They were a beautiful people, Strawl thought. His name was Raymond, and no one ever addressed him as Ray.

"We have done nothing," he said.

"I'm not here to accuse."

"You're not hunting a killer?"

"Are you killing?" Strawl put the gun barrel next to the man's temple.

Raymond drank from the whiskey bottle and handed it to a cousin or nephew, someone not young enough to be his son.

"Heard it was you," he said to Strawl.

"I heard that, too," Strawl said.

"That would mean you're chasing your tail."

"And that isn't like me," Strawl said.

"No," Raymond said. "It's not."

"Well, decorating bodies doesn't sound like you, either," he said. He raised the pistol and swung it around the room. "You others. I don't know so well."

The Indian now holding the whiskey bottle took a pull.

"Leave us," he said.

Strawl shot the bottle from his hand. The bullet creased a cousin behind him who hit the wooden floor and howled, then grabbed his bleeding arm. Strawl watched the blood soak his shirtsleeve, then tick on the floor as it had from Jacob, like time itself leaking away. Strawl bent and looked over the prone man. "Fuck pain," he said. "Fuck fear." He laughed. "Fuck your sister."

It was quiet. The wound was clean. "In and out," Strawl said finally. "You'll lift a glass again with no trouble."

"Killing us will do no good," the one still holding the bottleneck said.

Strawl turned the gun on him.

"It might," Strawl said. "Can't know for sure without going on and doing it."

"The law will take you."

"Law paid me for twenty years and all I did was kill and harass Indians. They'd be happy to have a few on the house."

He set his beer glass on the table and watched it wobble, then steady. Condensation ringed the wood under it. He inhaled a breath and studied his hands until their tremors slowed. Bullet holes pocked the back wall, and through them seeped a fainter light, like stars in early dusk. Casings clacked on the floor under his chair legs. The Indians stared at him, many wide-eyed, looking for openings to exit or furniture to duck under.

"Goddamnit," he said. This was nothing near what he'd intended.

He leveled his gaze at Raymond.

"We've been honest with one another, haven't we?" Strawl asked. "About the big things, I mean. You might have lied to keep from getting caught and I might have lied to catch you, but we never lied about what we were, any of us." Strawl tipped a beer bottle at the family. "I put Henry there in the guardhouse six months once. I'm just guessing, you likely pulled a couple over on me, as well." He paused.

"You have committed crimes, but most are justified by your ways. It's why I have not visited you."

Raymond and the others waited for him to go on.

"I have summoned devils within me all my days, and they have heeded my call. So much so, that they arrive now without prompt or cue and I have to beckon other devils to do them battle. I have spilled blood for no cause. I would like to be sorry for it, but for the most part I am not. It's a failing, I know." He paused. "It has made me strong and feared and it has ground me to a nub." He rested his eyes a moment. "But the things I have seen recently." He stopped and drank. "I hunt a man who is a man but something else, too. As brave as the Taker of Sisters died, this man I seek has more to him. He had the power to make such a man die, yes, but also the will to watch and appreciate such an end. There is something beautiful in blood, a thing past the beauty of the flesh, or a flying bird, or a painting or a song, even past a god's grace," Strawl said. "This man knows this thing. I will know what he knows. Then he can go ahead and take what he wants from me."

"What if it is your own face you see?" Raymond asked.

"It will be," Strawl said. "But it will be another's as well."

"Maybe your monster is lonely." The group laughed.

"Monsters are always alone," Strawl said. "But never lonely." He set his gun on the table and reloaded the cylinders, then held it up and spun the housing so the group of men could see it filled with rounds. He turned his back to it and the Indian men. "Here is my pistol. If you have done these things, you will kill me now, and I will die and many will be happy for me to be dead, but I will meet who it is that does these things and know him and be satisfied. Kill me, but only if you have killed the others." Strawl sighed. "And if you have done these things and do not kill me now, then you are not a man nor even a dog, but a snake slinking into his hole."

No one moved aside from Hurd, who ducked behind the bar for his scattergun.

They would kill him now, Strawl knew—he had neither the law nor the fear of the guilty to discourage them—but he would have his answer, nonetheless. And then perhaps death would be a relief, just a late Sunday morning with no chores and no church and no light flooding the room, no conscience to pester you into rising when you rolled onto your side and make out daylight in the window glass and determine the time, and then, just as you prepare to swing your feet onto the cold floor, you remember it is Sunday and your muscles unloosen and your head returns to your feather pillow and your eyes close and your head darkens once more, and you feel lucky, blessed even, for ten minutes of sack. And it was better alone, with no one to share it with, no one to wake you and ask if you wanted her to begin the coffee, or to start the coffee without your asking and then begin breakfast for which you would be grateful thirty seconds after rising, but those minutes before, resent as much as if a day of fence building stood before you.

The Bird clan whispered and smoked and mulled his offer. Minutes passed until the beer was gone and the cigars burned to stubs. The room emptied, two or three at a time nodding to the new barmaid on their path to the door, and with their departure, Strawl's fatigue returned. It was no relief being left alive and outside of it. Finally, only Raymond remained. He opened the cylinder and emptied Strawl's pistol of bullets and speared the burning end of his cigar in a tin ashtray.

"We have nothing to do with these killings," he said.

"I'm out of fight, Raymond," Strawl told him. "You should have seen them. The first had wings made of rib bone. And the last. Well, I told you about him. Both in their youth, still."

"None of us are young," Raymond replied. "Not even those just born."

Strawl handed Raymond a fresh cigar and sat in silence as the man left the tavern. He drank a little more from the bottle of beer in front of him, but it was lukewarm and bitter and didn't slake his thirst. Raymond and his band had not killed anyone. Strawl did not hold with the notion that eyes revealed the soul. Faces were another matter. He trusted them not for what they revealed, but for what they could not hide. Living animated each in a manner neither beard nor rouge could mask, and each differed in how it told of such living. Though Raymond had managed to maintain a lively wit, every muscle that wrapped his skull was tired. His skin draped over his face as loose as a serape. The narrative in him had ceased, and what remained was history severed from memory, no more alive than if read in a book. Killing was not in them any longer. They were simply witnesses that rumor and hearsay occasionally multiplied into more.

He'd failed.

He had no more suspects and a herd of red-assed police in a race to see which could take the most of his flesh the soonest. He realized he was tired and in want of sleep. He hoped Elijah had not dallied collecting the horses. It was a short ride to Conant Springs and the soft meadow that encircled it.

Strawl rose to square his bill. Hurd had left and the hired woman stood with her back to him, rinsing glasses. Her dark hair had been parted in the middle and tied with a beaded band. She stood in a familiar manner. The woman's face rose in the mirror then she turned to accept his money and he recognized it was Ida, his late wife and Elijah's mother. She counted his change, then let it sit on the blonde wooden slab.

"Alive," Strawl said.

She nodded.

"Did the current save you?"

"No," she said. "I was never in the river."

Strawl put his hands to his face and rubbed his brow. "Did Elijah give you the money?"

"He has money?"

"He sold half the ranch. I wanted to know what he squandered the proceeds on."

"He owns no ranch."

"I gave him half of mine," Strawl said. "After you died."

"I have not seen him since I left you."

"But he knows you are well."

"He knows," Ida said.

"Was living with me so awful?" Strawl asked.

"Yes," she said. "For me."

"Then why did you stay?"

"I didn't."

"You couldn't have left without deceiving me, making me think you were dead?"

"No," she said.

Strawl was quiet until she spoke again.

"I did not want to cause a mess in your house."

"Generous of you," Strawl said. He tapped the bar with his finger, rattling the coins and paper. "Though the funeral put me to some expense."

Ida set down a dried glass, then lifted another and toweled the inside, her dark hand flattened against the glass.

"I never chased skirts. I never struck you. I never left you hungry."

She ran some water and rinsed another glass under it.

"Well good luck to you," Strawl said.

He collected his money and stepped from the bar into the bright light of day. It blinded him, and he squinted. Elijah sat on the bench in front of the tavern.

"Same number went in came out. Still no killer."

"Nope," Strawl said. "Ran into your mother, though."

Elijah nodded.

"The money. Was it for her?"

Elijah shook his head.

"You knew she hadn't drowned."

"I knew."

"It would be a good reason. The money and her," Strawl said.

"I know," Elijah said. "But it wouldn't be my reason."

"Maybe I could stand being deceived a little."

"You've been deceived plenty."

"That so?"

"It was Dot that smuggled Ida off the place. That was her part of the bargain."

"Bargain?" Strawl asked.

"My end was to keep you from killing more Indians."

"Seems to me you got the lighter duty."

"Dot didn't know that."

"But you did."

"Yes."

"For certain."

"Yes."

Strawl noticed the grin on the boy's face, a strange smile, one he recognized though its expression was now not familiar.

"Jacob was about four days dead. That would put his death the night before you came back to the ranch, wouldn't it?"

"It would," Elijah said.

Strawl heard the meaty whack before he felt it. His knee bent in a manner it wasn't built for and he tipped clumsily onto his side. The pain was by now familiar: there was no beauty or wonder in it, only hurt, and he was not worthy of a glorious death or even a simple one after which people mourned, and rather than provoke him, the blow and the knowledge left him resigned. Another blow from the rifle butt to his injured ribs took the wind from him, and he imagined he was drowning, as he'd imagined Ida drowned. Then came another blow that cracked against his ankle and though it did the least damage it caused him the most pain, and he yelped like a wounded animal, enraged, finally, and once more.

| TWENTY ONE |

Elijah drove his feet into Baal's flanks and felt the air leave the animal. Outside of town he nudged the horse to a trot but Baal had never held that middling gait well, and, eventually, Elijah pressed his knees to the horse's withers and he smoothed into a lope. Ten miles later, he hobbled Baal near birch at the south bay of Owhi Lake. He hiked the basalt cliff above, halting at a serviceberry bush to load a handful into his shirt pockets. In his mouth the heavy skin bent and finally broke, and he tasted the sour juice and meat. He held one on his tongue a moment before swallowing and adding another. At the bluff's top, he studied the Nespelem's vague shape in the haze of dust and heat. The weather baked the country like summer still, but the aspen leaves had yellowed; instead of flashing like coins in the wind and sun, they tore from their branches and gathered in leeward depressions at the foot of the boulders strewn throughout the basin below him. He hunted the sky but saw nothing aside from two circling hawks. He watched them adjust their fanned tails in the quiet sky. A rising breeze elevated them, then broke, and they fell until boosted by another. Their wings barely beat the hot air, just tipped with and against it.

He had no doubt Strawl would follow. The old man knew nothing else. Elijah pitied him and that pity, he realized, had moved him to confess. No, that was not completely so. He knew vanity was the seed of his admission. The one person likely to appreciate his work was his faux father, and, like a son, Elijah had sought his approbation on the matter. And now the man was tracking him as he had so many men before and would likely kill him or surrender him to life in a cell, which was, in fact, the only form of approval he was capable of. But Elijah's acts could progress from rumor to fact in the world no other way. Blood and bone were simply sermons from the pulpit without a reckoning that included his own flesh in the game.

Elijah sighed and one of the hawks wheeled above, as if it might have heard the sound or felt the wind change with the breath required for the utterance. He was not bloodthirsty by nature. Each killing had turned food to ashes in his mouth for days after. He was relieved to be done with murder and to have confided his acts to Strawl, turning the matter over to him. Though Elijah trusted Strawl with little else, these were the duties for which the almighty had formed him and he could no more shirk them than shed his skin.

The Taker of Sisters, however, remained Elijah's burden alone. He'd permitted himself no art beyond the actions required for Jacob's death. Attending an end like Jacob's, however, was a duty beyond the ordinary. Decency required Jacob set the terms and Elijah permitted him the fullness of experience most don't earn in a hundred years of living, and, though the man screamed and cursed

and spat and bled those savage hours, he was completed by his pain
and his knowledge that one word from him would have ended it
with a bullet. Yet he never asked for quarter and Elijah, respectfully,
offered none. Still, if he'd had the means to stop his ears with wax
like Odysseus sailing past the Sirens, he would have done so.

And it was this compunction that troubled him. He should be
clear of the banalities of guilt and doubt. He saw them as useless
trappings of an infantile existence, and one steered by them as
pushed hither and yon on an ocean of tempests without a compass
or sextant and with no harbor or port or even rocky reach on the
horizon. Their lifetime passed upon a shabby, crowded vessel and
no track or windy utterance marked their passing. However, here
he was, the wind pressing his own sails away from certainty. And
instead of disembarking from his voyage, he found himself with
more distance to navigate.

Baal lifted his head. His ears twitched, and a coyote's tail sliced the
high grass a hundred yards away. Elijah descended from the promontory, patted the horse, and fed him some sugared raisins from his
saddlebag. He finished the serviceberries, then mounted. The hawks
had vanished into their perches to study the grass for field mice or
the occasional cottontail small enough to appear feasible.

Horse and rider ascended into the mountains through the Nespelem River's drainage and, when creeks slowed to a drizzle,
made a circling path around a triplet of broad-shouldered mountains, creased where they once joined. He watered again at Nanam-
kin's south creek, then covered more miles on a thin ridge until he
made a cold camp next to the north fork. Both drained east into the
San Poil. He was astride the spine of the country. Granite striped
with copper and gypsum, turpin and limestone lined with clay and
loam and pine needles and annual husks in varying stages of decay
composed the precipices beneath him. Pine and fir and tamarack
and an occasional spruce wrinkled the hills, thinning where the

ridges turned too steep to hold seed and water and in the softened creek banks and gulleys, where the hardwoods—oak and cotton-wood—had gained some purchase.

At first, killing had been little trouble for Elijah. He'd offered his plan to Marvin, who, in turn, had consulted Raymond Bird. They saw the philosophy in it and the religion, too, and admitted only a dire measure would do. Possessing no inspiration that ri-valed his own, they yielded. He collected the tools and thinking necessary to begin. To the initial victims, he offered simply irony. He had read some time ago of the Sand Creek Massacre. The in-dignities those militia visited upon Black Kettle's women and chil-dren would seem absurd if race were subtracted. He was pleased when reports of horrified women discovering their new hats were handed with skin and pubic hair reached him, but disappointed the news stopped there. None had heard of Sand Creek.

The Cloud boys proved more difficult. The early victims were practically strangers, either relative newcomers or so far lost that they seemed barely visible, even when sitting across from him at the Ketch Pen Tavern. If Elijah hadn't made a production of their deaths, they would hardly be missed. The Clouds, though, were pleasant enough acquaintances, and he genuinely admired their parents. These murders required less metaphor and more art; he wanted them to be questions asked by generations after but never answered. Elijah considered their deaths the best thoughts he'd ever conjured.

Then the Taker of Sisters became necessary. The word, necessary, gave him some comfort. He enjoyed repeating its sound, the e's and s's, wind in a tree, then the last syllables, waning like an animal's call. He appreciated its meaning, as well, and he bathed his doubt in its sound until, as night arrived, he finally felt a hard-earned calm approaching, one which he had expected earlier, one which he was disappointed not to have enjoyed already. He breathed and closed his eyes. He felt like he was floating in an endless lake of pine needles and leaves and soft earth, and the forest's clean, acidic fragrance encompassed him. In the sky were more stars than he could recall ever seeing, more light than darkness, like God himself was on the verge of returning the Lamb and ending night for good.

Half an hour after Elijah's flight, Strawl collected himself enough to give chase. His back ached so badly he had to find a stump to boost himself onto Stick. His knee swelled to half again its size and he felt the blood and pain pump through his pant leg. His head had cleared of romance and philosophy and meaning as all had somersaulted in separate directions.

He dozed riding and refused any thought's passage into his head. If Elijah's path had been less direct, Strawl would not have been capable of following. He camped ten miles beyond Owhi Lake and ten miles behind Elijah the first night, though he did not make the effort to determine the latter. He slept fitfully, the hard ground pressing him to change position to accommodate his injuries, past and recent, and the arthritis accompanying them.

The next morning, Strawl followed Elijah and Baal through higher country. The light spilled color over the green pine and yellowing oaks and grasses and warmed his back. He poked along the creek banks, allowing Stick to feed and drink. He stumbled on occasional signs of Elijah—horse droppings, his firepit, a feather pile from a grouse he'd snared. All along well-defined game trails, trod regularly by deer herds and horses and riders.

A magpie cussed Stick, and the gathered crows scattered through a birch's branches watched them pass. Stick dropped a nugget of shit and they cawed and swooped to it. Farther, a line of quail bent and quickened before him and farther yet, in the rock, a sage hen and handful of chukar drummed. As the afternoon progressed, sparrows and chickadees flitted from one tree to another hunting flying insects. Stick spooked a badger that hissed then dove for its den. Deer pellets and tracks dotted the path, but game of any size were bedded down in the heat.

Strawl halted finally on the lee side of a basalt chimney. His entire body seemed to ache, though the pains initiated in four or five distinct places. He rolled a smoke with shaky hands and another hour passed. He reclined against the stone and chewed on a piece of the jerked beef.

Half an hour later, a man on foot halted at the skyline and bent to catch his breath. Recovering his wind, the figure scanned the Okanogan Valley. Two rifles were slung upon his back along with an ancient military pack. Strawl recognized his frame but not until he began to descend in a lanky, stumbling gait did he make him for Rutherford Hayes. Two of his dogs followed, panting and staring at Hayes like he might part a sea if he were so inclined. Strawl whistled and Hayes halted until Strawl whistled a second time. Hayes and the dogs covered the distance between them. Strawl offered him a cigarette, which Hayes lit this time with trembling hands. His clean-shaven face and stunned eyes made him appear simpler than he probably was.

"You are a long way from home, my friend," Strawl said. Hayes didn't reply. Strawl watched him pull from the cigarette and drag the smoke into his lungs. Strawl fed the dogs a bit of sausage left from his breakfast.

"Where's the others?"

"Amos and Ahab are killed. Esther lit out and I couldn't wait without losing my hair."

"Indian cops?"

"And a couple white."

"I'm sorry they came upon you, Rutherford," Strawl said. "They're looking for me."

"You're one of them, ain't you?"

Strawl nodded. "Guess us skunks can't stand our own company."

"You running or just hunting good ground for a fight?"

"I'm not certain, Root."

"That don't seem anything like you," Hayes said.

They were quiet awhile. Strawl scratched one of the dogs' ears and felt its head loll against his hand, pressing him to continue.

"Excuse me being presumptuous," Hayes said. "I guess I have no manners."

Strawl chuckled. "I got a scad of people who want my scalp, some kin. I have no quarrel with you making an observation that is as true as the North is cold. To answer you, I guess running and fighting don't seem that far apart anymore. You run then fight, then fight then run."

"You can add hiding to that hoop," Hayes said. "Fighting nor hiding nor running, they don't do no good. I'm bound for Canada. Nobody pays much attention there."

"Sounds like a straight line to me."

Hayes spat. "It's quiet, I heard once. I ain't much with company, but I might learn. You could join me."

Strawl had never considered a simple exit, transplanted, and in another country to boot. It would require effort and paperwork and time if the authorities intended to uproot him, and he'd make it clear enough that if the law insisted on pursuit, his absence would be less trouble than his return.

"How'd you get to be the genius of us all?" Strawl asked.

Hayes stared at the horizon and didn't answer.

"Where you going over?"

"Chesaw."

"The Chink Road?"

"Bootleggers using it now. Got the Mounties spooked and the State Guard bought."

"Damned if you haven't thought it out."

He had considered calling an end to this ordeal and heading home. An angry collection of police would likely harass him, but on the ranch the BIA would have no jurisdiction, and as for Dice, angry as he may be, butting heads with Strawl had proven impractical and Dice was a practical man. The silverspoon would be bent but without recourse. It would baffle his pursuers. There was Elijah to consider, but if he had sense enough to keep Strawl in the dark, no doubt he could outwit his poor substitutes, and his crimes were his own business.

Hayes said, "You got family keeping you here, I suppose."

He wondered what he would return to: poverty and a dotage supervised by a child who saw fit to conspire with his wife to counterfeit her death and make him worse than a widower. And not without reason—he now knew she recalled her own mother's end. Arlen and his grandchildren would have no use for him.

Canada would be a blank piece of paper, and he could write what he wanted on it and leave out what he wanted, too. Still, Elijah would haunt him, he knew. He had no intention of turning him over for trial, and he doubted he had the stomach to shoot him. The boy was the only person he'd found entertaining enough to tolerate steady. Perhaps Strawl wanted nothing more than a conversation. Still it was a scratch that would need his attention, and sooner seemed more likely than later, considering the number of lawmen tracking them.

"I'm in, Root," Strawl said. "I have to close the books on a matter. Leave your name at every post office you hear of on that road or any tavern worth stopping," he said. "I'll come soon enough after you. We'll do it goddamnit."

Strawl loosed the rawhide straps on his saddlebags and withdrew the expense money he hadn't squandered and wadded it into Hayes's shirt pocket.

"Here's our road stake," Strawl told him. "You get us a start."

Hayes took a breath.

"I'll shoot you if you argue," Strawl told him.

Strawl rolled a cigarette and then another and they smoked in silence. Hayes nodded at one of the mastiffs. "That one's got a mean streak," he said. "She isn't the biggest, but she don't bark ever, just goes for the throat." He patted her head. "She's yours if you're inclined."

"When we meet up north I'll collect her."

Hayes said nothing more. Strawl watched him as he hiked toward the foot of the ridge. He filled his canteens in Harrison Creek and let the dogs drink, then threaded a path through the thickets and low brush beneath until he was out of view.

Strawl traveled two more days, remaining clear of the meadows and bald ridgelines, crossing country quickly and closing on Elijah, now only a mile or two in front of him. From the granite cliffs and basalt knobs he heard automobile tires hum over the paved San Poil highway and, later, axles rattle and gears whine while they fought the rutted logging grades that were their only other option.

The third evening a hound bayed. Strawl guessed the animal resided in Wauconda or Republic, twenty miles from him as the crow flies. The next morning over breakfast, he heard them once more, this time a chorus, on a scent. Dice and his minions were clumsy as three-legged mules, but that would likely make them all the more troublesome, so Strawl saddled and wound through the draws until he had moved within a mile of their soundings. He undid a handkerchief and looped it over a low branch and under piled a pound of Truax's peppered beef. He backtracked Stick to a shaded ridge, where he watched the hounds break brush and come upon the tree and the beef, which they ate greedily until their sneezes and hacks made it impossible for them to swallow. Horses followed, but he'd painted a tree trunk a hundred feet farther with

wolf scent a trapper had once traded him for a walk on a trespassing charge, and the horses raised and threw their riders as if
they had been driven into a fence.

Strawl recognized one of Dice's deputies, then Dice himself and
the silverspoon, in bandaged feet, who whipped his horse like it
had shit on his breakfast. Strawl was tempted to put a bullet between his eyebrows then and there and undo the tension pulling at
his own shoulders, but permitted the man another day of light to
cuss and night of darkness to suffer through.

Dawn woke Elijah and he rode on, letting Baal pick his way slowly
to keep from riding him to pieces. He diverted around Republic,
the Ferry County seat, then began the labor of serpentining the
broken mountains draining the Kettle River into the Columbia.
They watered at a series of clear cirque pools that headed nearly
every valley where, thousands of years before, snow had massed
into glacial crags that rivaled the stony heights. Their ice and
weight had extinguished the vegetation for millenniums and
welled the stone floors beneath. The water that remained from the
great thaws was a thousand years old and colored green or aqua or
nearly purple or jet-black, depending upon the rock and minerals
beneath. One pool, over gypsum, appeared the consistency of milk.

Wrinkled granite tables, each several hundred feet square,
littered one rise like children's scattered blocks, and he wound
through and over them with great care as the pitched rock was
sheer and the trails sandy and prone to collapse. Above, a long
ridge shadowed his path. At its crest, a mile of meadow spread
before Elijah, dotted with delicate white flowers for which he
had no name. Yellowing grasses, matted low shrubs, and squat
fir punctuated the clearing and lined its edges. The red cedar and
stately lodgepole pine were too demanding to endure this high,

and the lack of tall trees left the country looking scalped, and even more so the bald mountain above it.

Even midday was cool this far up and the air thin enough to require more respites for Baal. The pristine sky seemed to turn ten-mile distances to a stone's throw. In other pockets of these mountains, miners had uncovered enough gypsum or iron or gold or copper to make a meager go of their trade, but between the Columbia and the San Poil no one had taken an interest, and, as Elijah hiked the shale, leading Baal when he couldn't sort out a path, he encountered game one rarely did below, elk and a young bull moose standing in Timber Creek trailing water and tulle threads from his ruminating jaws and later a pair of bighorn sheep. Farther, he spied a scattering of caribou resting in a field below a hanging ledge, and, through his rifle's scope, a lynx trailing them—animals he'd only seen in books. Later, when he'd again moved lower, he stopped to study trees scarred with enormous grizzly nails and a sapling splintered by one of its blows.

A weather anomaly left this place warmer and wetter than most inland mountain ranges, and it was as likely to be blanketed by clouds, even in late fall, as snow. Evening, lacy mist collected in the fissures and dips of this strange world. The moon's blue light cast a glowing pallor over the trees, leaving them luminous, as if lit by white fire. That night, a lupine moan broke the quiet and stirred Baal enough that Elijah blanketed his eyes to settle him.

A day later and twenty miles farther north, evening arrived before the sun set, and Baal's breath smoked in the clear and freezing purple night. Elijah was prepared to bed down and collect wood for a fire when he heard a coyote yip, followed by two twitters from a bobwhite. He whistled an answer and when it was acknowledged, he stepped out of the stirrup and led Baal a mile angled beneath the mountain's shadow until he reached a rocky crag. There, he followed a shale slide over the other side. Baal's hooves clacked the flat rock and the sound rattled the animal. He battled the reins. Elijah settled him, then led on. Soon the smell of meat cooking on a spit beckoned him.

Off the rocks Baal stilled and Elijah rode him through the pines and yellowing tamaracks. The air sighed in the needles and their yellow pollen floated over man and horse. They jumped a pheasant and the pop of wings startled the horse. Elijah watched the bird light in a thicket where another stirred next to it. Soon he heard women's voices, too, and children harassing the female pup Rutherford Hayes had given someone in the spring. It woofed and scared no one. Firelight careened in orange and golden streaks against the darkened trees and pinched shadows.

Twenty heavy canvas military tents, staked and propped by poles cut from the surrounding woods, circled a common area. Eighteen were flapped down for families and privacy—eight for each of the pregnant widows and ten left for the families who volunteered to join them. The remaining two were open-walled to permit public meetings and religious services and meals when the weather required. Each family's tent had a chimneyed Franklin stove for heat, while the public tents contained a pair on each end and another in the middle. In the worst weather, the makeshift village's fifty inhabitants could gather their blankets and dogs and conserve fuel by crowding themselves together in one, as the Canadian tribes had done for centuries. Two other structures finished the circle. Both were metal and windowless and locked. One held food staples that would keep—gunnysacks filled with grain, flour, sugar, salt, canned fruits, baking powder, cornstarch, and some fodder for the animals; the other contained several thousand dollars in medical supplies and a small library instructing a layman how to use them. Together, the contents equaled half the proceeds from the ranch's sale.

At the center of the circle was a twenty-foot-long rock trough constructed for outdoor cooking. Atop the walls were metal grills and plates and cast-iron spits on which one could turn rabbits or game birds, and at the end was another, larger rod ample to roast half a deer or elk. Under both ends, Raymond's family had constructed brick-reinforced ovens to slow-cook wild vegetables, breads, and stews. Four cows and their calves lolled in a crudely wired square on the east edge of the camp, along with a half dozen sheep and a goat, which accounted for more of the ranch proceeds.

Stacked firewood six feet high formed three quarters of the compound's boundary, yielding only for the livestock. A hundred yards into the woods, Marvin, along with his grandchildren, had cut a root cellar employing rock to support the walls and crossed lodgepoles as rafters.

Marvin had determined Elijah's approach through insects' hush and the fluttering of birds. He tarried at the edge of the light to greet him with a strip of venison and a pipe of kinnikinnick. Elijah and he smoked, then Elijah ate the venison, stringy and coarse with muscle. It was gamier here than down below, where the deer browsed the wheat at night and tasted not unlike beef. Elijah sniffed, disappointed he preferred the other. He let Baal loose to feed on the clumped grasses that managed to grow despite the little light the trees permitted.

"I am finished."

"I know," Marvin said.

"Do you think I am a sinner?"

"Did you enjoy those things people would call sin?" Marvin asked him.

"No."

"It cannot be a sin unless you enjoyed it," Marvin said.

Elijah nodded and Marvin led him to a tipi outside the camp's boundaries, close to the stream serving the makeshift village, yet far enough to permit him his thoughts. Inside were a lantern and some oil and a copy of his good book.

| TWENTY-TWO |

Strawl rested a full day under the peak of Copper Mountain, eating the last of his frybread and the remnants of a salami stick. Elijah had not varied his trek, riding as if nobody was interested, or more likely, as if he knew those following and saw no reason to discourage them. The camp before him was impressive—enough so, Strawl determined Elijah could not have managed the project alone. Evening, he watched the pickets exchange, and through his spyglass he made out groups of women laboring at the long pit and silhouetted men walking alone or in pairs across the firelit commons into or past the tents, yellow wraiths where the glow ebbed and ended. Strawl heard stones scrape from the stream bank as another contingent of women and young girls cleaned pots or beat clothes with broom handles soaked in lye.

The encampment appeared comic. Even in this country no one
built villages or towns to hide them. They wanted businesses and
roads and railroads. They wanted to be found. A man like Rutherford Hayes might hermit himself. Even a family or two who believed in some smoky deity so strange and private that they could
only believe in it themselves if no neighbors existed to argue could
still be assured seclusion if they risked the most primitive corners of
the region. Any group larger, though, necessitated not company—
that would be the least of their concerns—but more than would be
accessible within walking or riding distance. That meant restocking
at stores and liveries, and those don't occur without people, and if
reduced to that, what was the point of going off?

As it grew later, Strawl made for the camp. He avoided the
pickets with no trouble, even with the horse in tow. At the creek
bed were seven women, each heavy with child. They scoured a
stack of pans and kettles with river gravel, chattering. He passed
without nodding and a quarter mile later arrived at the clearing
between canopies. Enormous trees had been pruned ten feet up
from the ground, the long phallic trunks appeared sins from the
uncharted country in people's minds. Squares of brown tarp were
tied fifteen feet high in the trees cinched tight with hemp rope to
the sturdiest limbs some places and tethered to the ground with
iron stakes in others. The group had scattered leaves and needles
atop them to make the place appear nothing unusual. Underneath, the hardpan was swept clean as a floor. In the center, the
firepit had high walls and a deep well to mute the light. Inez
stirred what smelled like a broth of some kind. A bruise remained beneath her ear. Her grandchildren scrambled toward
a tent upon seeing Strawl, and Marvin intercepted him, coming
from the darkness.

"You're a party to this?" Strawl asked.

"Yes," Marvin said.

"I thought you knew nothing of these doings."

"I lied."

Strawl smiled. "Well, the truth is overrated."

He decided to press no further. Marvin loaded a pipe with kin-nikinnick and lit it.

"I apologize for hurting Inez," Strawl said.

Marvin nodded. "No one can help who they are."

"You included?"

"Yes," Marvin answered.

"There guns on me?"

Marvin shrugged. "I can't speak for everyone here. If you came to shoot us, some will shoot back."

"I'm accustomed to those I shoot at shooting back," Strawl said. He sat on a flat boulder that looked like it was meant for the purpose. The camp had begun buttoning up. Mothers herded children to their canvas abodes, and several pregnant women tottered across the clearing, turning misshapen silhouettes as they left the fire's glow. Strawl watched two tents glow as lanterns inside clicked to life and flickered with their quaking oil feeds.

"Are you looking for a truce?" Strawl asked.

"Yes."

Strawl stared at the ground.

"You know who I'm here for?"

"He told me."

"You want this truce extended to him, too, I suppose?"

Marvin nodded.

"You know what he's done and who he's done it to?"

"Yes," Marvin said.

"I can't promise you anything on that."

"Is that why you're here? To shoot your son?"

"He's not blood to me."

Marvin said, "He is like you. He has no blood father. He is your son. You are his father. His deeds are yours. Blood is not necessary. He is why you are here."

Strawl shook his head. "I am not sure what's put me here, but unless someone throws lead my direction, I don't plan on shooting."

"Will you arrest us, then?"

"Who here would allow it without guns? And I already told you I'm not inclined to do that. Elijah, however, is excluded on both counts."

Marvin nodded. He steered Strawl up a trail to a rock outcropping that overlooked the camp. They sat and smoked a long time.

"One of those women wife to a Cloud boy?" Strawl asked.

"Two," Marvin answered. "One to each."

Beneath them, Inez organized the women into something resembling an apple-packing line at two split logs, which served as tables. There, some chopped roots and vegetables raised in a garden they'd passed climbing to where they now sat. Others gutted a stringer of trout, and two more plucked sage hens. They were preparing tomorrow's meals.

"Couldn't help but notice she was with child. A good deal of others seem in the same state. I'm guessing you're not building a home for wayward women out this far."

"No," Marvin said.

"No felony," Strawl said. "Impolite and a sin, but law doesn't reach that far."

"They are all pregnant with Elijah's children." Marvin tapped the pipe then struck a match and handed it to Strawl, who smoked then tried not to cough at the harsh mixture.

"But those Cloud girls, their husbands are barely cold."

"He had made them pregnant before."

"That why he killed them?"

Marvin shook his head. "He decided they would die before he made their wives pregnant, even."

Strawl handed the pipe back to him. The women below were separating the contents of their meal into pots to stew through the night. Inez ground some grain with a homemade pestle. Marvin studied their work. His hair was long and he wore it in a braid that he'd tied with a yellow handkerchief.

"You didn't stop him?"

Marvin puffed on the pipe and watched the smoke break in the cold air. "He asked permission."

"Permission to kill someone? Who from, his good book?"

"Me," Marvin said. "Though the book he listened to, as well."

"You told him it was all right to kill those Cloud boys."

Marvin nodded. "After he asked, I told him to copulate with their women and then to kill the men."

"Those other boys, too?"

Marvin nodded. "Except Jacob Chin. That was his own killing, though I am sure he thought it necessary."

"Marvin."

The old man raised his hand. "He did not kill without discrimination nor did we permit him to do so without caution and thought. When he asked about some, we told him no, and he did not go further. They are still living. They are sick, but they have life in them."

"All the years I have known you, you were a peaceful man. Why in hell would you grant him such a request?"

"The men were dead already," Marvin said. "Replacing them. It was the only way. If they lived longer, it would soon be as if they had not lived."

As Marvin told it, those boys were present a little less every day, senile in their thirties, but with no distant childhood to retreat into, their bodies and voices husks roused only by alcohol or blood for an hour or so, before sentience withdrew and they returned ghosts. Elijah couldn't tolerate witnessing their disappearance. They were bent on being forgotten, even by themselves, and Elijah had resolved to deny them that.

Strawl recalled Dot reading him from Shakespeare's play about the murder of Caesar. Let us not be butchers, Brutus said, but instead carve him up like a dish for the gods. And so Caesar was remembered, and Anthony lived and Brutus was killed. If Caesar had managed twice the years, until his back bent and his eyes clouded and his mouth drooled, he would not be remembered a tenth as well.

And Elijah had left them children, Marvin reminded him. Boys who would be fathered not by ghostmen, but by stories. And Elijah would be their great-uncle, breathing their fathers' stories into them like a man puffs an ebbing coal to renew a fire, until each child became a conflagration of his father's match-strike.

These children would hear of their fathers' strange deaths and consider them and retell them until they contained reason and God, and this would be the beginning of tales that would outlive all that was. They would be as resurrected as Lazarus recalled from the tomb.

"It's a generous idea," Strawl said.

"It is his."

"Do you believe it?"

"I want to believe it. I have nothing else to believe."

"Where is he now?"

"Sleeping. He is done with killing. Seven pregnant women," he said. "He's got all the story he can tell."

"Blood gets in a man's nature," Strawl said.

"It was not blood that killed them," Marvin said. "It was not anger. It was mercy."

Strawl was quiet. The crickets sawed at the night.

"You are not going to take him?"

"You think he is done."

"I am certain," Marvin said. "He is tired."

"The tired sleep and rise feeling froggy," Strawl said.

"Not those tired in this way. Sleep is not medicine for them."

Strawl nodded. "What would it change if I took him or didn't?"

Marvin didn't reply and Strawl didn't expect him to. They smoked a little longer in silence. Below, the mastiff announced herself to another yearling that belonged to the Birds. Five minutes later, the branches parted and Raymond Bird appeared. Strawl offered him the pipe and he smoked and smiled. They made room for him to sit. The bulk of the clan arrived half an hour later. They marched in four pairs, each packing a quartered elk strung to a pine pole. Strawl could smell the animal and the men and the blood and simple human residue from a day occupied with tasks enough to make a man feel useful.

"Rutherford Hayes left to Canada," Raymond said.

Strawl nodded.

"We asked him to stay with us," Marvin said.

"He's done with people." Raymond coughed and spat. "I put a deer's hindquarters on his porch once and he tethered that dog to my house a year later. Or paid someone to. Shame he's going."

Raymond unscrewed an army canteen and offered it to Marvin and Strawl, who drank deeply, then returned it to him.

The aroma of the ovens rose to them. Marvin stood. Strawl and Raymond watched him negotiate the trail into the camp. At its foot, he took two pie plates and extended them as if a penitent waiting for a blessing. The women loaded the tins with food, then he hunted spoons and returned.

Strawl thanked him for the plate. He and Raymond ate in silence and finished by cleaning the gravy and grease with a piece of flatbread. Marvin reloaded his pipe with kinnikinnick, but Raymond rolled cigarettes for himself and Strawl.

"There's law coming for him," Raymond said.

"A ways off yet," Strawl said. "And they're more likely hunting me. They don't know what for on this issue, and I've put the red ass on the lot of them recently."

Raymond watched his cigarette glow.

"How do you know how far they are?"

"Can't hear them," Strawl said.

"Hearing distance, they're already too close."

Strawl shook his head. "My ears are sharper than most."

"How good?"

"How far are we from that wolf?"

"What wolf?" Raymond asked.

"The one I hear howling," Strawl told him. He smoked his cigarette down.

Raymond looked to Marvin. "That bragging?"

Marvin shook his head. "They say it is so."

Raymond let that settle.

"I thought dogs could only hear like that."

"Maybe I am a dogman," Strawl said.

Marvin and Raymond chuckled at that. The dogs beneath hurried back and forth past the fire like the shadows of bats swooping, hoping for scraps or a chipmunk to chase. The owls hooted at them and the dogs yapped back until someone from the tents hit one with a stone. He yelped and the rest quieted.

"Someone is angry with your brothers," Raymond said. He set his plate on the dirt and leaned back so he could see the stars filling the sky.

"If you are dogman you should know the stories of Dog," Raymond said.

"There are a bookful of stories of Dog," Strawl replied.

"Know about the one where Dog sniffs his brother's ass because someone stole his salmon?" Raymond asked.

Strawl shook his head.

"He doesn't know the difference between food ready to eat and food shit out. Dog is stupid. Did you know Dog once went to the people to ask for fire for his people?"

"How did it turn out?"

"They fed him."

It was quiet a moment. "That it?" Strawl asked.

"If you know Dog, you know it is so," Raymond said. "Dog has no purpose. That's why he's ruled by people. I just wonder if what rules men has the same opinion of us."

"You think Elijah's done?" Strawl asked Raymond.

"I do," Raymond said.

"Convince me."

"Killing is work. They have to pay you to do it and put the weight of the law behind you, and it still wears you out."

Strawl nodded.

"Well, Elijah's got sense but he is like Dog in one way," Raymond said. "He is lazy."

Strawl laughed and pushed his cap back on his head. "A lawyer couldn't have made a case more convincing," he said.

<hr />

Strawl circled the firelight to Stick. The horse nickered at his smell. Strawl led him to a grassy spot beneath the rock promontory. Raymond and Marvin had offered Strawl a place among their blankets and tents, but Strawl had declined, preferring to bed near Stick in the case that Dice or the BIA turned ambitious enough to work nights.

Strawl collected twigs and pine needles into a depression and coaxed a small fire to burn, fueling it with branches from a bull pine halved with a lightning strike. The trunk had braided its new growth around what had been killed and in the darkness looked like a long neck twisted awfully, and above, half feathered with needles, half blackened by a blow of current and light and smoke; it trembled in the sky like a monstrous, dying head.

His tobacco pouch was empty. He undid the straps of his saddlebag and found a piece of jerky not completely ruined by Truax's pepper. He chewed and spat and sipped at the canteen, then poured water in his cupped hand and let Stick lap it dry. He repeated this until Stick's thirst had waned and then batted his nose lightly to announce an end to it.

The fire burned fast but low, fueled with the deadwood. Strawl withdrew a larger stick that had begun to catch and let it smolder on a stone, afraid the fire might be visible from above. He covered himself with his blanket. The sky was clear and had no bottom to it, just miles of light and darkness piled upon one another.

Elijah had managed to turn murder into art and philosophy and religion all at once. He'd not encountered anyone who'd equaled it, but he'd not encountered anyone interested in equaling it, either. It was as if the boy were attempting to take the cruelty out of crime and the selfishness, too, leaving only the blood and absence, making the pain that coincided temporary but the relief permanent, like pulling an abscessed tooth.

Ridiculous, Strawl knew, but an ingenious, thoroughly heroic, absurd epic joke, one so committed to itself that it had surrendered being funny and so had he. And Marvin thought them father and son. Strawl never possessed much humor, but the little he owned he'd never bargain for an idea. It was not that he valued laughter; he knew no ideas so worthy he'd drop a nickel into the offering plate. They were kin by means, not ends, because Strawl had none of the latter. What they had in common was blood. Strawl's talent lay there, and he'd bequeathed it to Elijah the same as the ranch, though he could not sell this inheritance to the neighbors. It was his.

Strawl lay back on the saddle and blew a breath into the sky that clouded in the cold, then disappeared. Still, he thought, the boy had promised an end to it and two good men believed him. Though he had committed his share of misdemeanors and the arson certainly had been a felony, he'd never hurt man nor beast before and he had had reason, no matter how unreasonable.

Below, one of the men banked the coals of the cooking fire. It smoked a moment at being disturbed, then did not. He fell asleep looking at the piece of sky over him, wondering if it was over Canada as well, and, if he were to lie in that land, if other things would be the same for him when he looked up at night.

| TWENTY-THREE |

Strawl rose and warmed the last of his water and put one of Elijah's tea bags in a cup, as he was out of coffee. He watched the steam rise from the steeping liquid, letting his face dampen in its wet heat. Stick nickered and Strawl rolled an apple he'd held back in the horse's direction. It popped in the horse's jaws as he snuffled and chewed. Strawl bridled him and brushed the blanket then set it across his back. He followed with the saddle. The horse puffed his belly to battle the cinch as he had since Strawl had purchased him as a green colt. Strawl tossed a rock into the brush, and when Stick turned toward it, distracted, Strawl tugged the strap and snubbed it tight. The horse wheezed at being bested once more. He shuffled and threw his head against the reins. Strawl scolded him and mounted. He circled the sleeping camp once more and splashed across the stream to the trail that brought him in. A half mile later, he came upon Raymond on foot. Strawl slowed his horse.

"Lighting out?" Raymond asked.

Strawl nodded.

Raymond shook his head. "These people. Us. We won't make it long."

"Think not?"

Raymond said, "We cook in pots and pans from the fort, sleep under dime-store blankets. It's not cold yet. Not like it's going to be. There's no seasoned wood to burn aside from deadfalls, and the snow will cover them. Even if we remember enough to get into winter, we're living so close together, typhoid or cholera or whooping cough or the flu will end us."

"There's some reasons others haven't put down here, I guess."

Raymond nodded. "And we're about to learn them. I'd invite you to stay, but that doesn't seem as friendly as allowing you your leave."

Strawl said nothing.

"We could use someone lethal to keep back those law folks. Whether they're pushing for you or him, they're pushing for someone, and they'll settle for who they find first and that will likely be fifty people who can't move like one. Maybe they will arrest us, and rescue us from languishing with disease."

"They may be due some ill fortune," Strawl said. "You never know."

"You think that might be so?"

"I believe if you're hunting a bear you better not neglect the likelihood the bear's hunting, too."

Raymond leaned upon a stick he'd trimmed to walk with. "You know, I was in those groups they shipped to the fort for schooling. I recall I enjoyed it. I could already read and they had history books that were nearly as entertaining as the old grandfather's stories. In those books, there were tribes of people, too. I remember the Huns were bad ones. They wiped out Rome. I never met one so I asked the Fathers, and they said there were no more Huns. They were rubbed out, I thought. But the Father said no, they just stopped being Huns and now were other things. Germans or Bavarians or Cossacks, maybe." He looked up at Strawl. "You didn't take anything from anyone they had not already lost. Neither did Elijah."

Stick tossed his head and snorted. Strawl patted him.

"He's up on the ridge," Raymond said. "Listening for those that are coming."

"No, he's waiting on me."

Raymond nodded. "Not unlikely that's so."

"You're staying on, I suppose," Strawl said.

Raymond shrugged. "If I don't get killed, the tale will be worth a bucket of beer every time I tell it. Never know when things will be that hard."

"One thing I'm wondering, what did he kill them with?" Strawl asked.

"He bronzed a donkey's jaw and teeth. He sharpened one end to a blunt punch and filed the rest sharp as a shaver blade. It appeared a lot of trouble to me."

Strawl shook his head. "He's had that around forever. I thought it was just decoration. Well, the boy took the long view with the few things he committed to."

"I guess this counts as one." Raymond did not look sad, but like someone who comprehended sadness existed in each moment of each day.

"Well good luck to you," Strawl said.

He sawed Stick's reins and pressed him forward. The trail wound through a bulge of ferns and yellowing serviceberry bushes.

At the top, he gazed over the forest and rock below. He could hear children speaking and mothers correcting them and then laughter from two men. Three hundred yards away in the shadow of a sheer slab of broken granite was Elijah aboard Baal.

⁂

Elijah had been waiting for Strawl since before light. His patience pleased him. He had risen above time. Like a storm, it passed, but it did not leave him wet. An hour in the freshening light was only an hour if he agreed that's what it added up to. If he decided it to be a year or a second, it was. He wanted nothing, not to live nor to die. He could not explain this even to himself and knew better than to attempt it. He built a cigarette and smoked it. Strawl remained on the skyline, Stick mincing steps, anxious to have his head and pick his way through the canyons below.

He had dressed this morning in fine canvas pants and a clean checked shirt. Over it, he wore an elk-skin vest that had come to him through his grandfather, worn thin and dark under the arms from sweat and hard rides and the raising of a rifle or bow and pocked with three tears, two fairly earned in skirmishes with the Entiats and one the result of being hooked by a shorthorn steer during cutting season.

Strawl remained silhouetted, frozen and black like a tree or a rock on the skyline. In Elijah's scabbard was his 30.30. He lifted the rifle over his head and yipped. Strawl returned neither the call nor the gesture. Elijah raised the rifle, pressed it to his shoulder, and fired a round. Dust rose ten yards in front of Strawl and the report echoed. Baal reared. Elijah fought him down. Stick spun Strawl in a full circle, and as Strawl regained his bearings, Elijah fired another round, this one splattering against a tree trunk ten feet above the rider and horse. Bark and pollen flew then floated then settled with the dirt. Once more Elijah beckoned. Strawl raised his hand, a gesture neither to halt nor encourage Elijah, just acknowledging he was there.

"Old man," Elijah shouted. "I heard them say you wanted to meet the one who had done this killing. You wanted to know him."

Strawl had dismounted to settle the horse.

"It will be fair," Elijah said.

"Like belting me with a board?" Strawl asked.

Strawl could hear Elijah laugh and he was glad for it. "Didn't like that much did you?" Elijah said.

"Not a very courteous way to treat an old man, especially one that financed your town here."

"Well, this is not the same."

"It's different because I know you're a killer."

"I've known you were a killer since we met," Elijah said.

"That make us even now?"

"Makes a square fight. One murderer against another."

Strawl spat onto the ground.

"You going to debate you're a murderer?" Elijah asked.

"No. I am inclined to argue your few scalps equal my many."

"Then I will probably lose," Elijah said. "But it will be square."

Strawl figured him true to his word. He wasn't sure if the boy hoped to be killed or to kill him or whether he didn't care how the matter ended as long as it was closed. But he would want it justly settled.

"There's others out there that won't be so fair to either of us."

"They will come when they come. You are here now."

"And I am leaving."

"You will not meet me, then?"

"I have met you," Strawl said. "Our business is settled."

He mounted and Stick wheeled, and he took one more look at Elijah. He was scabbarding his rifle and patting Baal's withers. He sat in his saddle straight-backed and carefully. One hand crossed his face, absent wrinkle or pock. It raked his hair, purpled in the dawning. He looked as young as he was and Strawl found himself feeling strangely relieved by this, as if killing had not stuck to the boy but slid off him like a tired skin and he was fresh with another.

He watched Elijah study the trail that would return him to the camp. Baal paused before descending and Strawl could see Elijah's face lose its animation for a moment. His skin and mouth slackened. His eyes, Strawl imagined, gazed sightlessly into the silt of the trail. It was as if he'd left himself and his flesh and bones were simply husk. He realized it would have been how Elijah's victims appeared to him and why he had decided upon them. Strawl studied the boy as he descended and nudged Stick forward to peer over the ledge. Strawl watched him pass through shadows and shafts of light, wearing the same countenance until a rabbit broke from the brush and hurried ahead on the path. Baal gave chase for a few yards and Elijah blinked and smiled and his face turned his own.

Strawl turned Stick south and townward, tired once more, though not yet ready for sleep.

| TWENTY-FOUR |

The BIA cops who had followed Strawl and Elijah into the mountains had foolishly left their weapons in their squad cars a quarter mile from their camp, as if automobiles weren't folly enough for such an endeavor. They huddled around the fire, arguing about who had made the coffee last. Strawl counted five.

He drilled a round in three as Stick galloped through the place they had cleared for their bedrolls. He shot to wound, but one named Elvin stood when he should have stayed seated and it was the last time he would without someone straightening his braced legs. The other two made for the woods. Strawl listened and when they broke brush he fired twice, hearing the thump of flesh and a groan with each report. He turned Stick and stood over those who remained, while they gasped and sputtered in the dawn firelight.

"Seek and you shall find, boys," he said. "Trouble is what you wanted, I am obliging you. Otherwise retire from the field."

He fired into one of their legs and listened to the fellow holler. Another stammered a pathetic plea and Strawl chose to leave them alive. "You heal and still feel inclined for more, come to my side of the river and we'll finish this hoedown."

Three hours later, tracking by sound, Strawl switchbacked up a canyon ahead of Dice and the silverspoon. He lay with a downed birch as a rest and sighted Dice's horse. It did not even rear, just stopped and fell, driving Dice into the ground like a fence piling. He did the same for the silverspoon's animal though it was a thoroughbred and he hated to waste good horseflesh.

Strawl scrambled down the hill for position while the silverspoon's head swiveled stunned by his sudden predicament. Dice remained under his horse—his ankle was broken as it turned out—allowing Strawl the luxury of patience. The silverspoon hopped on bandaged feet toward his rifle until Strawl shot out his left knee. The man fell in sections like a dynamited building, then propped himself to kneel. A second bullet destroyed his right elbow. He fell again.

Strawl reloaded and stepped into the clearing. Dice gasped and pressed at the horse, but the weight pinned him in place as if the hand of God. The silverspoon flopped like a fish on a stringer until his left hand gained some purchase in the dirt beneath him. He spat and swore. Strawl admired the man's spunk and shot out his shoulder and other elbow out of respect. It left him torn up as a kite in a windstorm.

"Please. Stop," he said.

"OK," Strawl said.

He took three steps—he counted them—and stood over Dice.

"You won't kill me," Dice said.

Strawl nodded. "I won't even shoot you." He stopped and rolled himself a cigarette and lit it, then put it between Dice's lips until Dice drew then exhaled. Strawl took the smoke from Dice's mouth with his fingers.

He nodded at Dice's saddle. "Your rifle's in the scabbard there," he said. "Might've made sense to reach for it."

Dice said nothing. The silverspoon could not move except to moan. Strawl turned to where he could see them both. "Your sheriff could've kept me off you," Strawl said. "You both have to live with that." He nodded toward Hollingsworth. "He may not die but he won't ever be himself, either. And he's got you to thank."

"It wasn't me that shot him to pieces."

"No, you just allowed it with a weapon twelve inches from your hand."

"You're just trying to keep yourself from being guilty."

"I have never been anything else," he said.

Dice's horse gasped and the bullet hole beneath his heart hissed red foam as his lungs fought to keep their prime. Its eyes were wide and adding and subtracting the way any dying thing does, hoping for a new kind of math. Strawl patted the animal's head and called it a good, steady fellow whose work was done well. The horse met his eye and blinked and Strawl saw his own reflection appear in the pupil. Strawl pressed his hands to his lips and then on its forehead and spoke to it one more time soothingly, before he stepped back and put it out of its misery.

| **TWENTY-FIVE** |

Most see hope as the opposite of fear, but Russell Strawl knew better: fear's opposite was certainty. Fear ends where knowledge begins, even knowledge of the worst kind. Strawl had no recollection of being afraid. The world had long ago lost its capacity to surprise him.

Several months later—it was nearing spring—Strawl arrived at the ranch house in the late afternoon. The air was brisk, winter's creeping frost still held the trees from budding. He put Stick up and loaded his manger with fodder, then poured what was left from a bag of oats into his feed pail. The horse nickered and ate.

Evening, he rocked on a porch swing and listened to its chain squawk and his grandchildren at play in the yard a quarter mile below. The girls shouted and chased each other with willow whips and the baby laughed once with so much delight that Strawl couldn't help feeling lighter.

That night, he slept a deep dreamless sleep and woke feeling the wounds with which he had marked the years and the past months. He dressed slowly and put on more coffee and drank it, then fried some bacon and basted two eggs and devoured them. They pleased him so that he cooked another half dozen and the last of the bacon slab and enjoyed them more than any meal he could recall.

Then he walked outside and climbed a bank behind the house too steep to plow, where he lay on the grassy grade. It was the first moment in his life he could recall having nothing pressing enough to need his attention.

Past Bird Mountain, light continued to break. An hour later, he searched his jacket pocket until he found a cigarette, which he lit and drew from until the ash caught. The burning tobacco popped in the wind. He laid his head back into the land that was, before his, no one's. He wanted to circle this place like weather, like the mists of each spring, to be only a shadow across the great rock walls, the yellow prairies, the few bear and cougar still prowling the woods, the pine, tamarack, elm, and white-barked birch that marked the canyon breaks, and the wiry creeks that unraveled into the thick gash of a river that had cut a thousand feet of basalt and granite to secure its place.

Arlen had hitched the plow to the tractor and turned the piece below the barn. Grey dust billowed on a light breeze and veiled man and machine. The earth parted before the implement, but it remained unchanged. Put your hands through it and it crumbles and returns to itself, as water will. Cross it with a blade and it welcomes the blow patiently, as if knowing the futility of any act to nurture or wound it. Its gravity towed the moon, but any farmer needing Newton to instruct him on its pull had acquired his vocation through accident or inheritance. Physics and fulcrums and formulas in a book possessed no wisdom next to an ordinary handful of dirt. In it was the only certainty and calm that existed. Nothing was more common than dirt, or more fair.

The emerging leaves appeared slick in the rays of the light. Rusty basalt and shale spills formed three of the four horizons, a few spindly locusts scattered among the sharp, volcanic rock. The steep canyons deposited earth and rock from the glacial floods along the canyon ridges and bottoms.

By noon, Arlen had finished turning the piece and moved on to another behind a basalt bluff that held an enormous bull pine the years and gravity had tipped dangerously over its steep bank. Dust lifted beyond the outcropping, smearing the sky, while the diesel motor's clatter receded to a tick. Arlen would cut those same waves and whorls through the same unknowing ground until he expired and the little boy replaced him on the seat.

In the past months alone, Strawl had read of a furniture delivery truck driver who'd chased his wife from her flowerbeds bordering their home with his rig, then, once she'd broken into the open lawn, gunned the throttle and put her under his wheels. When the police arrived seeking a motive, he simply said he loved her.

In the same newspaper was a brief account of two unemployed gypboard hangers, who after a day panhandling and a night drinking, backed their pickup into the water, then fell to an eventless sleep until, before dawn, the worn clutch holding the truck in gear slipped, and they coasted with the pickup under the current; a brief smell in their nostrils followed like dirty socks, then the exchange of air for water that in the reverse marked their birth, and then just quiet, until the sheriff's wrecker retrieved the bodies the next morning.

They were facts, he told himself, and a man or a woman absent from the world, well that was simply the absence of a fact, and life only a product of brain neurons spitting chemicals back and forth, making the time appear more. Hamlet misspoke, Strawl decided. It is consciousness that makes cowards of us all, not conscience. Right and wrong are venomless when compared to the simple awareness of being alive. The knowledge that existence can equal something past the sum of our circulation and digestion, that those corporeal purposes serve a galaxy of space between a man's ears, whose suns and planets obey his own peculiar science, but one in which he alone recognizes the order, and only in glimpses, epiphanies that melt before he can speak or even think them—and the knowledge even this distant self is not his possession but belongs to others weighing and judging the dim and distant light he emits. When a man who knows all this steps toward his doom despite it or because of it, he might be called heroic. And Strawl knew himself to be nothing of the kind.

For him, as for the vast, vast hordes, fate or accident ends their illusions with severed medullas and spilled spinal fluid, or impacts that separate their aortas from their hearts and empty their blood into their body cavities, or with clotted veins or arteries, halting some significant process, and life withdraws from them with the sensation one feels in a draining bathtub, all that warmth and time ended.

Time is too brief for philosophical musings to link absurd collisions of time and space and matter to justify a life that requires death. Finally only fear, useless fear remains. That is all there is to know. That is wisdom.

***

Arlen ended his work before dusk, leaving the discs in the field to collect again in the morning when he would finish the summer fallow. He parked the tractor on the hard-packed dirt outside the barn. He checked the fluids and tightened a nut holding the seat that continually vibrated loose. The girls clung to his legs as he walked toward the house. Dot and the baby met him on the foot of the porch where the girls worked the hand-pump so he could rinse his face and hands before coming inside. Strawl could smell a roast cooking—some kind of meat, at least, beef rather than pork, he decided. He had lit no lantern nor opened the curtains, so he was uncertain if they knew he had returned. He guessed not. Dot would find herself compelled to gather his news, no matter how ugly.

But then in an hour he saw her shadow moving up the hill, past the ranch house and corral, bearing his direction. He lay back in the grass and listened as her footsteps stirred the brush.

"I see you've done better than the others hunting me," Strawl said, his eyes closed. "I'd expect no less from you."

"You've been absent a long while."

Strawl nodded. "Dice been here?"

"And others. Daily for a month, then once a week. Now we see them stop at your place, but they don't bother to inquire with us."

"Sorry it was a bother."

"It wasn't," she said. "Not nearly as much as having you here might have been."

Strawl smiled at that.

"You been far and wide? They thought Canada."

"No," Strawl said. "I just been off the main road."

"Why not Canada? Seems the only safe haven."

"I don't seem to be safe anywhere."

"Well, you're unsafe company. That's easy to see."

"Enough said. I go to Canada, nothing changes but Canada."

"Are you arrogant enough to think you can corrupt a whole 'nother country?"

"You think I can't. I'd be happy to hear the argument."

"I don't have one aside from hope," Dot said.

"That's a prayer, not rhetoric."

Dot remained quiet; Strawl could hear her breaths from walking the hill.

"Seen Ida in my travels."

Dot said nothing.

"Seems the funeral was premature."

"How is she?"

"Healthy and happy and gainfully employed."

Dot was quiet.

"I guess you all made me the butt of that joke."

Dot's voice turned bitter. "It was no joke. Out was what she wanted and you aren't inclined to allowing people their own way." She sighed. "I thought it would be simpler than arguing."

"Simpler for her. Simpler for you."

"Yes," Dot said. "Because nothing is simple for you."

Strawl was quiet.

"Heard from your brother?" he asked finally.

"Not a thing."

"That's good."

"The police after him, as well?"

"I don't guess so."

Those that thought his ears were his only asset knew little about listening. Living alone had left him intuition like a woman's, which inclined him to listen and not just hear. At times the talent served him well. Others it hardly mattered.

"You let the law know I'm back in the vicinity, yet?" Strawl asked.

"Give me a reason not to," Dot said.

"What would be the use? You have or you haven't. I'm here either way."

Strawl listened to her walk away.

The following morning, he opened the door and in the hard-packed dirt yard was Dice—on a crutch, his ankle still cast in plaster—and five National Guard troops. Dot and the girls stood off a ways with Arlen, who stared into the dirt and dug a hole with his boot. A damned waste of time, Strawl thought.

"I'm unarmed," he said.

The guardsmen held rifles at ready, while the last approached and frisked him. Satisfied, he stepped back.

"I'd like to feed old Stick before I go," Strawl said. "He's my horse."

Dice shook his head, but the sergeant of the guardsmen said all right and they parted for him to pass. Inside, the barn was cool. Stick's head rose when Strawl slid the door. The light made geometry of the floor and walls, squares, octagons, rectangles with sides out of parallel. Rhombuses, Strawl thought, a strange word, one that ought to mean more. He hunted until he found another sack of grain and opened it with the pocketknife the guardsman had not seen necessary to confiscate. He added two bails to the feed box and cranked the hand-pump until water filled a halved barrel he'd fashioned into a trough for the horses left inside. Stick ate and Strawl pressed his ear below the horse's withers and listened to his stomach churn and the great bellows of his lungs pull in air and the steady hum of his passing blood, and the muscled heart drumming it. The Bible had no monopoly on miracles, Strawl thought.

At the other end of the barn were the double doors that led to the corral. Strawl opened them so the horse could exercise a little. Next to the outside wall, under a canvas spread, was the county's first threshing machine, used, but in working condition, certainly. Returning, Strawl passed the tack bench and his saddle upon it. He'd left the rifle in its scabbard and now withdrew it and opened the breach and filled the chamber.

Outside, it was bright and he blinked his eyes at the figures in his yard, just shadows until his vision adjusted. The guardsmen talked and Dice smoked by himself. The little girls stood under Dot, her hand on their shoulders, tethering them, and the boy rode in a wagon beneath. Arlen was the first to see Strawl return and he took two or three steps across the dirt yard toward him. In his eyes, Strawl saw the reassurances his son-in-law would offer, the devotion he would promise to his daughter and grandchildren, the good sense with which he would tend his work. Strawl knew, too, that Arlen's intents were not a false comfort; he was determined to follow through with them, right up to the moment he saw the rifle barrel, which Strawl had swung with each step to disguise it, rise and cough and then smoke, and Arlen felt the bullet split his chest and his eyes blinked and he thought no more of his responsibilities.

The guardsmen and Dice had their guns at their shoulders. Strawl tossed his in the dirt and continued walking toward Dice's squad car with his hands over his head. The shot's ringing silenced the grandchildren, even the baby. Strawl's ears were deaf with the bullet's report. Dot stared at him, mouth open as if she could not breathe.

Strawl opened the squad car door and Dice finally hobbled to him and cuffed his wrists, which he extended palm up to make the chore no more work than necessary.

EPILOGUE

Strawl died seven months later when a stroke paralyzed his left side and pneumonia congested his heart and lungs, a weight he finally decided he was too tired to lift. In that time he had no visitors and spoke to no one other than the guards for their counts. His body lies in the old prison cemetery, according to their records, though weather and age have worn all the stones from that time to blank, mossed slabs.

No one was charged with the reservation killings. They stopped, and that had been the intent of the investigation. They have passed from memory to tale to rumor to oblivion with remarkable alacrity, but that is the fate of stories in the time in which we live. Few are built to last.

The Bird clan is still a strong presence on the reservation, and many of that name are now Canadian citizens working ranches and pulp mills in Kelowna and Osoyoos. Marvin was sighted in Nespelem a year following Strawl's arrest, but then disappeared and was heard from no more. Rutherford B. Hayes became so devoted to Canada that once Britain entered the war and Canada mustered troops, he volunteered for duty and won the British Cross and the Queens Medal for Gallantry for his service at Juno

Beach, where he rescued a squad of infantry from a machine gun nest, clearing its gunners by hurling stones and shell casings upon them until they retreated. He then took the gun and turned it upon the retreating Germans and killed a dozen. After the war, he lit in Cranbrook, where he bred dogs and doctored horses until he was elected mayor by write-in vote, which incensed him to such an extent that he left the town for the mountains.

Dice, however, accepted the people's mandate and was elected State Senator seven times, until he retired to Spokane where he lost most of his pension on grain speculation, then recovered it and a fortune to boot when the Bureau of Reclamation, to add a third powerhouse, purchased a hundred acres he'd bought for near nothing thirty years before. He remained married to Karen, his only wife, until his death at seventy-nine.

Elijah disappeared. It was as simple as that. No one heard more from or about him. A month following Strawl's arrest, however, despite a wet April, fire consumed the woods of his encampment. The canyon walls, too severe for the smoke eaters to find purchase, became as embers in a smith's furnace, one heating the other and both the earth below. Trees exploded before the flames reached them and the basalt shone like the glass it had once been. Heat rose in surges and, when the wind pulled the smoke clear, even the blue of the sky shuddered against it. Nights, it bent the starlight and each morning, deer and elk and bear stumbled from the edges of the woods onto highways and into neighborhoods and the merchants' shop-lined streets of the outlying towns, blasting breath from their baked lungs and, in the adrenaline-fueled euphoria that is known to accompany the severest of burns, leaped and spun on their hind legs, dancing as if smoten spirits, while the moon, still hanging in the growing dawn, remained the color of blood.